The Chandelier Maker

A NOVEL ABOUT PEACE IN THE MIDDLE EAST

Four strangers, one room,

one day, one goal –

to save the world.

By Steve Maltz

Saffron Planet
PO Box 2215
Ilford IG1 9TR
UK

T: +44 (0) 7885 941848
E: contact@saffronplanet.net
Copyright (c) 2025 Steve Maltz
First published 2025

Typesetting: Michael Oakley

ISBN 978-1-9163437-9-5

Preamble

In 1929, after an Arab uprising in Palestine, the British rulers of the land instigated an inquiry into the causes, resulting in the Shaw Report, named after Sir Walter Shaw, who led the inquiry.

The findings were controversial and did not do justice to all parties. In fact, it all seemed a bit of a fudge.

One of the commission's members, Henry Snell, a Labour politician, certainly felt so. He issued a 'note of Reservations', an addendum to the report, listing his disagreements.

His summary was that "a few men of both races" should "meet together and explore the possibilities of common effort for agreed ends," to work towards co-operation in establishing inter-racial justice and goodwill. "Out of their efforts would grow a reserve of understanding," he proposed, "to unite Arabs and Jews in the task of building up a happy and prosperous land."

Now, almost a century later, they finally got round to it ...

THE CHANDELIER MAKER

Prologue

THE PROGRAMME

** Top Secret **

United Nations initiative: DRS12/45x.

A closed study of a small focus group brought together to
discuss the Israeli-Palestinian conflict
and explore the possibilities for peace.

Location: Secret.

Time: Early 2025.

Participants:

Mohammad (Mo) Hussein (Muslim)
– age 27, Haifa, Israel.

Abigail (Abi) Weiss (Jew) – age 25, Jerusalem, Israel.

Jacqueline (Jax) Botham (Atheist/Marxist)
– age 72, Highgate, North London, UK.

Joseph (Joe) Parsons (Christian)
– age 74, Cambridge, UK.

Convenor: **Newt Swinton**
– age 44, Euston, London, UK

*"This may well be our last chance.
Throw all the resources you have at this one."* D.B.

"Will do. I think we are good to go." H.G.

"Then let's do it … and may the 'gods' be with us all." D.B.

THE CHANDELIER MAKER

Chapter one

Four strangers sit in anticipation, ready for battle. There will be no quarter given. They are to fight for the truth as they see it. It will be brutal.

The room is square, with just a single window, slightly ajar but shuttered. The floor is expensively carpeted, and the ceiling is high. A few paintings adorn the wall opposite the window, all reproductions of the Masters. A single wooden podium in the centre of the room faces four desks spread apart in a semi-circle. Newt, the convener, sits behind the podium on a high chair. Behind him is a large circular area, surrounded by what looks like projector lenses, from floor to ceiling. Further back, on the wall, is a huge screen. Newt is expressionless, perhaps a little anxious. He has a challenging task ahead of him and breathes deeply to centre himself. The four candidates sit opposite him. They too show little expression, perhaps it is too early yet to emerge from behind their masks. Not a word has been spoken yet. The atmosphere is tense, as they all wait for the beginning of whatever is to come. It comes.

The lights in the room dim slightly and a growing jarring noise presses in from all four corners. There is a sudden activity in front of them all and the projector lenses flicker into life. Newt turns round to face it. It is the latest in holographic technology, the *holo-bubble*. It fades in and they are presented with a vast, noisy and colourful vista. Pandemonium, chanting, singing and shouting; discordant at first until things settle and images gradually appear that match the sounds. Firstly, a noisy chanting crowd pass through from right to left along a diagonal, a colourful sea of humanity brandishing Palestinian flags and banners declaring care for Palestinians, whilst heaping abuse on Israel. This is quickly followed on the other diagonal, from left to right, by a more sedate march of pro-Israel supporters, with their blue and white flags and gentler chanting. As both processions obliviously dissect each other over the heads of our small gathering, further images pop into view, tiny vignettes to add flavour to the developing narrative. A university sit-in, with angry students chanting from their make-shift tents. Noisy crowds outside the Israeli Embassy. An unseemly fracas in a TV studio. Shouty YouTube and TikTok videos, with extreme opinions from both sides of the debate. The overall message is clear. This whole situation is, in the words of Oliver Hardy, *'a fine mess',* although what he actually said was *"here's a nice mess."* There is nothing nice or fine about this mess, though.

Newt stands up. With a gentle wave of his hand the tableau freezes and there is a sudden silence. He speaks, with a curiously high-pitched voice.

"Scenes from the last couple of weeks, Ladies and Gentlemen."

He looks around from face to face. No one speaks. He continues.

"Much excitement, eh?"

Jax can't stay silent. She is quite agitated. "And with good cause too. Hundreds of thousands of people can't all be wrong. I'd be there too, if I weren't … here."

Joe speaks up. His voice is mainly controlled, but there is a tinge of emotion. "Don't forget there were others there too … supporting the … other side."

The other two are silent. In fact, they both seem embarrassed, as if they are witnessing a fight being fought on their behalf, by proxy verbal warriors. Neither feel able to say anything at this point. They steal glances at each other, not difficult as they are sitting opposite to each other. Abi smiles wryly. Mo stays expressionless.

Newt looks at them both in turn and decides not to draw them in at this point. He speaks.

"It's the biggest issue of our day ... Israel and Palestine ... and it's why we are all here today, Ladies and Gentlemen. This is a safe place ... an open forum ... somewhere where we can speak our minds without fear of ... well, let's just say, it's just the five of us here together ... five voices ... to talk about issues that others would rather not speak about ... without emotions and ..."

"... I'm afraid I have to stop you there ... Newt," says Jax. "We would not be ... human ... with real emotions ... if the sights we have seen in Gaza and Lebanon do not move us ..."Joe isn't going to let this go unchallenged.

"Of course, we are all moved ... not sure what you're implying here ... but ... we all know when this started."

"1948?" Jax is being provocative. Joe takes the bait with a passion that seems incompatible with his grey, ordered, austere features.

"October the seventh ... you ..."

He stops himself before mouthing an insult, which would have been totally out of character. He had promised himself that this woman, Jax, would not rile him. She had a fiery reputation as a very vocal activist and is already out to bait him. He considers himself unflappable. As a seasoned teacher and lecturer, he has seen it all, he thinks. His face has reddened and he is biting his lip. All is quiet for a few seconds and then, the scene changes.

The scenes are immediately recognisable. October 7th, 2023. The carnage at the music festival in the desert, with the abandoned cars. The devastation at the kibbutzim. Scenes that had shocked the world, paralysed a nation and instigated a bloody war. The sights and sounds combined to produce what must have been torture for Abi, the Israeli girl. *This is heartless*, thinks Newt, though he is powerless to affect the narrative, he is just a facilitator not a controller. Abi tries to hold it together, but her lips quiver and tears start flowing. She bows her head. Mo looks on, his face now slightly animated, a picture of compassion. Joe is quietly shedding a few tears too. The only person who seems unaffected is Jax, who actually appears to be fighting hard not to show any emotions.

"Yes, yes ... we've seen this before. Perhaps too much. They had it coming ..."

Her words are rudely interrupted by Joe, who can't hold back his anger this time. He attempts to rise from his seat but fails. What they didn't know, though one suspects that Newt was privy to this, was that a restraining force field was at play around the seating area. They are all effectively trapped in their chairs and Joe is the first to realise this.

"What, the ..." he cries. "We are ... prisoners? What kind of madness ...?"

"Yes, it is a bit extreme," says Newt. "But they really want us to see this through ... we are actually ... trapped ... until they, someone ... decides that we're free to move around. Bad form, I say, but ..."

"You knew about this, Newt?" hisses Jax. "How can we trust you now? What other surprises do they ... you ... have for us?"

"Trust me ... you must trust me ... without your trust I think we may be here a long time ... and ... no Jax ... there are no more surprises of this kind and, if there are, they will be a surprise to me, too." He knows full well that there will be plenty of surprises ... of a different kind but decides not to mention that yet.

Jax nods reluctantly, but Joe's anger has only been

delayed, not extinguished.

"They had it coming?" He speaks these words slowly and deliberately, facing Jax.

Jax is unfazed.

"Too right ... it had been coming for seventy-five years. As I said ... 1948 ..."

"... 1948? You mean the totally legal, United Nations approved, formation of the State of Israel ... accepted by the world, apart from the Arab neighbours ... who promptly invaded it from all sides. Tell me, Jax. Who were the aggressors then?"

"Looks like you need a history lesson, professor?"

"Professor?"

"Look at you ... with your neatly trimmed beard, your carefully combed hair, your half-rimmed glasses, your ... earnest expression."

"Newt! Can you ...?" exclaims Joe, pleading with the convener to intervene.

Newt interrupts. "I believe we must set some ground rules here, Ladies and Gentlemen. My fault for not bringing this up earlier."

He reads from some notes before him.

"Short list really ... No personal insults."

There's a silence as he looks up.

"And?" asks Joe.

"That's it," adds Newt. "No personal insults. That's all it has here. Apart from that, you are free to speak on whatever is on your mind."

He holds up a scrap of paper. He continues.

"I think the intention is that as long as we are ... civilised ... to each other ... then we can feel free to speak freely without fear of personal attack."

"Well, that's gone well so far hasn't it?" says Joe, with a

hint of cynicism.

"Don't see 'professor' as an insult. Quite the reverse really", adds Jax.

"OK then," says Joe, "Wizened old witch!"

"I can take the 'witch' part … I'm used to that, but … 'wizened'?"

She stares at him, but there is unexpected mirth in her eyes. She is not as insulted as the others imagine. It seems that she's had worse thrown at her in her life of activism. This insult is probably quite mild by comparison. Newt latches onto this temporary thawing.

"So, we have the Professor … and the Witch then. OK with you two?"

They both shrug their shoulders. The other two look on indifferently, as if they are thinking, *'let these dinosaurs play their games and get them out of their system.'*

"And Jax … the witch … is right … we need a history lesson. But … it is not up to Jax or, actually, any of you to give it. We must arrive at a history that we can all … if possible … agree on … even if there are minor disagreements."

"There can be only one … true history," interjects Joe.

"Correct," adds Newt. "So, let's see if we can find it then."

Chapter two

Jax is agitated. Newt can sense that she needs to get something off her chest at this early stage. She has some sheets of paper in her hand. He acknowledges this.

"Jax, is there something you wish to share with us?"

"Yes ... isn't it customary in debates for each to be allowed to make an opening statement?"

"This is not a debate. It is a free exchange of views."

"A debate by any other name."

"What is on your mind, Jax?"

"An opening statement, of course. I have one prepared."

"This is a bit ...". Newt looks at Joe. "... Joe, do you have an ... opening speech?"

"No, of course not. If I had been told ..."

"Would you object to Jax making one? She seems determined."

"Well, it's going to be a long day ... will I still be allowed to address her points, to challenge any ... fake news she may come up with?"

Jax glares at him.

"Of course. But perhaps over the course of the day ... there will be a lot to cover."

Joe shrugs magnanimously.

"And how about you two?" says Newt to the younger delegates.

They shrug and seem indifferent.

"We'll take that as a 'yes' from all three of you," says Newt. "Jax, the floor is yours."

"Thank you all ... and I mean that."

Then she looks at Joe. "But perhaps you won't be thanking me afterwards ... but, hey ho."

She sits up straight, grasping her sheets of paper.

"Before she starts," says Newt. "Please keep your comments until the end ... yes?"

He takes their silence as an assent. Jax starts to speak.

"What I have here is an actual opening statement from a debate at the Cambridge Union a year or two ago. It was not given by me but by a well-known Palestinian activist and I won't give the full text, just the pertinent points. Here we go ..."

She pauses to gather herself, then speaks.

"Where do I start? My heart is bursting, as I speak. So much to say to you dear folk, but so little time. I feel that time is running out for my people. Even as I speak there is a ferocious colonization of my people, ethnically cleansed by outsiders who have no connection with our land; European usurpers, planted by their colonial masters to supplant my people, the indigenous people of the land, who are forced to live in a state of apartheid. These usurpers, the Zionists, claim ownership on behalf of their political masters and in the guise of a religious so-called destiny, encouraged by Christians, mainly in the United States, who blindly support them, even to the extent of condoning the genocide they are conducting in Gaza and the West Bank, on a daily basis."

"Here's what they say to justify their evil actions. Chaim Weizmann, the English Jew, back in 1921, said this at the World Zionist Congress, that Palestinians are to him like 'the rocks of Judea, obstacles that had to be cleared on a difficult path.' We are not rocks, dear friends, we are living stones, with stories to be told and that will be told, stories that will make the world sit up and listen and condemn those who have committed such evil against us in the last seventy years and more. The Polish Jew, David Ben Gurion, the first Prime Minister of Israel, said 'we must expel Arabs and take their places.' Benjamin Netanyahu once complained about a missed opportunity during the 1989 Tiananmen Square uprising, 'while world attention was focused on China', to expel many Palestinians from their homes. Aaron Sofer, an Israeli political advisor, asserted in 2018 that 'we have to kill and kill and kill. All day, every day.'" Even their celebrated scientist, Albert Einstein, acknowledged the evil intentions of his own people, when he said, 'It would be my greatest sadness to see Zionists do to Palestinian Arabs much of what Nazis did to Jews'."

"Even people beloved by the Europeans acknowledge our plight. David Attenborough, the English naturalist, said 'I am not aware of any animal that is so cruel as the Israelis – not even crocodiles. They bomb schools, hospitals, refugee camps, orphanages, UN feeding stations, water works, power plants, ambulances, kids playing on the beach'. Lionel Messi, the footballer, said, 'As a UNICEF ambassador, I cannot play against people who kill innocent Palestinian children. We had to cancel the game because we are humans before footballers.' These are a few of many, far too many to recount. You get the picture, dear friends? They are less than human, these Zionists, committing genocide against our people, while the world looks on and ignores it. Are they trying to do to the Palestinians what was done to them in Europe by the Nazis, as if to say, 'what was done to us, we can do to others. The world cared little for us at the time, see how little the world cares for you now.' They have no conscience about the harm they do and yet, cry 'antisemitism' if they think others are persecuting them, playing the 'poor victims.'"

"I saw with my very own eyes when visiting Gaza of a young boy, his face and hands mutilated, through booby-trapped food left by Israeli soldiers. I was told that they had also done the same for people in Shujaiyya, and in the 1980s Israeli soldiers had left booby trapped toys in Lebanon to kill the children. Daily they snipe at our children with their 'kill shots' and indiscriminate bombing of entire neighbourhoods, burying families alive, destroying whole bloodlines, in order to snatch our future away from us."

Joe is incensed. "I must ..."

"No, please, Joe, let her finish," interrupts Newt. "Carry on, Jax."

She continues.

"Are my people not worthy of consideration? Are the works of their hands not worthy too? We, too, write books, create art and have dreams. We build schools and learning institutions and homes for our families, new houses to take the place of those stolen from us, homes wedded to the very soil of the land for generations. Instead, we have to witness the horrors that are inflicted on us, as our homes are stolen and we are oppressed, marginalised, vilified, expelled, poisoned, tortured, imprisoned, raped and killed ... an estimated 300,000 a year. No one is safe from this interference in our daily lives, they go after our journalists, our healthcare workers, our athletes, our artists, our intellectuals, our writers. They bomb our hospitals, places of learning, our museums, cultural and religious centres. They even set up observation platforms where people can watch our slaughter as if a tourist attraction! They force us into tents, then bomb us in places that are meant to be safe. They burn us alive, deprive us of food, water, and medicine. Oh the pain of seeing our children wandering barefoot with empty pots ... our babies dying in hospitals stripped of vital equipment ... of youths gathering the flesh of their parents into plastic bags ... witnessing them burying their siblings, cousins and friends ... making them sneak out from their tents in the middle of the night to sleep on their parents' graves ... making them pray for death to join their parents, to escape from the hell on earth they are forced to endure.

They fire on us as we approach the aid trucks in our hunger, that shows you the type of people they are. Are they even human?"

"Then there are the atrocities, ignored by the world's press. The sniper bragging about blowing out 42 Palestinian kneecaps in one day in 2019 ... the soldier boasting to CNN that he ran over hundreds of Arabs with his tank ... the systematic raping of doctors, nurses, patients, and other captives with hot metal rods and electrified sticks, sometimes raping to death ... women forced to give birth in filth, leg amputations without anaesthesia ... the world watches this, streamed in real-time ... and still denies the genocide that we see so clearly before us!"

"They have duped the world. We Palestinians offered them safety in our homes when the Europeans tried to murder them and everyone else turned them away and they arrived here in Haifa in their boats. We took pity on them and fed them, clothed them, gave them shelter and we shared our land with them. And ... in return? When they grew strong and with help from their British friends they kicked us out of our own homes, then killed and robbed and burned and looted our lives. They shattered our hearts because it is clear they do not know how to live without lording it over others. But now, perhaps, the world wakes up to this, finally glimpsing the terror we have endured for so long, and they are waking up to the reality of who they really are, evil usurpers. They watch in utter astonishment the gleeful sadism, the joy with which they break our bodies, our minds, our future."

Joe is getting increasingly agitated, but Newt gestures to him to hold off. Jax continues.

"But the land is ours, it always has been. Our tears have watered the soil for centuries, while they wander the world as outcasts. Whatever fables they weave, they have no past, present or future in our land, it is all a lie. Only we Palestinians are the true tenants here. Their heartlands are in Europe, in Poland or Ukraine, or further west, but not here. They will never have an attachment to this holy land but instead delight in destroying the trees and our holy places, destroying our ancient cemeteries, like the Anglican cemetery in Jerusalem or the resting place of ancient Muslim scholars and warriors in Maamanillah."

"The world is waking up to this travesty and responding to it. People all over are meeting in their masses – in universities, town squares, shopping malls ... everywhere - to show us their love and support, because they know where the truth lies. They want to be on the right side of history. The Jews will never know the feeling of having these masses all over the world pouring into the streets and stadiums to chant and sing for our freedom. They see through the lies of the usurpers, the depraved violent colonizers who think 'being Jewish' entitles them to the home my grandfather built with his own hands, on land that had been in our family for centuries. It is because Zionism is a blight on humanity. They can pretend to belong, changing their names and adopting our cuisines, but the world sees through these lies."

"We are not going away. We will never disappear, however much the Zionists want to wipe us out, no matter how many of us they kill and kill and kill, all day every day. We are not the rocks Chaim Weizmann thought you could clear from the land. We are the land itself, its soil, its rivers and trees, mountains and valleys. It has been so for countless centuries, since our ancestors, the Canaanites, Hebrews, Phoenicians and Philistines, from the River to the Sea. Others came and went, leaving behind carnage and disruption, but we remain, the trustees of the land, the only authentic voice. The stories of this land are in our blood and always will be. Our stories will be told, despite the despicable acts of our enemies and the world will see us the way we see ourselves, as authentic representatives of our land and heritage. Free Palestine."

Jax stops and relaxes. This has taken a lot out of her and it is clear that, although this has been written by another, she has believed and felt every word and shows it by her firm expression and the tightness of her jaw. She now waits for the fallout.

There is a stunned silence as they gather their thoughts. Joe has been listening with his head down, furiously taking notes. He is highly agitated, but is hiding it well from the others. Perhaps he is ashamed of the emotions that have been stirred up. But then he can't hold it in anymore and the volcano erupts.

"What a lot of ...", he says slowly and sternly. Newt stops him before he can say something he may regret later. He can also see Abi about to speak.

"Sorry, Joe, I must stop you there. And also you, too, Abi. This must have been so difficult for you to listen to and I thank you for not interrupting. I commend you both ..."

They both start to speak but Newt speaks over them.

"There will be a time for a response to what you've heard ..."

"I hope so ... because never have I heard such a tissue of lies and exaggerations ...", blusters Joe. "There are so many points to be made."

"As I said ... in time ... but first, let us consider where that speech was coming from. I know it came from Jax ... but it didn't originate from Jax ... it originated from a grieving heart of someone who has perceived a lifetime of hurts and has packaged it up and ... unleashed it like a guided missile. Remember our goal here, the pursuit of truth. What we must do is differentiate between what has created this grieving heart ... and what is the *product of it*. It was delivered with great passion and sincerity. But we must be forensic in our response, rather than be swept away by emotions. We are servants of the truth here and we must never forget that."

He pauses to allow this to sink in. Then he continues.

"There was a lot of poetry there – and, of course, poetic license ... and a lot of clever rhetoric. We must consider the audience and how it is often not just the words, but the feelings that carry the words, that impinge on us the most. My research has already shown me that this particular speech has gone viral, which means that, like it or not ... Joe and Abi ... it has spoken to many, irrespective of how much truth lies within the words. So ... respond we must ... but not yet ... but it WILL be responded to."

"This is difficult for me, Newt," says Joe. "But I will hold back for now."

Abi seems lost for words and stays silent, wisely picking her moment perhaps. Joe speaks again.

"No ... can I just say one thing, then I will shut up."

"OK," says Newt, just a tiny bit worried. Joe actually tries to stand up, as if ready to give a lecture, but then remembers the force-field.

"Oh no," groans Jax in anticipation. Joe ignores her and speaks.

"We can make all sorts of fine speeches, with poetic rhetoric and great passion but ... at the end of the day ... we must not forget God's promises. God promised the land to Abraham and his descendants. It says so clearly in the Bible and ..."

"Can I stop you there?" says Abi, her first words of the day. Joe stops.

"Best not go there," she says, quietly and clearly. Joe possibly wouldn't have taken this rebuke from anyone else, especially Jax, but Abi, of course, has every right to comment.

So he nods to her and doesn't continue.

'What on earth have you unleashed, Jax?' thinks Newt to himself.

THE CHANDELIER MAKER

Chapter three

Before anything more can be said, a new scene unfolds in the holo-bubble between them all. The sound of footsteps walking up a path to a small, terraced house in a dreary estate.

"That's my ..." exclaims Jax, shocked.

"Yes, it's your house, Jax. Just watch and listen ... all of you," instructs Newt.

The door opens and Jax greets a visitor. We are fast-forwarded to a cosy scene in a small living room. A male voice speaks, low and authoritative.

"So, Jax Botham ... why have you agreed to go on our programme?"

We see a thoughtful Jax lean back on her comfy chair, rest her arms on the armrests and then take a deep breath. Then she speaks. The 'real' Jax looks on, mouthing the words, because she remembers them so well, as it was a prepared speech.

"I want to be a voice for the voiceless, an advocate for the dispossessed Palestinians. It has been my life's work, for as long as I can remember, to fight their cause, to help right the wrongs that they have experienced and to bring back to them what was stolen from them in 1948 and 1967. I feel so humbled to be chosen from all the countless candidates and be assured that I will do the best job possible. Free Palestine!"

Abi mumbles something under her breath and Joe purposely and ostentatiously pays no attention. Newt notices both and wonders how bridges barely under construction anyway will be rebuilt after Jax's opening speech. The voice continues.

"And how will your involvement in the programme achieve this?" says the voice, a little mechanically.

"I've just answered this, haven't I? Do I need to tell you more,

*young man?" She is peeved, as if the man hadn't been listening
to her.*

"Noted ... anything more you wish to add?"

There is a silence. She is confused.

"Yes ... but ... do you really want to hear more?"

*She isn't very impressed. She is bursting to speak again but
her visitor does not appear so keen. She holds back, it's best to
not seem too keen. He does say one thing, though.*

*"We have what we need ... you will get ample opportunity to
express your opinions if you attain the role ..."*

"Unfortunately!" declares Joe, a little too loudly.

The scene fades out. Newt speaks.

"So, Jax. The others here have learned something
about you."

"Hardly a full disclosure! I think they have already made
their minds up about me anyway."

Newt then changes the subject.

"OK, folks. We're now going on a little tour. We will start
at a fixed point in history and go wherever our discussions
take us. Is this good? Are we happy with this?"

There are nods from all except Jax, who is still peeved
and seems distracted, as if she doesn't entirely trust Newt.

"Jax?" asks Newt, noticing this. "Yes, fine," is the
answer, spoken with some irritation.

"OK, then. Let's begin ... 1948" says Newt suddenly.
"The significance of that year?"

Abi looks around and notices that the others are not
forthcoming.

"The formation of the State of Israel," she says, clearly
and proudly. Mo looks away, as if insulted, mouthing
something under his breath.

"Mo?" says Newt, looking straight at him. "Can you
speak louder?"

"The Nakba" was the answer, a little louder. "The Catastrophe."

"Noted," replies Newt. "We'll address that too. But first ..."

A scene unfolds before them. It is a video, an old black-and-white video. We are in the United Nations building, in the main chamber. Men in dark suits and ties are sitting at a large desk. A date scrolls across the screen.

'On November 29, 1947 ...' then the words, *'The United Nations voted ... to partition Palestine into two states ... One Jewish and One Arab ... 33 Countries voted in favour and 13 against.'* Then there were scenes of jubilation in a large crowd of Jewish people, one brandishing a flag. *'Many Jews consider it a landmark achievement ... and celebrations broke out in the streets of Tel Aviv and Jerusalem.'* Then there was a view of an Arab leader, in full headdress. *'However, the Arab countries rejected it and vowed to resist. Then scenes of war. The vote led to the outbreak of war between Jewish and Arab communities ... and six months later to a broader war ... between the newly established State of Israel and five Arab armies ...'*

The video stops at that point, but the words linger in the air.

"Comments, anybody?" Newt watches and waits. And waits ... and waits. He waits because he sees from the faces that they all have something to say but, for some reason, none want to be first. Eventually Joe speaks up.

"That's how I see it. An accurate account, though perhaps could do with more commentary."

"Commentary you say? I agree – probably the only time I will agree with you, professor. For starters ... what about the stitch-up at the UN?" remarks Jax coldly.

"What are you talking about ..." retorts Joe. She interrupts.

"... The fact that, although there were over twice as

many Arabs as Jews in the land, they were only allocated 43% of the land. No wonder they rejected it."

"And have you seen the maps?" retorts Joe.

"What maps?"

"The ones that show the *actual* allocations. How much of the land given to the Jews – in fact, most of it – was desert. Uninhabitable ... at the time of course."

"Land is land!" is Jax's final word, her arms crossed defiantly.

"And that was justification for an invasion?" is Joe's response. He too sits defiantly. Newt feels that this is a good time to intervene.

"So, 1948 is the crunch year then, we'd all agree with that?"

He notices that Mo is agitated and he understands why.

"Mo?"

"The Nakba." The young Palestinian repeats what he had said earlier.

"Yes, the Nakba."

"The Nakba!" repeats Jax, but with firmness. "What you going to say to that ... professor." That last word was spat out with venom. Newt calms things down.

"Now we're getting to the issue. The Nakba - I'm sure you know this, though I confess I didn't before I did my researches – I must say I found the Wikipedia description very ... let's say ... inflammatory ... it's Arabic for 'the catastrophe', which they define as: *'the ethnic cleansing of Palestinian Arabs through their violent displacement and dispossession of land, property and belongings, along with the destruction of their society and the suppression of their culture, identity, political rights and national aspirations.'* Phew ... heavy stuff. ... but true ... in every way, I ask?"

"Of course, "says Jax, smugly. "In every way."

Newt continues. "Because … as a neutral here … if every word of this is absolutely true then … yes, you can see their point … But …"

"But? Of course there's a 'but' … a big but!" retorts Joe, angrily.

"Speak for yourself … and your big butt" says Jax, still wallowing in her smugness and trying to inject humour, which is lost in the growing emotional atmosphere. Mo gives a very slight smirk at the innuendo. Joe ignores her.

"Mostly wrong on just about every point!" he adds.

"I thought you might say that," says Newt. "Would have been surprised if you hadn't as, to me, it sounds like carefully constructed propaganda rather than an observation from an independent news source. I'm not confirming or denying its content, just reacting as a neutral. 'Ethnic cleansing' is a very emotive term!"

"Some neutral you are", says Jax, angrily. "Already doubting our narrative and …"

"And there you have it," interrupts Newt. "Narrative. That word tells all. It tells me that we are seeing things from one perspective. I think we're all very clear about your perspective, Jax, from your opening speech. I'm sure the other side has its own … narrative. Is that so, Joe?"

"Of course," he replies. "We have a totally different view of this … Nakba."

"Which is?"

Joe leans back, very much taking the poise of a professor about to lecture his students. Jax looks the other way, trying to stay as disengaged as possible.

"Where do I start? Ethnic cleansing, violent displacement, disruption of their society, suppression of their culture … what absolute nonsense … and as for the lies we heard earlier …"

He grasps a piece of paper, where notes had been scrawled.

"...expelling, oppressing, imprisoning, poisoning, torturing, raping, killing ... this makes sense if she was speaking about the Palestinian's *own* leaders. They have killed far more of their own people than the Jews ever did!"

Both Mo and Jax, clearly incensed, attempt and fail to get out of their seats. Jax is the angrier of the two, by far.

"Joe ... please ... your choice of words? A bit of sensitivity is in order here I think," says Newt.

"What ... to that old ... Marxist? She has absolutely no stake in the argument!"

"But neither have you, Joe ... and what about him?"

Newt points at Mo, visibly upset, but holding back his anger with admirable poise. Joe looks at him and stops, thinking better of carrying on his tirade.

"Do you have anything to say, Mo?" asks Newt, gently.

"A lot ... I think. But I want to choose my words carefully, not allow my heart to rule my tongue."

"Well said."

These words came from a surprising source, Abi, the Israeli girl. She continues.

"Listen. I feel like ... and perhaps Mo too ... performing cocks or crazy dogs in one of those staged fights ... it's like you're all watching us ... talking *at* us ... it's *our* history ... it's *our* lives. Now ... please show us some respect. We both live in the land ... you two ... have you ever visited?"

"Of course!" blusters Joe, ready to say more but then thinking better of it.

Mo nods and smiles. There is a silence for a long time until Newt recommences.

"I feel I really have to choose my words carefully here too, Mo ... so please, all of you, hear me out." He continues. "I know I have no stake in this discussion either, I have been chosen for my neutrality ... but I'm not entirely ignorant here,

I have some experience in these matters. All that interests me is the truth … but I also know that these days there seem to be *many* truths or narratives … Yet history only forges a single path …"

He let those last words hang. He is proud of himself, as they only just came to him but they seem to sum up the situation well: '*History only forges a single path.*' He continues.

"So, we have two narratives … and the key disputed issue seems to be what actually happened in 1948 when Israel became a nation. The Palestinians … did they leave … or were they pushed? … Joe?"

"I think the situation is clear, Newt … they left … clearly not of their own accord … but their own leaders encouraged them to leave their homes … to return when the Jews were defeated. They were so certain of victory. And we, of course, all know what happened next … they lost … and as it is with wars … there were no homes to return to …"

Jax interrupts. "… I object. That is a false narrative!"

"Oh, yes? So, every Palestinian was ethnically cleansed by a people who, mostly, have just been ethnically cleansed themselves by the Nazis? That's 'ethnically cleansed' in the proper sense of the words, by the way!"

Jax is about to respond angrily, but Newt holds up his hand to stop her.

"So, there we have … the two narratives. Now the question I ask is this. Where is the truth? Is one right and the other wrong … or, perhaps, as I am inclined to believe … there may be elements of both?"

There's a lull in the proceedings and then Newt hits them with a different perspective.

THE CHANDELIER MAKER

Chapter four

"I've given this a lot of thought," says Newt. "Fresh ideas perhaps, a new perspective maybe from someone ... me ... who has no axe to grind except one ... to see if there is any possibility of a peaceful solution. That is my only desire here."

"Some hope!" exclaims Jax.

"Wish you well on that one," adds Joe, with a sigh.

Newt realises that he really has his work cut out today. Nevertheless, he ploughs on.

"I have some ideas for you to think about. But, first ..."

Newt clears his throat and stands up, stretching his legs, flexing his arms and neck muscles too. The others look on, helplessly, watching him with growing frustration, while they are still trapped in their seats. There is suddenly a mechanical sound, a soft clanging, followed by a slight shuddering as if a short sharp breeze is blowing across the room.

"It seems, Ladies and Gentlemen, that ... the powers that be ... wish to grant you a degree of freedom."

They are puzzled.

"Come on," he adds. "You can join me."

Mo is the first to realise that they are no longer trapped, followed by Abi, who leaps to her feet and immediately embarks on a stretching routine to get blood back into her limbs.

"Treating us like adults?" she says.

"Looks like it," answers Mo.

The other two are not quite so animated. Jax stands up for a few seconds, then sits down again. Joe stays seated. Newt wanders over to Mo and Abi, who are standing near to each other, but not really together.

"We've a long way to go," he says, "But hopefully we'll understand each other a lot better afterwards. Thank you both for agreeing to take part in this ... project. I hope you are not ... regretting it now?"

"I'm not sure, sir," replies Mo, respectfully. "I fear we're all going to hear things we'd rather not. Am I right?"

"Frankly ... yes. Is that a problem?"

"I'm not sure, sir. But I do feel a sense of purpose being here."

"OK, that is good, Mo. And you don't have to call me 'sir.'"

"No, I'd rather ... that's how I've been brought up."

"Then your parents have done a good job."

"Yes, they have. But it's been ... hard for them."

"I'm sure it has ... Perhaps you can tell us all about your background a little later?"

Mo nods his head and walks back to his seat. Newt turns to Abi.

"And you?"

"Not so respectful, I'm afraid. I'm a sabra, Newt ... Israeli born. Not known for our politeness."

"And you're still happy to be here?"

"Sure, yes ... let's see."

She turns on her heels and returns to her seat. At that moment Newt feels very alone, very much as the odd one out here. All eyes are on him, not particularly friendly eyes as he, too, returns to his seat. He speaks.

"OK, Ladies and Gentlemen. I hope you enjoyed your little 'stretch'. These will become more frequent from now on. There will also be food and drink ..."

"... and toilet breaks hopefully," says Jax. "A lady must powder her nose ... frequently at my age. Aged professors too ... more so, I believe", she adds, cheekily.

"Of course."

At that moment he could have kissed her. The most unlikely person has lightened the atmosphere a little and possibly has made it easier for what he has to say next.

"I've been thinking …" he says. "Thinking back to 1948 … but also thinking about now, how our world has changed. Looking especially at Europe, particularly the UK … so this is of particular interest to you two."

He nods towards Jax and Joe.

"Though," he adds, "it will also be familiar to you other two … the digital world has shrunk the world so much, hasn't it?"

The other two nod slightly.

"So … here it is. I'm looking firstly at 1948 in general terms … what actually happened, rather than the mechanisms that drove the events … what we see first is a population, Arabs and some Jews, living in the land, quite peacefully for a number of years … until we hit the 20th Century … then we saw migrants, from many backgrounds, settling because of economic needs, but many because of persecution elsewhere. All was going well, until the end of the First World War, when some leaders decided to stir up trouble and the situation became toxic and, from then on … those who suffered most, the Arabs in the land, were encouraged … by their own leadership … to foster bad feelings towards the Jews, who they were encouraged to call usurpers. And out of that we see strife, war, terrorism …"

He pauses, for this to sink in. He could see that Jax was agitated.

"Hold on, Jax. Let me continue, then we can discuss."

Jax settles, reluctantly, as Newt continues.

"Then I look at now, nearly eighty years later. And my focus is on the UK, though it could equally be France, Germany, Italy and so on … Here too we have an indigenous population, faced with a severe migrant situation, people seeking refuge because of economics or persecution. But in this case ... they are welcomed in by the leaderships and, in fact, encouraged in many cases and, by and large, they add value to the culture and integration happens. We now call this multiculturalism. There is relative peace even when the newcomers create their own enclaves, bring in their own cultural baggage etc. The landscape changes, particularly in many inner cities. Also, some towns and cities end up with more migrants than natives. But there is no war or hatred – apart from a minority of nationalist hotheads – they learn to tolerate each other, even integrate with each other in most cases ... Just some food for thought."

Then he stops again and makes his final statement, giving them time to absorb what he's just been saying.

"I will finish with a question. What is the basic difference between the two scenarios? The leadership ... not the people. People, whether Jews and Arabs, or English Christians and foreign Muslims, tend to want to get on with each other and live lives in peace. The leadership can make or break this, and my contention is that, from 1948 until now, the Arabs, in particular, have not been blessed with the best leaders ..."

Jax stands up. "I object ... with extreme prejudice." Interestingly Mo seems unperturbed by this analysis. She continues.

"How simplistic and naïve can you get, Newt!"

"I can see where you're coming from, Jax, but it's just an observation and of course it's not taking into account all of the complexities of the situation on the ground."

"To put it mildly!"

"Yet it's a fair summary," says Joe thoughtfully. "Very interesting indeed."

"You would say that!" shouted Jax, clearly riled. "Any reason to bash the Arabs!"

"How am I bashing the Arabs?"

"By insisting that it's all their fault."

"I think you must have misheard, Jax. Newt was talking about the Arab *leadership*."

"And what about the Jewish leaders … and as for the British!"

"Good point," interrupts Newt. "There's a lot of blame that can be put at their feet, too, but the lion's share is firmly with the political and religious leaders of the Arab nations at the time."

"Who wanted a war … who wanted to drive ALL of the Jews out. They didn't want to live with them … they wanted to exterminate them!" adds Joe, forcefully.

A softer, more reasonable voice speaks up. It is Mo.

"This is all new to my ears and quite distressing too. May I interrupt, sir?"

"Of course you can, Mo. You have the floor."

"Thank you, sir," he says, pausing for a few beats. "This is not my family's experience. I am shocked."

"Then tell us about your family," says Newt.

THE CHANDELIER MAKER

Chapter five

"My family go way back. We have been in Palestine for centuries. Not one of the wealthy clans. If we had been richer, perhaps we may have sold our land to the Jews as many did. No, we were poor, humble *fellaheen*, workers of the land, but never owning any of it. You have a word for it, *peasants*. Not a pleasant word, but an honest word. Barely living, always at the mercy of others, whether Turks, Jews or our fellow Arabs, but surviving, going about the daily tasks that sustained us, while the world revolved around us. We were unconcerned about such things that concerned others. As a family, we just lived our lives as best as we could."

He pauses as if expecting an interruption. Joe raises his hand to speak but Newt waves him away and gestures for Mo to continue.

"We lived in a small village just outside Haifa, to the south, *Wadi Nisnas*. There are about eight thousand living there. It's still there, a tourist destination these days I believe. Hardly any Jews there, mostly Christians, about two-thirds I think."

He stops. He is getting emotional and takes deep breaths before continuing.

"You mean it escaped Zionist demolition, then?" Jax can't stop herself. Joe glares at her angrily but Mo answers her.

"No. Far from it ..."

He pauses. This time for effect. There is an element of grandstanding here and Newt, for one, is most impressed, but keeps that to himself. He is glad that Mo has the confidence to speak so openly here, with such assertion. This was obviously why he had been chosen above so many others.

"In our village, Jew and Arab ... also Christians and Muslims ... we all got on with each other. So, no ... madam

... it still stands as it was. It has changed ... but it still stands. In fact, in 1948, the biggest increase we had in population was other Arabs relocating to our village."

"Having been driven out of their homes elsewhere by the Jews?"

"I suppose ... But it didn't seem a big deal at the time."

Jax seems peeved at this but has sufficient grace not to interrupt.

"My grandfather's family worked in the bakery there. It was the biggest employer and they were so grateful for this work. It took them away from the back-breaking toil of working on the land that his father was unable to do any more after his accident. He had damaged his back in a freak accident, the very worst injury for a fellaheen, but Allah was merciful and he was offered a desk job at the bakery – thankfully, he was good with numbers when not many were. Otherwise, I feel my family would not have survived. You see, my grandfather was an only child and far too young for meaningful toil."

Mo nods to Newt as if to ask for permission to continue. *'He really is a polite young man'*, thinks Newt, who then speaks.

"Any questions ... or observations ... at this stage?" Joe is the first to respond.

"And you know this for sure ... your family history?"

"Insensitive, or what!" declares Jax, incensed. "This is his family he's talking about. Come on now ..."

"It's just that we hear so many conflicting stories about the ... Palestinians ... and their claims to the land. You know that most of them have no history in the land, they were mostly migrant workers from Egypt, attracted by the opportunities created by the Jewish settlers ..."

"Rubbish!"

"... rather than ... as the lady activist we heard earlier

seems to believe ... the Jews being kindly let into Palestinian homes, to be fed, clothed and sheltered ... sharing the bounty of the land ... No, no, no ... It was the Jews who bought uncultivated and empty land from the Turks and it was they who made it habitable ... and then employed the locals and Arab migrants to work on it with them! That is the truth!"

"More rubbish!" shouts Jax.

"Jax!" exclaims Newt. "Please ... let's have some decorum. And ... anyway ... I have done some independent research, Joe, and yes, there was some immigration from Egypt and other places in the early 20th century ... but not at the levels you're perhaps suggesting. The consensus is that 20% is a realistic estimate."

"And that's the issue," growls Joe. He flicks through a notebook in front of him and continues. "No one knows anything for sure, who do we believe? Winston Churchill himself said '*Far from being persecuted, the Arabs have crowded into the country and multiplied until their population has increased more than even all world Jewry could increase the Jewish population*' ... and he is someone I am inclined to believe."

"The Patriarchy rules OK," says Jax with contempt. "Rich white males clubbing together!"

"Utter nonsense!"

"Let the boy speak, eh?" A voice drowns them both out. A slightly accented voice. Abi has had enough of their bickering. "I want to hear more ..."

"Yes, thank you, Abi", says Newt. "Things are getting a little heated. Mo, do carry on."

Mo hesitates, glancing at the two aged adversaries and gently tutting. Then he continues.

"In April 1948, my grandfather was eight years old. He had a good childhood. A happy home, though they were poor, but then everyone else was poor too. He saw no hatred, he met with, spoke to and even played with, Jewish kids without any bother. He wasn't taught to hate, as many were … on both sides I believe. He was a good son. He helped his dad in the bakery and was rewarded with delicious *ma'moul* cakes … baked cookies stuffed with dates. Delicious … a family favourite even now. But … everything changed … in April 1948."

"Don't tell me … Irgun, the Stern Gang …" pre-empts Jax, referring to the Jewish terror groups.

"No you are wrong, madam."

"Arab terror gangs? Jihadi fighters?" growls Joe.

"Wrong, too, sir. Please … let me tell you the story of Haifa, April 1948 … can I?"

"Most certainly you can," says Newt, encouragingly. The room is shrouded in silence as Mo continues with the story of his family.

"Everything changed on April 22nd,1948 … but at the same time nothing changed for us as a family."

"The Battle of Haifa", mutters Jax, knowingly.

"Yes," says Mo. "But more like just a few local skirmishes, according to my grandfather. It only lasted a day or two."

"You sure about that?" adds Jax, "it was the Jews breaking all resistance, before sending the Arab population into exile – the biggest one of all and the beginning of the Nakba."

Mo looks at her for a few beats, then shrugs his shoulders. "I think you better check your history books on that one, madam … or find one that tells the truth …"

"… No, I must …" she interrupts. Newt then interrupts her.

"… let him speak, Jax. This is HIS family history he's talking about, after all. You were quick to rebuke Joe earlier, weren't you? … Go on, Mo."

"It didn't touch us, my family remained in our home. So did many, though some left and had their homes ... reoccupied, often by other Arabs. But none were driven out."

"What are you talking about, boy?" says Jax arrogantly. Newt glares at her and Mo ignores her.

"As I said, check your history books. I have heard it first hand and I have checked. The Jews offered a truce and implored the Arabs to remain in their homes and build a future alongside them. Even the Jewish Mayor begged them to stay ... and ... by the way ... I am not your 'boy'."

Mo is a little red-faced and peeved at these constant interruptions. There is a silence, even from Jax. This is unexpected and not the story they are expecting. He continues.

"The Arab leaders chose to leave ... they weren't driven out. Thousand left, adding to the thousands of the more well-off families that had already left in the previous few months ... of their own accord."

"Walid Khalidi said that they left as a result of Zionist terror and psychological warfare" declares Jax.

"Khalidi? He would say that!" This is Joe, finally breaking his silence. "Hardly a credible source!"

"And I suppose you think your hero, Benny Morris, is more credible."

"Yes I do, as, especially in his earlier writings, he was no friend of the Israeli establishment."

"Until they bought him out!"

"What on earth are you talking about? And, anyway, some of Khalidi's research has proven to be flawed."

Newt can detect an escalation and a potential trading of insults, that would not exactly be helpful. He speaks.

"I have done research too. I have read both Khalidi and Morris and even a police report of the time, even a report from a meeting in the British Parliament. Jax, we must respect Mo and his observations, his eye-witness account. Surely, he has no incentive to speak lies here?"

Jax harumphs. Joe holds his peace. Mo speaks.

"I speak only of the experience of my family. For us personally, there was no Nakba, though it for sure happened elsewhere. I speak truth here. Otherwise ... what's the point of all of this?"

"Well spoken, Mo," says Newt. "Now's a good time to hear more ..."

The holo-bubble flickers into life again. Mo faces the camera and looks very relaxed as he sits on a wooden chair in front of a huge and colourful wall rug. He is answering the same question put to Jax earlier.

"I live in a bubble I suppose. My experience seems different to most. My family have lived in Palestine for many generations. Always poor but always happy. Since the Nakba, my grandfather and his family continued to live here in our family home in Wadi Nisnas, on the southern edge of Haifa. I had a good childhood, despite the feeling of being a stranger in my own land. Nothing major, just a few things here and there. And that's my reason for being here. I want to know more about life in Israel as a Palestinian Muslim, or Israeli Arab, however you want to define me. I want to know more about the forces that seem to tear others apart and, at the same time, do what I can to offer myself, inshallah, in any way that helps ..."

"Thank you Mr Hussein. We will be in touch."

The scene fades and all eyes turn to Mo, who looks down shyly. He feels that he has said enough for now. Newt realises this and turns to Abi.

"Abi, you've said little. Is there anything you wish to say?"

"Yes ... lots."

Chapter six

Before she can speak, the holo-bubble again flickers into life and we hear her story.

"My name is Abi Klein. Born and bred in Jerusalem. My family moved to Eretz Yisrael at the beginning of the 20th Century from Russia. But I'm native born, a **'sabra'.** *My folks live in the Old City, Jewish quarter of course. They are Zionists, but also quite religious and spend much of their time at the 'Kotel' – Western Wall. No idea why, it's just where they find peace.*
I moved out as soon as I could, straight after my IDF stint, on my twentieth birthday. In fact, I went straight to a shared apartment with some friends and have been living there ever since. Why am I here? No idea, actually. Seemed like a good idea at the time ... someone has to do it!"

There's a silence while she stares at the camera, expressionless, before a smile breaks out.

"Let me explain. It started off as a joke, or a dare. I'm quite a loud person, by nature and up for anything. When the call came to be considered for this ... thing ... my friends pushed me forwards. At no time did they think I would get this far. Me too! I've no idea why I've come this far, either."

The scene fades and Abi continues talking.

"I still don't get it. That's why I've spoken little so far, though that's really not my nature. I've heard you all now. Two bickering old fossils who have been getting excited and het up about things where they have no personal stake. And this Muslim boy ..."

She pauses and points at Mo, who looks down, embarrassed.

"Now I've had a very closed life. I've always lived in Jewish circles, the only Arabs I see is at the felafel stall, or road sweepers and stuff. I wouldn't willingly speak to one

43

... they're my enemy aren't they, eh? They all want to kill us, even those who look like butter wouldn't melt in their mouths. That's what we're taught. We join the army for two years, learning of different ways of killing them or protecting our families against them. And then ... there's him ..."

She points again to Mo.

"I don't get him. We are told all Palestinians are liars. Are you a liar, Mo?"

Newt speaks up for him.

"No, Abi, he is not a liar. And not all Arabs are liars, in the same way that not all Jews are liars."

"Shame we can't say the same about ... certain others," sneers Joe.

"Look at yourself, professor," is the sharp response.

Newt pauses to let that sink in, then continues. "Can we have a truce, you two? ... Anyway, I'm hoping that none of us here are liars, or even truth-twisters or truth-manglers. It's the truth we are trying to get at here and, despite appearances, Abi, everyone here has been selected ... even you, of course ... as someone who has a sincere desire to arrive at the truth ... even if it may not always seem so."

He looks at Joe and Jax as he says this. They both have neutral expressions, though *who knows what's going on inside their brains!* Abi responds.

"I still don't know why I'm here. I don't know much; I don't know how I can add to what's been said here. A lot of it is already over my head."

"Then perhaps you're just here to respond?" suggests Joe.

She shrugs and tuts, then remains silent. After a while, Newt speaks.

"So, Joe. I think it's time we heard a little about you."

The holo-bubble cranks up and we see Joe. He is standing behind a dais in a lecture hall that seems to be empty. He has evidently just given a lecture and has that air of proud self-satisfaction about him as he answers the interviewer's question.

"I believe I'm the best man for the job. I have been a Bible teacher for over forty years now and God woke me up to the importance of Israel and the Jewish people around thirty years ago. So, you could call me a gentile Christian Zionist. I speak on this all over the country, indeed all over the world. Yes, I would be more than happy to take part in your proposed programme."

The tone of his voice implies the opposite, namely that the proposed programme should be more than happy to have him play a part in it! That was probably what he was thinking at the time.

The display flickers off and all eyes wearily move to Joe. This little speech was a little too arrogant for their tastes. Even Newt notices this.

"So, you're the best man for the job, Joe. You still believe this?"

"Of course. Why not?"

Joe looks around and judges the mood of the room, a skill honed through decades of experiences with audiences varying from indifference to outright hostility. This little group is no different. Abi is doing her best to show indifference, Mo is uncharacteristically displaying the hint of a sneer and Jax is showing a full-blooded sneer, dripping with hostility and contempt. None of this fazes Joe, but he does adjust to it.

"OK. OK. So I'm a confident person and it may come across as arrogance. I can't help the fact that I have a lot of experience, but here I am. I will do my best to express my views with humility and patience. All I ask is that you ... receive them in the same way ..."

"Well spoken, Joe," says Newt. But the others are still not impressed. Jax can hold back no longer.

"And I will listen to every word you say, professor. But don't expect agreement ..."

"... don't expect it. Of course, that works both ways."

"Indeed."

"For sure."

They slip into silence, like two snorting bulls standing their ground, waiting for the commencement of battle. Newt breaks the silence with an announcement.

"I think it's time for a little break. Anyone hungry?"

Many nods are forthcoming and, as if on cue, there is movement in the area between Newt and the others. A chasm appears in a semi-circular section, as the floor lowers down in just a few seconds. In its place a single curved table raises up to ground level, then a few feet more. The table is bedecked with a crisp white cloth and on the table is a variety of food and drinks, placed strategically to cater to the palettes of the four of them. So Arabic cuisine occupies the area in front of Mo with plates of lamb kebab and musakhan, with bowls of humus and maftoul with taboon and rice. Abi is presented with bowls of falafel and humus, with shawarma and various bowls of salads and beans. Less exotically, the other two are supplied with plates of steak, chicken and sausages, accompanied by bowls of boiled potatoes and green vegetables. Beer, wine and fruit juices are distributed around the table. The smells are intoxicating and enticing. You could almost hear the taste buds springing into life and drool factories commencing production.

"Now this is what I came for," says Jax, leaping from her seat, grabbing a china plate and stacking up the food with an indecent energy. By contrast, Joe stays in his seat and closes his eyes, as if meditating. The other two are a little more polite but aren't going to see this feast go to waste, each sticking to their cuisine, though Mo 'borrows' a felafel or two with Abi's silent permission. Newt stays in his seat in silence while this is going on. Perhaps he's already eaten.

They eat in silence, their hunger trumping any attempts at socialising. Even Joe ventures one trip to the table, for a plate of meat and potatoes. The only comment made is an effusive thank you from Mo and some hearty burps from Jax once they have finished their desserts, a smorgasbord of fruits that appear on a lower table that again rises up from under the floor at the appropriate time. Once they have settled down again the tables disappear with a rattle and the odd spill and all is back to normal.

The battle is ready to recommence.

THE CHANDELIER MAKER

Chapter seven

"So, Ladies and Gentlemen," announces Newt. "Now we are going to do something interesting and a little different."

There is no reaction. It seems that the participants haven't yet caught the vision of what they need to accomplish here. They hadn't really got into the swing of things yet. Newt perseveres, knowing that this is about to change. The holo-bubble switches on and we are in a desert, the hot sun casting stark shadows in the meagre vegetation. In the distance, one or two figures on horseback are slowly approaching.

"Omar Sharif?" mutters Jax. Joe actually responds with a chuckle. This does not go unnoticed.

"No," says Newt, "this is not Lawrence of Arabia ... Edward Mitford. Ring any bells, Joe?"

Joe shrugs negatively.

"One of your forbears, I believe," adds Newt, "perhaps a great uncle, twice or thrice removed, so I didn't expect a reaction. Mind you, the Mitford name ... ring any more bells?"

"The Mitford sisters? Pair of horrors!" exclaims Joe.

"One a friend of Hitler, the other the wife of Oswald Mosley. Not the best legacy."

"Quite."

"Same family I believe but perhaps a hundred years earlier. What you see here is Edward Mitford and his companion Henry Layard crossing the Syrian desert, about to enter Palestine in 1840, as part of an epic journey to Ceylon, where a job awaited him."

"And?" says Joe, without too much enthusiasm.

"Sit and listen."

The scene shifts to the two riders now at the edge of the desert. Behind them is the town of Acre. Edward speaks.

"Well, that was a strange visit. That convent was rather odd.

Did you notice the skull and bones at the dinner table?"

"Yes, but it would have been far too impolite to comment."

"We are English gentlemen, after all."

"Quite. I also heard that the monks wear leather girdles and fast all week."

"Yes ... mmm ... but the food was rather good, I would say."

"And we must feast when we can. I sense that such meals will be a rarity in this troubled land. Yes, that was quite some feast."

"The Turks really have let things go here, I sense. The monks spoke of great persecution at their hands. Thankfully, the French have the convent under their protection."

"That's heartening. But, anyway. Look ahead, what adventures we have in store ..."

"Quite, Henry, my good man. We finally reach the Promised Land."

"Yes, we do, Edward. Not exactly adorned with visual riches is it, though?"

"No. But let's not be swayed by first sight. Come ... there's a whole land to explore. I am so looking forward to this. I even have the handbook ready."

He lifts up a well-worn Bible from his saddlebag. They both smile, then spur their horses into a rising gallop. A few days later, they are travelling south, having visited the town where Jesus grew up.

"So, what was your impression of Nazareth, Henry?"

"Not what I expected. One grows up with ... the stories ... but when the reality is so different, it can be a bit of a blow, I suppose."

"Yes ... did we really see the original dining table for the Last Supper? Shouldn't that have been in Jerusalem?"

"I have a sense of profiteering here, don't you think? Preying on the pilgrims."

"Also, the well where the Virgin Mary drew water ... really?"

"Distasteful."

"Yes, rather."

The scene moves to one of them on the approach to Bethlehem. An old Arab, mounted on a sorry horse, has joined them for a short while and Edward asks him why most of the villagers they have met on their journey don't seem to be prospering.

"It is corruption, my friend. Our overall ruler, Mohammad Ali, he is draining us. Soon we will all be nomads; our villages will be no more."

"It's really that bad?" asks Henry.

"We have sold our carpets and our ornaments. We have even sold our horses to meet their demands. We cannot plough as our children are taken as soldiers. None are left to work for us. We pay the Modar of Acre and, his superior, the Pacha. The Turks are taking everything, our villages have no future. These men are meant to be fellow Muslims, yet they show no concern for us here! Many of my countrymen are abandoning the villages and becoming people of the desert. Even in Bethlehem, where they are people of your faith, they are considering leaving because of the taxes of the accursed Turks!"

"This country has such potential, but no will to drive it," muses Edward to himself. "These Turks are such poor landlords. I wonder ..."

Edward spends the next few minutes in private thought, as the other two exchange niceties. After the Arab has left them, Edward speaks to his friend about something that has been on his mind for a long time.

"While I was British Consul in Morocco, I was privy to many unsavoury sights, but there is one that still lives in my memory and I just cannot purge myself of it. In fact, it is very much in the front of my mind now as we make our travels here."

"You have intrigued me. Do go on."

"It was a young Jewess, from a respectable family in Tangiers. She had committed the 'crime' of not proclaiming Mohammed as the apostle of God and so was sentenced to death after withstanding the most awful pressures to recant. An acquaintance of mine witnessed her end, her throat cut and then her body burnt. She went to her death with such innocent grace that hardened men were reduced to helpless tears on beholding this atrocity."

"You must have come across that scenario countless times, surely?"

"Yes. True. But often it's with the criminal classes, or hardened vagabonds, not with ... such innocence. Not with the ferocity and hatred I saw in this instance, just because of her race."

"No love lost between Jews and Muslims, Edward."

"Of course, but you had to be there and actually ... feel ... this hatred, Henry. I saw it many times in Morocco ... and it got me thinking."

"More thoughts? You intrigue me more, my friend."

"I have been thinking ... much over the last few years ... of these people, the Jews, to whom we Christians owe so much , yet ... seem to care for so little ... in fact, it seems that often we Christians have been more of an enemy than a friend ... and that can't be right, that's not what I see when I read the Bible."

"That is certainly something to ponder, Edward."

Joe feels the need to comment at this point.

"Alas, he speaks the truth here, this Mitford fellow. My love for the Jewish people is not shared by so many of my faith these days."

"Then that must show you the ... inadequacies of your faith, eh professor?" teases Jax.

"No it doesn't ... but it does show me the inadequacies of some who profess to follow my faith. And that is so sad."

"Wasn't Isa, Jesus a Jew?" remarks Mo.

"You are quite right. But you try telling that to some Christians!"

"For us he was a great prophet."

"For us, too, Mo. And more."

Abi interrupts. Her voice is strident.

"Hold on, let's rewind a bit. The point here is what this Englishman witnessed. That horrific death!"

"Yes, of course ... sorry, Abi. Of course that must be addressed. Convert or die!"

Jax speaks.

"So, this white male colonialist has the cheek to question Islamic religious practices ..."

"Religious practices? Slitting the throat of someone who refuses to convert?" retorts Joe.

"Read your history books, professor. You Christians have been doing this for centuries. Haven't you heard of the Inquisition? Well, I have and what you lot did then was just as bad as what we've just heard here."

Joe is muted as he responds.

"I can't argue against this, Jax. There have been ... shameful times."

"If that's the price of living as a Jew in their country then that ... Jewess ... could have kept her head down or perhaps chosen to live elsewhere."

"How dare you..."

This is Abi, clearly offended by such insensitivity.

"You really have no idea ... old woman!"

"I agree", says a surprising voice. It is Mo. "This is not the Islam that I know."

"That's a separate issue. What we are witnessing here is someone who is trivialising the life of someone living in a society that hates them." Joe is speaking, looking directly at Jax.

Jax is silent, perhaps surprised that the whole room has turned against her. She realises that she has to address this if she wants to be taken seriously from now on.

"OK. OK. Folks. Perhaps this came out wrong. I apologise ... Abi ... I'm not sure what I was saying. It's been a tiring day ..."

Abi grunts and looks away. Newt decides to intervene.

"The reality of antisemitism was very real to this Englishman. He witnessed it first-hand in Morocco. He had a lot more to say about it. In Morocco Jews were confined to ghettos, forced to wear distinctive clothing and were not even allowed to ride horses, or even donkeys or mules. They had to perform any jobs required of them by Arabs, were not allowed to complain and were certainly not protected in any way by the legal system. It was a horrible, precarious existence."

"That's awful," mutters Abi, to no one in particular. Mo is visibly shocked.

The scene continues. There is now a voice-over to accompany it.

'Our Victorian travellers are now approaching the city of Jerusalem. The approach is through lower hills filled with debris and rubbish, the remains of earlier settlements, now ruins. Not the introduction to this hallowed place that Edward had hoped for. All of his Christian life he had conjured up this idealised city of life and light, the city of his Saviour, of his hope. But the reality is very different and he is a little choked up as they get closer. The high walls now face them, with numerous Islamic domes of all shapes and sizes dotting the view, with the massive dome of the mosque of Omar dominating and adding to his feelings of wretchedness.

Jerusalem is a mix of Arabs, Greeks, Jews and Turks, as well as monks and pilgrims from all over Europe. Order is kept by

Turkish thugs, rejects from their army in Egypt, sent there as a punishment for mutineering. They rob people at the gates and in the markets. Two such soldiers had confronted our travellers at their entry at the gate. A flash of gleaming steel brandished by our two travellers was enough to thwart their intentions.'

"Let us sit and ponder for a few moments, Henry."

They rest on a large boulder, indented conveniently for their comfort.

"I have for so long treasured this moment, visiting the very place that our Saviour inhabited and from where his word went out, breaching the centuries."

He holds up his Bible as he says this. He continues.

"I look around and I think, 'Did those feet touch that spot over there, did those hands grab the earth that is piled over there?' It is all so overwhelming and I feel so privileged, Henry. Yet, my mind snaps back to the present and ... I don't see a holy place anymore."

"I can understand that. That dent in the wall of the via Dolorosa, that we saw. They say that it was there that Jesus stopped and leant on his cross. Now pilgrims are obliged to kiss the spot and, through these actions, contribute to the indentation. I am very sure that money changes hands too."

"A sacrilege. How things have fallen!"

"Yes, indeed. There is so much of this fraud around. It is awful. Remember that convent we passed through yesterday?"

"Oh yes, the tree!"

"To actually say that it was built around the very tree from where the Cross was fashioned."

"That stump among the fruit trees."

"Quite ... then there are the houses ... of Pilate, Caiaphas, Mary, the rich man and Lazarus ... I could go on."

"We've come thousands of miles just to witness a crooked circus, a sideshow ..."

"Then there are the Turks."

"Let's not talk about the Turks. Mind you they do a worthy job at the sepulchre, Christ's burial place."

"Yes, what a disgrace. All of those Christian sects fighting over the place, claiming ownership. It tickles me that the Catholics, Maronites, the Armenians all have their own chapels and keep themselves separate from each other."

"And at Easter time? I heard that the pilgrims get so unruly that the Turk guards have to bash them on their heads with sticks to keep them from killing each other with knives."

"I would laugh ... if it wasn't so sad."

"So, many illusions shattered. Enough to make one waver, I fear."

"Only in my view of our fellow man. We have seen much kindness on our travels, usually from those who have little, but ... all in all ... there is also such madness."

"How God must weep."

"Surely."

Edward's countenance drops further as he observes an aged bent-backed Jew shuffling along the path in front of them, grasping some weather-beaten scrolls and muttering under his breath.

"I have not felt such despair for a long time," says Edward, his eyes clouded with tears.

"The way I see it, Edward, is that this is no different to any of the other places we have visited in this run-down land. Everywhere has seen better days."

"I know, Henry, but it's not just that, though it acts as a symbol for ... deeper things."

Henry pauses before replying.

"The Jews?"

"The Jews. I am sorry to keep at this, but ... on the one hand I see these people, full of creativity and accomplishment, struggling for existence with fortitude and perseverance, demonstrating the miracle of their survival against all odds, with no place to settle in the world where they can find peace ... and then I see this land, the land of their ancestors ... a land dying a Turkish death ... can you not see?"

"Tell me more."

"A lot of them are indigenous, been here since Biblical times I believe. But others have come from Europe, some because of persecution, but others of a religious persuasion have come out of tradition and a longing, they seek to be reunited to the land of their birth."

"I can imagine that just by looking at us, proud Englishmen. We have conquered the world – not you and I, but you know what I mean – but all we seek is, at the end of our days, the rolling hills, polite manners and quiet comforts of our mother country."

"Yes, we all yearn for our origins, I suppose that is a very human thing. 'Lest I forget you, O Jerusalem ...'"

"Quite. You are already creating a thirst within me ..."

"Within your soul?"

"Not quite ... but I could really sink a good pint of ale served up by a buxom wench at my local hostelry in my home village."

"Less of that, Henry ... but I do get your point. Back to the Jews ..."

"Tell me more."

"I have seen much of the Hebrew nation on my travels and I do consider them, intellectually and physically, some of the best examples of humanity, despite the deprivations and persecutions they have endured in their long history. We British are in a good position to help them ... and for them to help us in return. Their gain will be our gain. This land cries out for them, that's my belief, though I may be wrong ..."

"Yes, I do see where you are coming from, my friend ... but

this is a grand vision you are describing. What, pray, are you going to do with it?"

"Oh yes ... I plan to do much with this. I have the ear of Lord Palmerston after all."

Henry looks at his travelling companion and sees a face set in fortitude.

The screen freezes and Newt addresses the room.

"So, what do you think happened next?"

"I must say I've never heard of this chap, Edward Mitford. He's one of my forbears you say?" says Joe.

"Oh yes, I have done the research" responds Newt.

"Then you're better at it than me. And I thought I had the full account of my family. One of them was a friend of John Wesley, you know, the man who started Methodism."

"All you have seen in our reconstruction is a correct account. It was taken from an obscure book by his great-great-grandson. It's a story that history seems to have forgotten, but it was true nonetheless."

"But I must return to my question," says Newt. "What do you think happened next?"

"Well, it's clear that he had some firm views about the Jews and their relationship to their ancestral home," says Joe, before anyone has a chance to respond. He immediately looks at Jax, who says nothing. She is clearly bursting to say something but is perceptive enough to keep schtum for now. Newt looks at her and nods gently at her. He speaks.

"It may surprise you to know – especially as history seems to have overlooked this completely – that Edward Mitford completely prefigured the Balfour Declaration of seventy years later."

He is met by silence.

"Can you explain this?" asks Jax, trying her best to seem unconvinced and disinterested. Newt complies.

"The Balfour Declaration ... now this is something that we will discuss ... eventually, Jax ... but for now let's just see it as a British promise in 1917 to the Jews to facilitate their return to the place of their ancestral birth ... the land known now as Israel and the 'occupied territories' though – to be accurate – also including the Land of Jordan."

He continues.

"What he proposed to the British Government, in the 1850s, was a two-point plan. Firstly, that there should be the re-establishment of the Jewish nation in Palestine, protected by Great Britain. Secondly, that, when the new nation was of sufficient maturity, Britain would withdraw."

"Of course, there would be nothing in it for the British then?" says Jax, sarcastically.

"Alas you are correct. At that time it would help restore Britain as a key player in the Middle East and also help her in their communications with India and the East."

"So no different to the manoeuvrings behind Balfour then?" adds Jax.

"But I do believe there was a difference here," says Newt. "I am convinced that Mitford primarily was motivated personally by the plight of the Jews as he saw it."

"So you say."

"I agree and disagree," says Joe. "I also believe he had good intentions but tend to agree with Jax – God help me – that Britain did not act very honourably after producing the Balfour Declaration."

"Well that's a surprise, professor," exclaims Jax. "We actually agree on something."

"Progress, indeed," exclaims Newt, an actual smile on his face. "For the benefit of the other two, let's sit back and see exactly what Britain did to mess up the Middle East."

A holo-bubble scene explodes into life in front of them.

Chapter eight

A simple map of the region appears. It covers the land now known as Israel and the 'occupied territories', including Gaza and the Golan Heights, but also includes Jordan, east of the Jordan River. Across it is the word, *Palestine*, with *Southern Syria* in brackets below it. An authoritative but flat voice speaks.

'*Let's go back to a vital decade – the second decade of the 20th century to the area known as Palestine, or Southern Syria. There was much immigration to this area at the time, by Jews and Arabs. Perhaps if left in peace we wouldn't be in the mess we are now in. However, Europeans, mostly the British, had their eyes on this territory.*'

The map is now accompanied by two figures in conversation, an Arab in full desert garb and a formal-looking English diplomat.

'*In 1916, while the Turkish landlords had taken the side of Germany in the First World War, two men started to correspond. The Sharif of Mecca, Hussein bin Ali of the Hashemite family was a real mover and shaker in the Arab world at that time and no friend of the Turks. He was targeted by the British who saw him as an ally against the Turks. Sir Henry McMahon was a British High Commissioner in Egypt and in a series of letters to the Sharif, he encouraged the Arabs to revolt and thus hamper the Ottoman Empire that controlled the land. A promise was made ... if the Arabs would revolt against their Turkish masters ... the UK would recognize Arab Independence, though significantly no specific mention was made of Palestine in this secret agreement.*'

We now see an actual famous scene from Lawrence of Arabia, of Omar Sharif riding out of the desert to meet Lawrence.

'*This Arab Revolt was made famous by the activities of*

Lawrence of Arabia who came to their aid fighting alongside Emir Faisal. So, this was a promise made to the Arabs – the first promise.'

Jax interrupts.

"Told you! The British! I'm so ashamed of our colonial past."

"So you keep saying," mutters Joe. "Though, as I said … you do have a point here."

Newt looks from one to the other and grins. *I wonder how long this is going to last?*

Some new scenes are overlaid over the map. We see two very European figures appearing, a dashing young Englishman in uniform and a smart Frenchman with the obligatory flamboyant moustache. The voice continues.

'It's a shame the British never mentioned this agreement to the French who also had major interests in the region. They soon put that right with more secret negotiations with not just the French, but also with the Russians. The Sykes-Picot proposal of 1916 was a secret agreement between the governments of the United Kingdom and France and also with Imperial Russia. It was a plan to carve up the land, when the war with the Germans and the Turks was won.'

"Did I tell you I hate the French too?" remarks Jax.

"And the Russians? They were part of the story too," offers Joe. She doesn't answer him.

The map expands and is annotated accordingly, as the voice progresses.

'The Europeans carved up the whole area, from the coastal strip between the Mediterranean Sea and the River Jordan, also Jordan, Southern Iraq and a small area including the ports of Haifa and Acre, to allow access to the Mediterranean. France was allocated control of Southeastern Turkey, Northern Iraq, Syria and Lebanon. Russia was to get Constantinople, the Turkish

Straits and the Armenian areas.'

Jax can't hold back. "Colonialism at its very worst!" Joe nods but says nothing. Newt switches off the display and speaks.

"Which brings us to the Balfour Declaration."

"Wondered when we were going to get to that hoary old chestnut", sneers Jax, ready for a fight that she had evidently planned for.

"Well, I'm up for it," says Joe, with a surprising confidence. If he had loose sleeves on his starched and rigid suit he would be rolling them up now, ready for a fight. Newt exhales dramatically and repeats the word.

"Balfour."

"What is … this?" asks Mo, unaware of the controversies invoked by that single word.

"OK. Let us watch and listen … then we can debate."

Newt re-activates the holo-bubble.

We see the full letter, addressed to Lord Rothschild, the acknowledged leader of the Jewish community containing the Balfour Declaration, with some mug shots of the main players in the story, including Lord Balfour, Chaim Weizmann and Rothschild himself.

The soundtrack continues.

'This piece of paper gave official British recognition of the need for a Jewish homeland in Palestine. Arthur James Balfour was the British prime minister in 1902. He wasn't very good at the job and was replaced in 1905 but bounced back when he became foreign secretary during the First World War. Politically, he had made friends with many influential Jews such as Theodore Herzl, the first Zionist. But his most significant friendship though was with Chaim Weizmann, the Jewish chemist.'

When they met in 1914, Balfour stated that the Jewish question would remain insoluble until either the Jews here in Britain became entirely assimilated or there was a normal Jewish community in Palestine. In the meantime, Uganda was offered as a possible homeland for the Jews. This was rejected. It is said that Balfour asked Weizmann why the Jews were so hung up on Palestine. Weizmann responded by asking why the British were hung up on London. Balfour replied that the British currently had London but the Jews did not have Jerusalem. Weizmann then replied 'We had Jerusalem when London was a swamp!' That was enough to persuade Balfour to begin to argue for Palestine for the Jews.

The focus changes to a notice pinned up on a Scout hut.

The following is the content of a notice that would have appeared on the walls of classrooms and Scout Huts during World War One.

'Collecting groups are being organized in your district. Groups of scholars and Boy Scouts are being organized to collect conkers. Receiving depots are being opened in most districts. All schools are involved. Boy Scout leaders will advise you of the nearest depot where seven and six per hundredweight is being paid for immediate delivery of the chestnuts without the outer green husks. This collection is invaluable for war work and is very urgent. Please encourage it.'

So the question arises as to why the War Department urgently needed conkers as the First World War progressed. Chaim Weizmann made himself invaluable to the British war effort through his discovery of a process to produce synthetic acetone - a chemical needed to make cordite, a naval explosive - he cleverly discovered a process that made acetone from conkers and that's how school kids did their bit for the war effort. He was rewarded with the Balfour Declaration.

A map of the area re-appears, containing the area now covering both Israel and Jordan.

Here are the words:

"Lord Rothschild, I have much pleasure in conveying to you on *behalf of His Majesty's government the following Declaration of sympathy with Jewish Zionist aspirations which has been submitted to and approved by the cabinet. His Majesty's government views with favour the establishment in Palestine of a national home for the Jewish people and will use their best endeavours to facilitate the achievement of this object, it being clearly understood that nothing shall be done which may prejudice the civil and religious rights of existing non-Jewish communities in Palestine or the rights and political status enjoyed by Jews in any other country. I would be grateful if you would bring this declaration to the knowledge of the Zionist Federation. Yours sincerely, Arthur James Balfour."*

Jax raises her hand to speak. Newt nods.

"So much that is wrong there!"

"I object", says Joe immediately, without even giving her a chance to expand. She ignores him.

"What right did the British have to make such a promise, especially after their promises to both the Arabs and the French and Russians? They even hedged their bets and made promises to the Turks, in case they actually won the war! Outrageous!"

"With you on everything except … the first point," responds Joe. "The British were acting purely out of Christian love for the Jews, who had suffered so much and desperately needed a place of refuge."

"So, you've forgotten the conkers? Would they have made promises if it weren't about the conkers?"

"It's never about the conkers."

"Never about the conkers? What on earth are you saying?"

"The conkers were irrelevant. The British Christian establishment had been canvassing for a Jewish homeland for a century by then. We heard about Edward Mitford earlier …"

"… Oh yes, your beloved ancestor who you've only just

heard about."

"True … but nevertheless he could see even then, just on humanitarian and practical grounds, the need for the Jews to return to their ancestral home."

"Shame the land was already full up."

"No, it wasn't. You heard that Mitford account earlier …"

"Oh yes, your glorious colonial great grandfather thrice removed."

"Listen, he wasn't the only witness. Plenty of explorers and visitors speak of the contrary. Mark Twain …"

"… Mark Twain, Mark Twain. You Zionists always bring up the same quote, as if it were the only thing he wrote!"

"… A desolate country given over wholly to weeds... we never saw a human being on the whole route...."

"We really don't need to hear from Mark Twain, professor. He wasn't particularly impressed with Greece either …"

"OK. How about … Sir John Dawson, 1888, 'No national union, no national spirit …' De Lamartine in 1835, 'No living object, no living sound, we found the same void …'

"Oh stop reading from your little bit of paper. It's just words."

"These are not just words, they are history, madam!"

Newt had had enough and put a halt to it, turning the holo-bubble back on, with the remark, "We'll get back to Balfour later. But this is also important."

We see a picture of an Arab and a Jew, together, looking comfortable and at ease with each other. The voice continues.

'Here were a Jew and an Arab … and they actually got along with each other. The Jew was Chaim Weizmann and the Arab was Emir Faisal, the son of the Sharif of Mecca - the Hashemite who had made secret agreements with the British just a few years earlier. They met at the end of 1918. The interpreter was Lawrence of Arabia and the first thing they did was dismiss the Sykes-Picot

agreement that carved up the Middle East between Britain, France and Russia. Then Weizmann talked about the rights of Jews to live in Palestine under British trusteeship, allowing for up to 5 million Jews to immigrate, with Arabs looked after and Muslim holy places respected as the basis for the agreement. Faisal agreed and it was duly signed off.'

"Can't say I ever heard of that one," says Joe. "Sounded like a good deal though. Obviously, something got in the way of it."

"Perhaps the needs of the Arabs?" suggests Jax.

"No," says Newt. "The Europeans got greedy." The voice continues.

What they didn't allow for was the meddling of the European Colonial Powers who sought their reward for removing the Ottoman Turks. The British and the French thwarted any plans for an independent Arab Middle East by carving it up to suit themselves!

Newt stops the holo-bubble and speaks.

"We will return to this later, but it is clear that, in the current conflict, Britain and France have a lot to answer for!"

Jax starts to speak but Newt stops her.

"One last thing on this. I want to read out a letter from Mark Sykes, the British man partly responsible for these manoeuvrings. It was a letter he wrote to Emir Faisal at that time. 'I know that the Arabs despise, condemn and hate the Jews but passion is the ruin of princes and peoples. Those who have persecuted or condemned the Jews could tell you the tale of the Empire of Spain in the old days and the Empire of Russian in our time, that show the road of ruin that Jewish persecution leads to. You say to yourself, what is this race, despised rejected, abhorred, that cannot fight, that has no home and is no Nation! Oh, Faisal, I can read your heart and your thoughts and there are counsellors around you who will whisper similar things in your ear. I believe I speak the truth when I say that this race, despised and weak is universal, is all powerful and cannot be put down!"

"Yay, Jews!" mutters Abi with a clenched fist, but with mischief in her eyes.

"Yay, Palestinians," responds Mo in like manner. They smile at each other briefly.

Newt looks at them, also with a smile and says, "Thank you for your considered opinion, you two! ..."

Before he could say more, Jax interrupts.

"... back to Balfour. It's a nonsense. The Brits broke their promises to the Arabs and even their own partners, the French ..."

"... they also broke their promises to the Jews ..." adds Joe, quickly.

"So you say ... but we still have this ... Balfour thing!"

"Yes ... but it was never fully implemented ... as you well know! Also ... just to show you that the British weren't as one-sided then as you insist ... when Allenby rode into Jerusalem, having taken it from the Turks, who does he hand the keys of the city to? To the Arabs! And that one act led to the rise of one of the worst Jew haters in history ..."

Before anyone can respond, there's the sound of music. Not Julie Andrews galivanting around an Austrian hill, but the rising chords of a tune, familiar to all of them.

Chapter nine

It is *'Yester-Me, Yester-You, Yesterday,'* the 1969 hit from Stevie Wonder. Apart from Newt, every person has a look of incredulity on their faces. This would have been very surprising to an outsider, but not to Newt. He knew that this particular song was significant, for every person here for very different reasons.

"Thought this would grab your attention," he says, looking at them all in turn. The volume is turned down to just play in the background.

They are speechless.

"Who's first?"

Jax, unsurprisingly, is the first to speak.

"Well, Newt. If you're going to play one song to shut me up ... then you've picked the right one."

"Why is that, Jax?"

"Stevie Wonder ... I was in love with the boy. 'Little' Stevie Wonder they called him at the time. He was still a teenager then. I was really into Civil Rights, more Malcolm X than Martin Luther King but, for me, to see this black kid make it in the 'white' world. It was fantastic. This is the song that I'll always associate with him. Perhaps it was because we were more or less the same age. Great memories."

"And you, Joe?"

"How could you have known this? Are there no secrets anymore? Can't believe you would have known that ... I was a secret Tamla Motown listener in the day and Stevie Wonder in particular and this one ... my personal favourite. It just made me feel good. Goodness ... I don't think I've heard it since ... this is weird ..."

"Just live in the moment, Joe", says Newt. "You're overthinking. Just enjoy the memory."

There's a silence as there are two more stories to tell, surely the most intriguing ones. Abi is the first to speak.

"When that song first started playing I really thought I was imagining it. I could hear my mama's voice, not this ... Stevie Wonder. Who is he, anyway? This is mama's song, the song she sang to me every night to get me off to sleep. Always in English, my mama was from the USA you know. The words ... they were a comfort to me ... though I think she may have changed them slightly. We kids ... those were frightening times ... the second intifada ... many Jews killed by suicide bombers ... 'what happened to the world we knew, when we would dream and scheme ... but peace is not far away ... Yester-me, Yester-you, Yesterday' ... she would point to herself, then to me ..."

Her voice cracks a bit and then she stops suddenly. After a few seconds she looks over to Mo.

"And you?"

Mo is also slow to speak. His words come out haltingly.

"My grandfather. I spoke of him earlier. He loved music. All music. Not just Arabic and Palestinian music, but Western music too. The Beatles, Simon and Garfunkel and ... the Strolling ... Rolling Stones. He had one of those old record players, with the record turning round and round in a small box and a terrible tinny sound. He only had a few records though. But this was one of them ... Stevie Wonder ... and he played it over and over and over ... I grew to hate it, but now it reminds me of him ... and that is a good thing, no?

This brings a poignant smile to the others. Newt speaks.

"So, Ladies and Gentlemen, you have more in common than you realise."

The music returns to full volume. Jax immediately gets out of her seat and starts dancing ... of sorts. It is clearly a forgotten art for her. Still, considering the stifling atmosphere, doing so is probably very therapeutic and releasing for her. She dances jerkily and with full abandon, totally in her own world. She is smiling and her eyes are closed. She is in a different place, probably a far nicer place. It is awkward for the others, though.

Joe taps his fingers on his desk. That's probably the limit of his self-expression at this moment. Abi sits eyes closed soaking it in and Mo appears unaffected by the music but seems to be dealing with things inwardly. Newt watches them all and makes notes. About half-way through the song Abi leaves her seat and starts swaying gently and elegantly to the music without moving from her spot in front of her desk. The two ladies, each in their own space, in their own worlds. The two men, sitting there, a trifle embarrassed. More than once they glance at each other as if to say, *'yes, I don't know what to do either.'* Then the music fades out and the ladies return to their seats.

"What was the purpose of this, Newt?" asks Joe. "This was all very contrived, there must have been a reason for it. I feel ... manipulated."

"Right ... fess up, man!" agrees Jax.

Newt shrugs his shoulders. "Just thought I'd provide some light relief. It was getting a bit heavy, Jax and it looked like you were about to go on a rant ..."

"... was I? Well, perhaps I can find a new one coming on. Rent-a-rant, that's me! Is that a full argument you want? Quoting from Monty Python, by the way. Satire from the Sixties, in case you didn't know."

"No, I apologise, Jax. I was trying to be facetious. Not very good at it," replies Newt, his voice softer and tinged with contrition. "It all came up in my research. I was amazed to discover how this ... one song ... featured so heavily in all of your stories."

"But how were you to know?" asks Abi. "This was a private memory ... just me and my mother."

"I'm a good researcher."

She is not convinced and shows it by a Hebrew phrase whispered under her breath, probably not one that could be repeated here. Newt is momentarily destabilised, feeling that there is every possibility of losing them, so he acts quickly and reactivates the holo-bubble.

The voice soundtrack returns. Pictures show a group of men huddled together on the steps of an impressive building.

It is 1920 and the Europeans had convened a conference at San Remo in Italy to make sense of all the promises the British made in the previous decade. By this time Emir Faisal had fallen out with the Europeans and the British were losing sympathy for the Jews ... and also the Arabs in places like Jerusalem were starting to revolt, frightened at the thought of a massive influx of Jews. David Lloyd George represented the Brits. Faisal wasn't there and Weizmann came in a dispirited mood, particularly as the issue of Palestine was relatively low on the agenda. Syria had already been created as a new nation with Palestine as a province of South Syria. Emir Faisal had been put in charge before the French kicked him out and decided to rule the place directly. Also they decided to incorporate the Balfour Declaration and produce what was known as the Palestinian Mandate which passed over to Britain to govern there as the British Mandate.

So the declaration gave birth to this mandate for Palestine, which was a historical League of Nations document that laid down the Jewish legal right to settle anywhere in Western Palestine, the area between the Jordan River and the Mediterranean ... but not the whole territory indicated by the Balfour Declaration as it never included the area to the east of the Jordan River.

In summary, Britain made three Promises ... to the Arabs, to the French and the Russians and to the Jews. The McMahon-Hussein correspondence with the Arabs, the Sykes-Picot proposal with the French and the Russians and the Balfour Declaration to the Jews.

"Imperialist bastards," growls Jax, clearly incensed. "This is our country, professor. Aren't you ashamed?"

"Yes, frankly I am, for what they did a century ago. Different times, though", responds Joe.

"And things are different now? We have inherited a terrible legacy and it is our duty to put it right."

"Oh yes? How do you propose we do that?"

"Give the Palestinians what was promised to them."

"And what about giving the Jews what was promised to them?" replies Joe. "At San Remo, they lopped off 78% of what they had promised and created Jordan, or 'Transjordan' as they called it then and gave it to the Arabs. So, in fact, the Arabs received more than the Jews ... and they still weren't happy! And do you know who was responsible for that decision?"

"No, but I'm sure you're going to tell us, professor."

"Winston Churchill was the one who came up with the plan ... and Lord Balfour himself who announced it!"

"So, he came clean?"

"No ... just doing what he was told to do by his political master."

"Bah, politics!"

"Bah, indeed!"

Newt interrupts.

"Joe is correct, Jax. Jordan was given to Abdullah, the first son of the Sharif of Mecca. And Iraq was given to his other son, Faisal."

"Yes, but what about the Palestinians?" responds Jax.

There's a lull before Newt declares, "Time for a refreshment break. Stretch your legs, Ladies and Gentlemen and we'll resume in twenty minutes." As if by magic, the tables appear from below, laden with hot and cold drinks and a variety of sweets and cakes to suit all the palettes represented here.

Chapter ten

Two carrot sticks hit the same bowl of hummus at the same time. Accidentally of course. And embarrassingly, most definitely. The offending veggies belonged to Mo and Abi. Both hands immediately retract as their owners fix their eyes on each other properly for the first time.

"S ... Sorry," babbles Mo. "You first, um, Abi."

She complies, expressionless and re-dips her carrot, scooping out a huge dollop of hummus and thrusting it into her mouth in a single action.

"Impressive", he says, intent on receiving even some sort of response from her. "You're a seasoned hummus-eater I see."

He smiles with both his mouth and his eyes. She curls her lips slightly, but her eyes remain detached. In fact she now has her eyes fixed on the cacik bowl, the Turkish yoghurt and cucumber. He is undaunted and follows her with his carrot stick, beating her to the cacik and showing his dexterity too.

"We are both ... masters of the dip", he boasts, smiling and dripping the yoghurt down his lip. He must have seemed faintly comical as Abi finally breaks into a grin. But she stops herself and walks away, her eyes now on the cold meats. He follows her.

"You can't escape, you know? We are trapped together here," he says.

"Why are you following me?"

"How can I be following you? We've been trapped in this room together for hours already. I'm just being ... friendly."

She offers her hand to him and gives a brief, ironic curtsy, then speaks sarcastically in a mock English accent.

"Good day. My name is Abi. Nice to know you. Have you had a good day?"

She looks away and grabs some salt beef, places it on her plate with a pickle and starts to make a sandwich with some rye bread. He is a little put out.

"Have I offended you in any way, Abi ... or ...?"

He pauses and this attracts her attention.

"... is my presence here an offence to you?" He points to himself.

She could see where this was going and, in that moment, lowers her defences and allows her true self to break free. Some tiny barrier within her has been breached and she is secretly glad because he really does seem like a pleasant boy, not what she was expecting, not the 'sly Arab' her friends told her to expect.

"No ..." she says, putting the plate down. "It's just me ... I'm a sabra. Hard on the outside ... but soft on the ..."

"Really?"

"Oh yes. I'm as soft as they come. If you want 'hard' you should meet my room mates."

"Are they pretty?" He has a gleam in his eye.

"I suppose so ... if you like gay men."

He looks shocked and she laughs. She finds his innocence quite endearing, but she isn't going to show it yet, she still feels the need to keep some distance. She sits down, her plate on her lap. He pulls up a chair next to her, ignoring his food. She carries on eating as he talks.

"This is a strange place, isn't it?" says Mo.

"Strange place, strange people. I'm not comfortable with ... old people."

"I'm OK with them generally – I have a large family – but these two ... well ... I'm not sure."

"Then perhaps we two should stick together, then."

"Agree."

They shake hands. Mo feels emboldened enough to ask

a personal question.

"Just one question, Abi. You don't have to answer it, but I feel compelled to ask it anyway."

"Go on … spit it out."

He hesitates, unused to her directness.

"When you spoke earlier about your mother singing that song to get you to sleep … I detected a … sadness there. Was there a …"

"That's it!" she declares, standing up, dropping her plate to the table and walking back to her desk. Mo is startled and thinks about saying something then looks over to Newt, who has been observing them. Newt raises his hand to stop him and Mo nods in compliance. He grabs an egg sandwich and returns to his desk too, his tail between his legs.

After a few minutes, mostly spent in silence, Newt calls the meeting back to order.

"I hope the spread was satisfactory."

"Yes it was … most satisfactory," says Joe, who had again only made a brief visit to the table and seems to have spent most of the break in the toilet cubicle. Everyone is too polite to ask if there were problems in the 'plumbing department', it's not the sort of thing an English gentleman feels comfortable discussing, of course. Jax has been just sitting there, seemingly out of sorts. No doubt getting ready to cross swords in the next session! Newt continues.

"Just to finish this history lesson, just one more short sequence." He turns on the holo-bubble. The voice starts up.

'So, the mandate gave Western Palestine as a home for the Jews, rather than all of the area promised by the Balfour Declaration. Article 25 of the Palestinian mandate gave a bit of leeway for the British to do what they liked over the area to the east of the River Jordan.

They weren't obliged to offer that to the Jews too so they didn't, instead they gave away 78% of the land through to one of the sons of the Sharif of Mecca. This was Abdullah the first king Hussein of Transjordan and Iraq was given to his other brother Faisal. In this way the McMahon-Hussein correspondence was honoured within the framework of the Sykes-Picot proposal by diluting the Balfour Declaration.

In this way Palestine was broken up into two regions divided by the River Jordan,

Transjordan ruled by the Hashemite King Abdullah in the East and Palestine to

the West. The latter becomes the British mandate for Palestine, a legal commission for the administration of Palestine or, rather, west Palestine as instigated by the San Remo conference and the League of Nations.'

It stops abruptly and Newt speaks.

"That's enough information for now. A bit of a necessary history lesson I think, to show how European dabbling in the Middle East created so many problems that are still playing out through to this day."

"How do you mean, sir. I don't understand?" says Mo, genuine confusion plastered over his face.

"The British made three promises that it couldn't possibly keep – to the French, the Arabs and the Jews. All promises were responses ... for the Sharif of Mecca instigating the Arab revolt against the Turk, to drive them out of the Middle East; to the Jews for helping them in their war effort and to the French, because they were supposedly friends. They couldn't keep all three happy, so they fudged it. They carved up the Middle East and created all of the nations that you see there today. They gave Palestine to the Jews, Syria to the French and Iraq and Jordan to the Arabs. But they kept a tight hold on things, to protect their own interests, mainly Arab oil and a safe passage to their far eastern colonies. None of this was really to benefit anyone apart from themselves."

"Pretty harsh," says Joe, "but mostly true."

"Vindicated!" growls Jax. "So, now you all agree with me?"

"Not quite," responds Joe. "They may have been the architects of the problems, but the main problem was, and is, something very different."

"Which is?" says Newt.

"Palestine."

There's a silence while they all draw breath. The elephant in the room is awakened and Jax is the first to respond.

"About time we mentioned this. Surely it's the key issue here?" says Jax.

"Why should that be?" responds Joe.

"Because stolen Palestinian land is at the heart of the issue ... it's why we're here?"

"Is it? Have you forgotten what Newt just told us? The 'Palestinians' were given land – over three times more land that the Jews were offered ... Jordan, or Transjordan as it was then, or Eastern Palestine according to the Mandate. If they had taken it, there would be no problem now."

"What you mean just force them out their homes, just to let the Jews in?"

"Yes, probably the shortest migration in history! They would have only travelled a few miles! Think of the Jews kicked out of their ancestral homes in the Arab countries at that time ... over 800,000 of them. We don't hear of them, do we? They lost everything, had to leave in a heartbeat in 1948! And what about the 18 million Hindus and Muslims who moved home in India at that time?"

Jax is uncharacteristically silent. Newt speaks.

"This is a good time to summarise, I think, to get a realistic perspective of the situation. We start with this small strip of land – the size of Wales - once populated by the Jews of old but conquered again and again, by the Greeks, the Romans, the Crusaders and, finally, by the Ottoman Turks. We know that the Turks had allowed it to go to ruin, there are so many eyewitness accounts of this and we've already heard some of them. People were living in the land, yes. Mainly poor land workers. There were Jews, but not too many, until they started arriving later in the Nineteenth Century, fleeing the pogroms in Eastern Europe. There were also some rich Arab families dotted around, but most of the land was owned by absentee Turkish landlords. When the Jews arrived in larger numbers, bought tracts of land legally from the Turks, organised themselves into communities and started to work on the land to make it habitable, other Arabs started to arrive, from Egypt and such places, to work alongside them ... in peace. The Hope Simpson Report acknowledged in 1930 that there was an "uncontrolled influx of illegal immigrants from Egypt, Transjordan and Syria" ..."

"... and you know all this for sure?" says Jax.

"Oh yes. I am a good researcher," is the response. Newt continues.

"At that time there was no real Palestinian identity. The Arabs saw themselves as living in Southern Syria, the legal designation for that region ..."

"... Palestinians have a rich history ..." insists Jax.

"I can vouch for that," adds Mo. "My family ..."

"I am not saying that no people were living in the land," says Newt. "It's just that they were just clumps of people dotted around. There was no organisation, no corporate identity, no government ... they were a people under Turkish subjugation."

"Yes, times were certainly hard for my family" admits Mo. "The Turks were harsh and uncaring."

Jax has no answer. It seems that her knowledge of those times is a bit patchy. Joe decides to 'stick his oar in', reading from notes.

"According to his memoirs, King Abdullah of Jordan wrote '... the Arabs are as prodigal in selling their land as they are in useless wailing and weeping'". Mo glares at him.

"Yes, Joe, "says Newt. "But not helpful." He continues.

"Palestinian identity for the Arabs at that time was simply not a 'thing'. In fact, in the first half of the Twentieth Century, it was the Jews who actually identified as 'Palestinians'. Hence the newspaper, 'The Palestine Post', now called the Jerusalem Post and there's a picture circulating of the 'Palestine Symphony Orchestra' of the time. All Jewish."

"I feel that I'm losing the thread here," says Jax. "Are you manipulating me, Newt?"

"Certainly not. Just the facts, just the facts. As I said earlier, it could have been so different after the San Remo conference. The compromise offered could have solved everything. But then ... the trouble really began. In 1929."

Chapter eleven

"It is time to return to some eye-witness accounts ... Abi, I hope this will not be too difficult." Concern is immediately painted on her face as she stares intently forward, not knowing what to expect.

We see a scene in Jerusalem Old City, in the narrow corridor that faced the Wailing Wall. A group of around 300 young Jewish men and women have arrived. They are boisterous, carry the blue and white Star of David flag and sing the *Hatikvah* (the hope). Some are chanting "The wall is ours ... we will sacrifice all for the Western Wall." This may have been youthful exuberance, but it was to have dire consequences. A voice-over speaks.

'It is August 1929, the 9th of Av, a particularly solemn day in the Jewish calendar. These young Jews are excited at being at the holiest site in Judaism. Someone else is excited too as he watches from the window of his home. This is Haj Amin al-Husseini, the Grand Mufti of Jerusalem. He is happy as he now has a pretext for indulging his most abiding impulse, his total hatred for the Jewish people.'

The focus moves to the Grand Mufti, who now sits at his desk, dictating a letter to his secretary.

"This needs to be sent out to every community as soon as you can. Are you ready with your pen?"

"Yes, your eminence."

"The Jews are attacking our holy mosque, Al-Aqsa in Jerusalem. They have invaded our neighbourhoods, raped our women and cursed The Prophet. We must take arms now and rid our land finally of this accursed race."

His secretary raises his eyebrows as he knows this is a falsehood. Still, the Grand Mufti is not to be disrespected. So he writes down the words, regardless, and shuffles off to get them printed and distributed.

'The Grand Mufti was an Islamist who believed in direct action. For him, the issue was never the land of Palestine, it was the Jews in the land. Total annihilation of the Jews was all he would contemplate. The Hitler of the Arab world, he eventually moved to Nazi Germany and became a friend of Hitler. The first riot he instigated, with the death of five Jews, was in Jerusalem and was actually a few days before the San Remo conference. His actions today are going to have terrible consequences. It has been said that these are the actions that initially ignited the Israel-Palestinian crisis itself ... the first Jew killed as a result of this action was on the road leading out of Jerusalem. Many are to follow.'

Some text appears. 'The town of Hebron, soon afterwards.'

Abi gasps. She knows the story that is about to unfold. It is the story of her family, on her father's side.

We are in a meeting room of the Anglo-Palestine bank in Hebron. Two young men arrive, Aharan Cohen and Saadia Kirscenboim, from the Haganah (early IDF) to meet a group of town dignitaries, the bank manager himself, as well as elders and the chief rabbis Slonim and Franco.

"You must listen to us," Cohen implores. "There is an Arab mob baying for your blood."

"Don't be ridiculous, the Arabs here are our friends", says Slonim.

"Believe us, there is a riot coming ... you must either allow us to protect you – we can bring more men ... or you must leave immediately all of you."

The dignitaries are unimpressed, possibly because of the age difference between them and these 'young upstarts'.

"Neither this nor that is necessary" says Eliezer, a tall, imposing dignitary. The others nod.

"The Arabs here are our friends," insists Slonim. "No harm will come to the Jews of Hebron."

The two leave, exasperated. We see Cohen enter a small house, where he changes into Arab gear, then walks over to the home of Sheikh Marka, one of the hostile Arab leaders. Marka is speaking to a small group of Arabs. They think Cohen is one of them so they ignore him.

"The Jews are attempting to seize Al-Aqsa," growls Marka. "I have heard from the Grand Mufti. Their next target is the Ibrahami mosque here in Hebron. The Jews here will betray us ... unless we slaughter them first!"

Cohen leaves and returns to the bank, having changed his clothes again. The group are still there. He barges in.

"I have just heard it from their own lips, Sheikh Marka himself ... they plan to kill you all. Please allow the Haganah to come and protect you."

Slonim points to an elderly Sheikh in the corner of the room, who speaks.

"Even if all the Jews in Palestine are killed, not a hair will fall from the head of a Jew in Hebron."

Cohen leaves in frustration and Rabbi Slonim follows him. They meet up with a small group of Haganah fighters, who follow them into the Rabbi's house.

"If there was a need for men like you I would ask for them", insists the Rabbi. "The Arabs won't raise a hand against us. We have lived with them for years; they are our friends."

Shortly there is a knock on the door. An English policeman is there. Slonim greets him.

This is Raymond Cafferata, the British chief of Police. He is young and inexperienced. He knows only a few people in Hebron. He has a force of 33 policemen, all but one is Arab.

"Who are these?" asks Cafferata.

"We are hikers" says Cohen.

"I know who you are – Haganah. Please go back to Jerusalem,

we don't need you here."

He holds the door open and they leave, their faces full of sorrow. There is a flash of doubt and fear on Slonim's face.

We see the other rabbi, Franco, in an Arab shop. The shopkeeper is friendly to him and gives him a leaflet. It is one of those printed by The Grand Mufti. Franco reads it and looks worried. Two Jewish ladies notice him from outside and rush into the shop.

"Rabbi, rabbi, we have just overheard something awful from some of the Arab market traders … they didn't realise I understand their language … awful, so awful …"

"Go on," says Franco, frustrated.

"These are his words … oh … I just can't speak them. Shifra, you tell him."

"This Saturday … every one of us will have a Jewish woman … they will have their Sabbath but we will have the pleasure."

"And this is from the man I have bought fruit from for years … Ali's his name I think … he's my friend … or so I thought …"

The ladies collapse into sobs.

The two Rabbis meet the district governor, Abdullah Kardous, an Arab Christian, who worked for the British.

We see them meet in a plush office.

"The Arabs are preparing to attack us," says Franco.

"And there are very few police here to protect us," adds Slonim.

"Don't worry yourself," Kardous assures them. "The British government knows what to do."

"And if they attack? Where are the policemen?"

"If it comes to that … we will protect you …"

None of the three look particularly convinced. Kardous is particularly worried. Perhaps he knows more than he is admitting to?

Outside the Ibrahami mosque, a preacher addresses a mob leaving the mosque. They are armed with clubs, sticks and daggers.

"The Jews have killed a thousand Arabs in Jerusalem," he shouts. "They have taken the Wailing Wall and the Al-Aqsa, soon *they will be here to take our holy places!"*

Rabbi Franco is looking out of the window of his home in the Jewish quarter. Sheikh Marka is addressing a small, armed and emotional crowd.

"Allah and the Prophet Muhammed are calling on you to avenge the blood of your brethren that has been shed in Jerusalem ... slaughter the Jews."

The crowd begins to move away and further into the Jewish quarter. We hear chanting and, very soon, screams as well.

Rabbi Slonim looks out of his window and sees the mob approaching. It is clear that they have already begun the massacre and have tasted blood. He is sad to see some of his Arab neighbours leaving their houses and joining the mob. He leaves his house and tries to stop them and gets pelted with stones. Police chief Cafferata appears on a horse, with four Arab policemen, also mounted.

"Thank goodness," exclaims Slonim. "Will you help us now, police chief Cafferata?"

Incredibly Cafferata confronts Slonim.

"Go home, old man. You are making things worse here."

The policemen gesture for the Rabbi to go back. More stones are thrown at him and he is now physically attacked, while Cafferata looks on. An irate Jewish lady storms out of her house to help. She shouts at the policeman.

"This is the Chief Rabbi. Aren't you going to help him?"

"Go inside, both of you ... You Jews are to blame for all of this."

Slonim looks up at him in disbelief.

In the next scene Eliezer, the dignitary, looking bloodied, arrives at the office of Kardous, the district governor.

"You must take charge," he shouts. "A yeshiva student has been killed. Another has been stabbed in the back. Nearly every window of Jewish homes are shattered."

"Stay in your homes and don't go outside ... and you won't get hurt."

"And what if they come into our homes ... district governor ... eh?"

There is no answer.

Cafferata is at his desk on his phone. He makes a phone call.

"We need reinforcements here … it is getting out of hand … what do you mean no-one can be spared … from Jerusalem … Jaffa … oh, so you can send some from Gaza? … When are they available? We need them now!"

He slams his phone down. He is shaking. He is evidently very weak and helpless, rather than an evil person. He is totally out of his depth.

All goes black. There is a faint sound of a slow heartbeat. The atmosphere is dark and foreboding. A sign appears. 'Saturday August 24th the next day.'

A family cowers in a small, dingy stone-walled house. The father has his back to the door, while the mother kneels in the opposite corner, her two small children shaking either side of her. There are screams, apparently coming from the house next door. Suddenly there is a frantic pounding on the door. The pattern of the knocks must be familiar as the father opens the door and a scrawny young man stumbles in. He is bleeding from a head wound.

"They are going from house to house … with their clubs and knives", he says, breathlessly, before sinking to his knees.

"Who?" cries the father.

"The Arabs. They have lost their minds … they are baying for Jewish blood, Mordechai."

He covers his face with his hands, smearing blood all over and weeps.

"But the British … they protect us … where are they?"

"Why is this happening?" cries the mother. There is no answer.

Mordechai starts to gather furniture, piling it against the door. Tables and chairs, all are thrown into a heap to create a barricade. He then grabs the knife that he had just used to cut up the chicken, holding it tightly.

"I am a scholar, not a fighter" he mutters. His hand is shaking.

"Every life is precious, Miriam ... I will do what is necessary."
He waits.

*He will kill if it comes to it, though deep down he is not sure if
he is capable of such an act. You can see this on his face. There is
loud shuffling outside his house and unworldly yelping, the insistent
sound of bloodlust. The door is slowly pushed open. Mordechai
rushes forward, screaming, his knife thrust in front of him.*

*Everything goes black again. The heartbeat returns. We hear
a testimony, a young girl's voice.*

'We could hear the mob approaching, with their religious war-
cries and demonic chanting. It grew louder and louder and we
knew that ... very soon ... it would be our turn. Suddenly there was
a knock on the door ... we all jumped in shock ... a soft voice could
be heard ... 'do not be afraid' ... My father peered through a crack
in the door. It was our Arab neighbour, Abu-Eid Zeitun. He held
a stick and a sword hung from his belt. He had his brother and
son with him. They had worried faces and we knew we could trust
them. So, Father opened the door ... 'Come come' said Abu ... 'You
must be quick; they will be here very soon ... I have a cellar; I will
hide you there.' ... my parents and younger brothers followed them
out of the house ... I just held back a little, to gather some important
things ... we knew that our house would be looted of everything
valuable ... but ... but ... I took too long ...'

There is much commotion and sobbing, then silence.

'Now I am helpless. I am held down while my neighbours loot
my house and I thank God that there are good Muslims like Abu,
who has saved my family ... But, alas, too late for me. Another
neighbour, Attu ul-Zeer, stands over me. I have known him my
whole life. We have shared childhood adventures, even a shy kiss
behind the stables an eternity ago ... he now looms over me, his
face contorted in a spasm of evil intent. His intentions are clear ...
He violates me to the cheers of my other neighbours. I am blanking
this out with thoughts of my family and better times. He takes out

a knife ... I start reciting the martyr's prayer ...
    ... Sh'ma Yisrael, Adonai Elohay ...'

Everything goes black. You hear the Sh'ma sung by a cantor in the soundtrack's background. In the foreground is uncontrolled sobbing. Jax, Joe, Mo and, in particular, Abi, are bereft and their grief pours out unashamedly. Only Newt seems unaffected by this. A voice returns.

'Sixty-seven Jews lost their lives in Hebron, including twelve women and three children under the age of five. Of the dead, twenty-four were yeshiva students. They were killed by a mob of 3,000 (including boys as young as 8) from Hebron and surrounding villages, armed with swords, daggers, knives, hatchets, iron bars and wooden sticks. They were led by Sheikh Marka with the instruction, "in the name of Mufti Haj Amin al-Husseini, we inform you that the day has come to annihilate all the Jews, young and old, and take their women and property." Babies had heads smashed against the wall, many rabbis were tortured and castrated, wives and daughters were raped in front of their families, and fingers were severed. Among those killed were Eliezer the bank manager, killed by those he had helped for years.

But many Arabs were heroes that day. We heard of Abu-Eid Zeltun, but others, also, either confronted the mob or hid Jews in their homes. It was estimated that around two dozen Arab families risked their lives to save at least half of the Jews in Hebron.'

The display fades. Newt speaks.

"Hebron, 1929 ... not Southern Israel 2023. The same intention, though."

Abi has seen enough. Suddenly she leaves her desk and rushes out of the room without looking back, whimpering as she goes. Mo looks horrified and stands up to follow her, only to be stopped by a look from Newt.

"Her great grandfather's brother was one of the sixty-seven Jews killed in the Hebron massacre. He was just a child. He was beheaded."

"Why put her through that?" demands Mo, full of concern for this girl he barely knows but feels such empathy for.

"Life is cruel," answers Newt mechanically and surprisingly with very little sympathy in his voice. "It's just how it is. There is much cruelty in our story here and it is important that you all experience it fully ... only then can you understand each other."

"Poor girl," mutters Jax. Joe nods. There are tears in his eyes. Newt continues.

"This horrific episode was the climax of a decade of Arab riots. It all started after the talking ... at San Remo and the League of Nations ... stopped."

"But why?" asked Mo. "I don't understand."

"No need to feel guilty, Mo," says Newt. "Evil men have the power to create bad history. And, I'm afraid to say, one particular evil man bears much responsibility for this."

Joe nods his head, knowingly. "The Grand Mufti of Jerusalem. Remember when I said earlier that, by handing the keys of Jerusalem to the Arabs, the British set a process in motion that led to the rise of one of the worst Jew-haters in history? Well ... here's your man!"

"Correct. Full name, Amin al-Husseini. An absolute horror."

"Thought you're meant to be impartial?" says Jax.

"For him I will make an exception. Let's say ... here was a man with his own agenda, a hateful one."

"That's not my reading of the man," says Jax. "I see him as a freedom fighter."

"Just like Hamas are freedom fighters too, eh?" snarls Joe.

"Let's not go there ... yet," responds Newt, not wanting that particular trigger to instigate a fully blown argument. He continues.

"Let me tell you something more about the Grand Mufti. He was just as bad as Hitler, who made him the spiritual leader of the Muslims in Germany. He did his best to lobby leaders of the European countries that had been conquered to stop them from sending their Jews to Palestine, but rather to the death camps. He even tried to get the Nazis to bomb Tel Aviv. The saddest thing was when he avoided prosecution after the war."

"Absolute horror," admits Joe. "And we all know who he was mentoring after the war, the man who was going to replace him … Yasser Arafat … and we all know about him, don't we?"

"We will discuss him a little later, Joe, but let's not jump the gun here. Back to the Grand Mufti and his religious crusade."

"Poor choice of word," says Mo. "Crusade … did you know …?"

"… Sorry, Mo, we will cover that a bit later. I do know where you're coming from and good point. Anyway … It was a worrying development with the Grand Mufti. Before then there was a sort of peaceful co-existence, but now the 'religious card' came to the fore … and there was no going back."

"Religious card?" asks Mo. "Islam?"

"Yes, I'm afraid," responds Newt.

"I follow a religion of peace," says Mo.

"You are one of the good guys," responds Newt. "Not everyone sees it the way you do."

"I have a story about the Mufti," says Joe. "You reminded me of it when you mentioned his plan regarding Tel Aviv. Did You know that he did instigate an action against Tel Aviv? A small team was parachuted in, with the aim of poisoning the water supply with arsenic."

"No!," says Abi.

"It's sadly true. They didn't succeed, of course. They were shopped by an Arab, funnily enough, who saw them falling from the sky. They had enough of the powder to kill a quarter of a million people. Incredible! They were caught. One of the Arabs got away and became a rebel leader ... his son was one of the terrorists at the Munich Olympics."

"Really?"

"Newt ... fact check?"

"Yes, he's right. All true."

"You researched that so quickly, Newt", says Mo.

"Told you before ... my secret skill," smiles Newt.

Abi had returned quietly just before this exchange was taking place. No fuss was made, although she had evidently been crying. Mo gives her a sympathetic glance but she looks away. She sits down. "Have I missed anything?" she asks.

"Nothing you don't know already, Abi," replies Newt. "I know that you have researched this period because of your family connection."

She nods and says nothing more.

"The Grand Mufti followed an extreme version of Islam that, sadly, is now very much at the heart of the current conflict, especially as it has taken on board some very troubling features from Marxism."

"What an oxymoron," declares Joe, perhaps intent on showing his cleverness through his knowledge of obscure words. He is met with blank faces.

"Two concepts that should never go together."

"Like British Intelligence?" ventures Jax, with a chuckle.

"Yes, yes, yes. We can start sparring if you want, but the point I am making that there should be absolutely nothing in common between a theocratic belief system and an atheist philosophy ... that's all."

"But when you add the Nazis into the mix, it gets even weirder," says Mo.

"That's the nature of antisemitism ... it brings together the oddest of bedfellows," adds Joe.

"Yes you are correct," says Newt. "But, back to Amin al-Husseini ... he was, at that time, in effect the leader of the Palestinian Arabs and was considered an important ally by the British Mandate authorities, who gave him the Grand Mufti title. The British rulers, at that time, were very much veering towards the Arab cause, despite what you may have been told."

"I would query that," says Jax, but offers nothing more, so Newt ignores her.

"From 1921, Amin al-Husseini began to organize larger-scale riots to terrorize Jews. Colonel Richard Meinertzhagen wrote in his diary that British officials 'incline towards the exclusion of Zionism – the movement of Jews back to the land - in Palestine.' In fact, in many cases, they even encouraged the Arabs to attack the Jews."

"Hold on there," shouts Jax, incensed. "You have proof of this? Because my sources tell me a very different story."

"Go on, Jax, let's hear your story."

"Well, for a start, the British arrested Amin al-Husseini after the Jerusalem riot."

"And allowed him to escape to Jordan," replies Joe.

"Then sentences him to 10 years in jail."

"Which he never serves. In fact it was during this phase that they gave him the Grand Mufti title – hardly the act of an enemy! – then of course he goes on to instigate more riots, in Jaffa and Petah Tikvah, I believe."

"I see you've done your homework, professor."

"I see you haven't!" replies Joe. Newt continues.

"More of the same in the 1920s, culminating in ...

Hebron". He looks over to Abi, who nods slightly. "Again instigated by the Grand Mufti by circulating rumours of a Jewish plot to seize control of Muslim holy places. It was a nasty one and eventually the British evacuated the 484 survivors, including your family, Abi, to Jerusalem."

"The sad thing is that, despite the horrific events in 1929, the British tried to sweep the real causes under the carpet. They held an investigation – the Shaw Commission – and their findings were that, somehow, the Jews were ultimately responsible for the riots against themselves! In their words they concluded that 'the violence occurred due to racial animosity on the part of the Arabs, consequent upon the disappointment of their political and national aspirations and fear for their economic future.' The Jews were seen as a threat and so, apparently, it was understandable that the Arabs would riot against them."

"So, a massacre is a natural consequence of ... economic fears?" says Joe. "You couldn't make it up!"

"Apparently so," replies Newt.

"The British again! Meddling in other people's lives and getting it wrong again!" declares Jax.

"Wait a minute, here we have the British acting against the Jews! Have you changed sides, Jax?"

"No. Perhaps my disregard for the British is greater than my disregard for the Zionists, professor."

"You are a complex being. I would hate to be inside your head."

"Likewise."

"Children behave," says Newt, exasperated. "Let me continue ... it's not all bad here."

He has their interest.

"One of the commission, a Labour MP called Henry Snell actually disagreed with their findings ... and made some very enlightened observations. He switched blame for the riots, rightly, to the Muslim religious authorities, particularly the Grand Mufti."

"Good for him," says Joe. Newt continues.

"Here are his words … 'I agree that the animosity and hostility of the Arabs towards the Jews were the fundamental cause of the outbreak of August last, but, as I have already indicated, I believe that this feeling was rather the result of a campaign of propaganda and incitement than the natural consequence of economic factors.'"

"And the rest of the commission didn't see this? Were they blind?" exclaims Joe.

"Blinkered is the word, I think," adds Abi. Newt continues.

"He also said the following … 'the Arab population have been encouraged to believe that they have suffered a great wrong and that the immigrant Jew constitutes a permanent menace to their livelihood and future. I am convinced that these fears are exaggerated and that on any long view of the situation the Arab people stand to gain rather than to lose from Jewish enterprise. There is no doubt in my mind that, despite errors of judgment which may have resulted in hardship to individual Arabs, Jewish activities have increased the prosperity of Palestine, have raised the standard of life of the Arab worker and have laid the foundations upon which may be based the future progress of the two communities and their development into one State' …"

"He also said, 'The two peoples were thrown together under quite unusual circumstances, without any unifying influence of language, religion or race. The impact upon an undeveloped people, fatalistic in their outlook and devoted to their ancient ways, by a highly-gifted and progressive race, burning with great ideals, would in any case impose a great strain upon both. It is probable that the leaders of both races failed fully to appreciate the circumstances and the necessity for an enduring effort to establish good relationships.' … and, finally, 'it is my view that, notwithstanding their failures, the achievements of the Jews in Palestine in the last decade are as significant as anything that has happened in our time. In spite, therefore, of racial differences and of last year's tragic events, I believe that there exists, even now, a sufficient basis of goodwill on both sides upon which racial cooperation may be built'"

Newt seems to be recounting this without ever looking down at his notes. "Is he reading this, or does he have a fantastic memory?" whispers Abi, to no one in particular. "Incredible!"

"We need more politicians like that, don't you think, Jax? People who see things as they actually are and can be, rather than spinning things for their own political advantage," says Joe.

"That's not surprising, professor. He was a socialist, after all," says Jax, proudly.

"In the days when socialists actually cared about their people … the workers," remarks Joe.

"What do you mean, professor?"

"That was before your lot came in and started following causes … like Palestinians, animal rights, black power, gay liberation … rather than people!"

"I object! Newt please correct him!"

"But there's truth in what he said. The 'New Left' appeared in the 1960s, as a development of cultural Marxism …"

"… how do you know this stuff?" says Abi.

"I'm a good researcher."

"Oh yes … good researcher … of course."

"Bah, humbug," says Jax. "Can't be bothered to argue

with you."

"Hallelujah!" exclaims Joe.

"Praise the Lord!" adds Abi, ironically.

"Amen to that!" adds Mo, in the same vein. They all laugh, even Jax.

Newt adds a postscript to the conversation.

"Sadly, Mr Snell was ignored and his comments were just added as a personal addendum to the report. I believe history could have been so different if he had been listened to. He said a lot more in his 'Reservations', too much to read out now – perhaps you can do your own research later on … In fact, perhaps there would not have been a need for … all this."

"I disagree, actually," says Joe, quite firmly.

"Oh yes, professor. So you know better than … brain box here?"

"All I would say," replies Joe, "is that there would still be hatred in the heart. No amount of words can take that away. There needs to be a real intent to change, to want peace …"

"Well spoken," responds Newt.

"Quite", says Joe.

Jax surprisingly nods in agreement.

Chapter twelve

Newt pauses and gives a very slight nod of his head. All of sudden, the whole room turns black and darkness shrouds everyone. Even electronic devices switch off completely. Gradually light filters in through the window, so at least they can still see each other. Newt seems to have disappeared.

"Power cut?" suggests Jax.

"Or more surprises, perhaps?" suggests Joe, perceptively, but with a huge dollop of cynicism.

Silence continues for a short while, though they can hear some shuffling sounds. Suddenly the room is bathed in light, a huge screen fills the back wall and Newt has lost his desk and is now standing before them in a gold lame suit, a colourful shirt and cowboy boots, brandishing a diamond encrusted microphone.

"There's something different here," suggests Jax jokingly. "Newt, you look ridiculous. Have you gone mad?"

Newt just stands there with a huge grin (which really doesn't suit him) and the screen behind him explodes into multicoloured life. A gaudy logo spins into view, with the words 'Spot the Fib' cascading from top to bottom, before exploding into green, red and white sparks. Before anyone can speak there is a whirring sound and they find themselves held into place in their seats. This is for a good reason, as the seats themselves move along tram lines and the four of them are re-assigned positions. To the left are Mo and Jax, and to the right are Abi and Joe. Between them a glass barrier thrusts upwards from the ground. Two teams ... in a ... quiz show?

"A ... quiz show?" gasps Joe. "Can someone please explain what is happening here?" He tries to leave his seat but is unable to, just like before.

Garish music explodes from hidden speakers, playing some kind of theme song, while Newt makes peculiar leg movements, in some attempt at a quirky dance. It ends with a clumsy flourish as the music stops and he speaks.

"Ladies and Gentlemen. Welcome to 'Spot the Fib'. This is the real reason why you are all here. As for all that you have experienced and the selection process, it has all been a clever ruse to bring you here. I bet you are … shocked."

He speaks that last word with a comic inflexion, as if he is performing to an audience. In fact his voice has changed in timbre, accent and volume. Is this the same person? Wasn't Newt meant to be a trusted, sensible person, not this … crude parody of a game show host?

The screen behind him changes to a view of an auditorium packed with seats, all filled with smiling, cheering, happy people. There were people here that they recognised. Mo's extended family are in the front row, from grandparents down to baby brother. His local Imam is even there, beaming. Behind them are Abi's housemates, her gay best friends and even her landlady. Further back are some of Jax's fellow urban warriors, dressed appropriately as 60s throwbacks. All were carrying small Palestinian flags. Joe, sadly, seems to have no one to represent him. It doesn't seem to bother him at first. But enough is enough!

"WHAT?!" Joe is particularly incensed. He would never have signed up to such a … frippery. Newt picks up on this. He knew that Joe would present a problem.

"Well, all your families and loved ones knew all about it and approved … apart from yours, Joe, apparently your loved ones wanted to have nothing to do with … such a frippery."

This is some relief to Joe, but he is far from happy.

"This is a joke, yes?"

"I don't think it is, professor, although I am as surprised

as you are," says Jax. "But my posse wouldn't be here if it was just a ... frippery."

"But why ... what?" Joe is totally disorientated. He has no coping mechanism for such a development and is so out of his depth. Abi has reacted similarly and her delayed explosion of discontent is no less forceful.

"This is madness. I would never sign up for this."

"Even for $100,000, dear?" suggests Newt in a voice that has gone suddenly very camp.

Abi goes quiet as if contemplating something new. She could certainly make great use of such a sizeable sum. And her friends in the audience seem so supportive. To be honest, she was always a reluctant delegate for the event she thought she was coming to, though she had been warming to it and had already learned so much. *But $100k is $100k, after all. Mmmm!*

Mo is speechless. He doesn't know what to say or do, so remains silent and gives a shy little wave to his family in the front row, who all wave back frantically! Newt continues.

"You had all been nominated by your families or friends for this show. All in total secret, of course and in the knowledge that none of you would willingly have ... cheapened yourselves so!"

He makes a comic grimace and there is a ripple of laughter from the audience.

"I find this VERY hard to believe" growls Joe.

"Perhaps it's because you have NO friends?" suggests Jax. Joe glares at her.

"Good healthy banter, this is what we like," says Newt, prompting more applause.

"Your best way to get back at her ... is to win that £100k" says Newt.

"Then perhaps I will," replies Joe, his voice a little more

stable now. He didn't actually mean it, of course, but it was the only thing he could think of.

"OK, then" says Newt. "Then let us begin. Let's play 'Spot the fib'. It's an easy game to play, with very few rules. You all have a button in front of you. All you have to do is watch the sequence we will play in a moment and, every time you think that what is being said is a deliberate lie, just press your button."

"That's it?" asks Abi. "What if I just press the button continuously? That way I'll pick up all the lies, as well as the rest of the stuff?"

"You think our system is that stupid, Abi" says Newt. "Perhaps that's how it would work if you had created it … no … every lie is time-coded and the marking system is very accurate. If you press when there is no lie, you will have points deducted, which will do you no good at all, young lady. All very straight forward. Is that OK, Abi?"

"Yes … but you don't have to be so rude."

"I'm a game show host, dear, I'm here to entertain, not empathise." More laughter.

"Then we shall begin."

Some more music and then the holo-bubble bursts into life. "Spot the fibs", says Newt one last time, in the campest voice he could manage. He then sits down and faces forwards, towards the delegates rather than towards the display.

What follows is a series of video clips from various sources. Some are just a few sound bites long and some are extended interviews, from both sides of the conflict. None of them are conciliatory or even-handed. All the views expressed are strident, from both sides. The delegates are getting worked up and pressing their buttons, often with great venom, as if the mechanism is registering not just their actions, but also the strength of their feelings. All eyes are continuously fixed on the screen, concentration is paramount and no 'lie' must be allowed to go by unnoticed. Some of the 'lies' are blatant, others are more subtle. But not everything is a lie, some of the truths are hard to take, depending on your perspective. There are many instances of what some see as firm 'truths', but which for others are outright 'lies'. It was clear that, once the show had got started, thoughts of the cash prize had probably faded into the background and that partisan and strongly-held positions had come to the fore, even if the veracity wasn't always apparent.

The video lasts around twenty minutes, with a three-minute gap in the middle, presumably for advertising messages to the audience. It finishes with a final flourish, the holo-bubble fades out and Newt leaves his chair and faces the delegates. Curiously, the screen on the back wall had disappeared, so there was no audience to cheer them on or encourage them any further. Even more curiously, Newt had lost his game-show host garb and was now dressed as before. His demeanour has even reverted to the 'old version'. Something weird is going on here and the delegates feel it. Mind you, nothing surprises them anymore, so they just sit politely, waiting for what is to follow in this strange surreal world that they had entered just a few hours earlier.

"I can see you have guessed," says Newt, "that things are not as they may seem."

"You're telling us," groans Jax, "I suppose you're going to tell us that we've just had a massive communal group-dream and we have now woken up ... mind you, our chairs have definitely moved, so something real has happened ... please ... Big Brother ... pray reveal all." Her cynicism is shared by them all, judging by their faces, all quite content to allow Jax to act as spokeswoman.

Newt nods slightly and the chairs slowly move back

to their original positions, as the delegates make weary and ironic hand gestures to themselves or each other, as if this was some fairground attraction. Eventually everything is reset and all that remains is to figure out what has just happened in the last thirty minutes or so. Newt starts to enlighten them.

"Of course ... there is no game show."

"Oh really," groans Joe. "So, what was the point?"

"Coming to that."

"And the audience ... I saw my family," says Mo, utterly confused.

"Just a clever simulation. Computers are very clever, you know."

"And no $100k, then?" says Abi, unable to hide the disappointment.

"No, sorry ... just need to grab your attention really."

"Oh manipulation ... thy name is NEWT" says Jax, a little too loudly.

One thing that has happened is that the four of them have drawn closer together, in shared contempt of what has been happening to them, with their bile focussed totally on Newt. He doesn't care and can see the advantages of this strange new bond they now have. He starts to explain things.

"It wasn't totally a pointless exercise and, let's face it, you were all pretty angry at the time."

"I came round," says Abi, quietly. "So, no one has won?"

"Oh yes, there is a winner here", answers Newt. "You're all a winner ..."

"Oh yes?" asks Jax. "How come?"

"You have spent twenty minutes or so concentrating on your prejudices, on critiquing your perceived 'enemies'. Perhaps it has taught you something."

"Really?" says Joe, unconvinced. "Just to let you know

that I never actually pressed my button once."

"Yes, we noticed," replies Newt. "Why?"

"Because it was all nonsense and I wasn't going to lower myself."

"So, you weren't tempted to react to any of the 'lies' you heard?"

"No."

"No engagement at all?"

"No."

"Then ... Joe ... perhaps that has taught you something about yourself? Something to think about, eh?"

Joe starts to respond, then thinks again and pauses.

"Perhaps ... you're right," he mutters, eventually, before waving everyone away and closing his eyes in contemplation.

Jax breaks the awkward moment.

"Well ... it didn't teach me anything."

"We noticed that you hardly pressed your button at all," responds Newt.

"That's right. I noticed that the clips were dominated by Palestinian viewpoints and that they were obviously biased to get a reaction, seeing that we mainly heard ... let me say ... extreme opinions."

"So," replies Newt. "You accept that they were extreme ... but you didn't accept them as lies."

"It all happened so quickly. I'm an old lady. It takes time to think, to evaluate ..."

"Even when ... as you well know ... some of those lies were very blatant."

Jax is silent. Newt turns to the other two.

"You, Abi, were very busy with your button. I don't think it was totally because of the prize money. I could see by your face that you were very engaged."

"Yes, "she replies. "So many lies!"

Newt doesn't answer her and turns to Mo instead.

"And you, Mo, you were like a rabbit in the headlights."

"A ... what ... in a what?"

"An English expression. You seemed shocked. Am I right?"

"You are truly right, sir. I have never heard of such things. Perhaps I have had a ... sheltered existence?"

"There's nothing wrong with that, Mo. You have been brought up well."

Newt smiles at him and Mo attempts one in return, but it is weak.

Newt now addresses them all.

"So, Ladies and Gentlemen. Not a complete waste of time then ..."

He is interrupted by Joe.

"... I have now thought more. Yes, I have learned more about myself. I allowed my pride to trump my passion. I'm old too, Jax. An old Englishman. Very unteachable ... I suppose." He falters, then stops. His face is sad.

Jax looks over to him, with what could be seen as a measure of compassion.

"Well said, professor." She says no more.

"I think it's time for another comfort break," announces Newt.

More drinks and snacks suddenly appear. Jax walks over to Joe. She pats him softly on his arm, then moves away and carries on walking to the ladies' toilet. Abi also approaches Joe. She is not quite so conciliatory.

"So, we both saw the lies, yet you chose not to acknowledge them. I thought you were on my side." She turns away from him in disgust, grabs a soft drink, then returns to her seat. Mo stays in his seat, lost in his thoughts.

Chapter thirteen

After the short break, Newt continues with the programme, switching on the holo-bubble. Images of British rule in the mandate years fill the display and the voice speaks.

After the massacre in Hebron, the British appointed Sir William Shaw to head an inquiry into the causes of the riots. He found that the violence occurred due to 'racial animosity on the part of the Arabs, as a result of their disappointment of their political and national aspirations.' The conclusion was that the conflict stemmed from different interpretations of British promises to both Arabs and Jews. It was a fudge and the Jews were not happy with this.

The Hope Simpson report of 1930 recommended a limiting of Jewish immigration, a body blow to the Zionists. Released at the same time, the Passfield White Paper emphasised the need for Arab interests to be to the fore. Some even argued that this effectively overturned the promises of the Balfour Declaration, essentially saying that Britain should not plan to establish a Jewish state. This greatly upset the Jews and necessitated a letter from British Prime Minister MacDonald to Weizmann, reaffirming the commitment to create a Jewish homeland.

The Arabs rioted even more, particularly between 1936 and 1939 and the British made little or no effort to prevent them. After each incident, a commission of inquiry would try to establish the cause of the riot, with a predictable conclusion that the Arabs could only be satisfied by making further restrictions on Jewish immigration.

With the sinister developments in Nazi Germany, the Jews in the land had to take action. Jewish terrorist groups, Irgun and the Stern gang, appeared to counter the Arab aggression, alongside the official Jewish response, the Haganah, founded in 1920. However, even the Haganah reached the limits of their patience with the British in 1939 due to the White Paper that year. This new policy proposed a Jewish National home but within an independent Palestinian state. It also further restricted Jewish immigration, a poignant decision considering developments in Germany and, to cap it all, ruling that the Arab majority would determine the number of Jews allowed into the country.

The display ends with Jax feverishly waving her hand for attention. Newt speaks.

"Yes, Jax, I know you have a personal interest here and have a lot to say about … events. Let us roll on and see … a story you will be familiar with."

The holo-bubble returns with the view of a newspaper, The Palestine Post, with the headline, *'Army seize Jewish Agency, hold leaders, 1000 others in dawn swoop."* A sign gives the date, Saturday 29th June 1946. A voice explains.

'It was called Black Sabbath by the Jews and Operation Agatha by the British. It was an extensive operation against the Jewish defence groups, what they called the 'Jewish Resistance movement', namely the Haganah, but also Irgun and the Stern Gang. 17,000 British soldiers were involved and more than 2,700 individuals were arrested and sent to detention camps. The offices of the Jewish Agency were raided and many documents were seized, in an attempt to find proof that key Jewish leaders were plotting violence. These documents were stored in the British military headquarters, at the King David Hotel.'

We see the front view of the hotel, with military staff, as well as Jews and Arabs coming and going. We then move to a small smoky room, where two men are meeting.

'Two men meet to discuss what can be done about this. They are Menachem Begin, head of the Jewish terrorist group, Irgun and future Israeli Prime Minister and Amichai Paglin, codename Gidi, chief planner of Irgun.'

"*The Prime Minister was all in favour, but I think he's lost his* nerve," says Gidi.

"But not now ... surely. It's not just a response ... they bomb our headquarters ... we bomb theirs ... it's not just that ... Ben Gurion wants those papers destroyed. They are ... compromising."

"Well... he's happy for us to go alone on this."

"For us to take the rap if it goes belly up?"

"He's a politician ... no?"

"And you're confident that our plan will work, Gidi?"

"Oh yes. I've created this timer mechanism that will give enough time for evacuation."

"That's key. The objective is not to kill anyone ... just destroy those papers ... and ... of course ... to show them that we mean business and we're not just going away."

"You know about my little chat with Sadeh of the Haganah? He wanted fifteen minutes before the big bang; I said forty-five ... we compromised on thirty. Hope it's long enough!"

"We've got good men going in, they will do a good job ... and the plan is foolproof you say ... remind me?"

"Milk cans."

"Milk cans? I tell you what, Gidi ... I don't need to know anymore ... just get it all ready for the 22nd of July."

We see the front of the King David Hotel. A drone's-eye-view from the entrance, through to the lobby shows smartly dressed people are drinking tea and the bar packed with the well-off, Jew, Arab and British, all mingling together. It then flies down to the basement in the southwest area, to the La Regence cafe, which is almost empty, where Irgun operatives, dressed as hotel workers, overwhelm the café staff, locking them in a room. Two British soldiers are suspicious and there is a small gun battle, with casualties. The operatives then place the 50lb bombs hidden in seven large milk cans, before setting free the café staff and fleeing. Signs are placed next to the milk cans, 'Mines, do not touch.'

They leave the building and their leader shouts 'Get away, the hotel is about to blow up' to all who are present. A small explosive device outside the hotel then detonates and the operatives are able to escape under the cover of the smoke.

Next we see three scenes simultaneously. Three phone calls are made at the same time. One to the Palestine Post newspaper, one to the French consulate office and one to the King David hotel management office. All three are answered. The third one is taken by a clerk, who immediately makes another phone call.

The drone flies upwards to the offices of the British military command. A phone rings in a small office on the top floor. A secretary answers it and listens intently, before dropping the phone and rushing into the adjoining office.

"Sir ... a bomb threat. Over the telephone."

Her commanding officer seems unimpressed.

"What were the exact words of this ... message, Miss Jones?"

She had a good memory and recited the message, word for word.

"This is the Jewish Resistance Movement; we have planted bombs in the hotel. Please vacate it immediately. You have been warned."

"Thank you, Miss Jones ... back to work now, there's a good girl."

"But ..."

"Off you go. Leave it to me."

She reluctantly returns to her office, where she gently places the telephone handset back onto its receiver.

Corporal Blake leaves his office and strolls over to his commanding officer, Captain Fanshawe-Styles, repeating the message.

"Another hoax call, Blake. Leave it with me."

The Captain wanders down to the first-floor bar, where he meets up with two others of equal rank. He repeated the words of the telephone call.

"Jewish Resistance Movement? Never heard of them."

"Anyway, we don't take our orders from the Jews. Just ignore it. Mine's a whiskey, George."

A voice-over can be heard, over a picture of the devastation.

'Another officer, Brigadier Dudley Sheridan Skelton, was listening in the bar. Something must have prompted him in his spirit as he immediately dropped everything, left the bar and the hotel and was just a few yards away when there was a mighty explosion ... all six stories of the southwest corner of the hotel collapsed. He lived to tell the tale, one that he told in 1979 to Greville Janner, a British MP, as proof that a warning had been given, something that had been denied for decades by the British authorities ... this is despite both the Palestine Post and the French Consulate testifying that it had! The telephone operator at the newspaper swore on oath that she had immediately passed on the message to the police.'

"I must stop you there," says Jax, forcefully.

The holo-bubble immediately pauses.

"I contest that. My family were heavily involved in that massacre. You probably know that my aunt was one of the secretaries there and died in the blast. The head of command – a man we all trusted, though I've forgotten his name – insisted that no warning was given by the Irgun savages. This MP ... Jewish was he?"

"The official records state that not only was a warning given, but they even contacted the Palestine Post newspaper and the French Consulate" says Joc. "And yes he was Jewish ... why does that matter?"

"Of course, it matters and, anyway, you're wrong ... and that's that! This was the biggest terrorist act that Palestine had suffered. Ninety-two people were killed, I think. It was just plain evil, inexcusable!"

"So, you're saying that the objective was to kill everyone, even the Jews in the hotel?" says Joe. "That's a lie, Jax and ... I think you know it. You and I both know the real reason behind the bombing ... and it wasn't about killing people."

"Terrorism, pure and simple!" Jax is adamant. Newt interrupts.

"I think what Joe is alluding to are the very sensitive documents seized by the British on a raid a few days earlier. They were being stored in the King David and contained information very prejudicial to the Jewish cause. The action, we were told, was to destroy those documents ... and half an hour was easily long enough to vacate the building ... those British officers were condemned by their own arrogance."

"So you say," says Jax, unimpressed. "People were still killed – including my aunt – TERRORISM!" She sits there, impassive, her arms folded. "And that's all I'm going to say on the matter."

Joe knows when to shut up and so does Newt, who changes the subject.

"It is so hard for us, so many years in the future, to be able to examine motives and even the facts of what actually happened in those turbulent times. All accounts are always going to be prejudicial. Sometimes we just go with the truth that ... seems right to us. And ... of course ... this brings us back to 1948. We talked about this earlier. It's time for a revisit I think."

The holo-bubble starts up. We see the United Nations building, in Lake Success New York. First outside, then inside for the meeting of the United Nations General Assembly meeting.

The facts tell us that, on November 29, 1947 the United Nations voted ... to partition Palestine ... into two States ... one Jewish and one Arab ... 33 countries voted in favour ... and 13 against ... The actual story is not quite so straightforward. Many countries needed to be convinced. At the beginning, the Jewish Agency came up short. Three countries needed to be worked on, Liberia, Haiti and the Philippines.

The Philippines' vote hinged on a conversation between a man in London and the President of the country. The conversation hadn't taken place when it should, so a nudge was made that ensured that the President spoke with his Ambassador at the UN, who then voted in favour. Haiti was the last country to vote. It needed a two-day excursion by a Protestant minister who loved the Jews to convince the Haitian leader!

Some people promised to vote, then changed their minds. Others were pursued and voted at the last minute. One delegate from an unnamed South American country was found in a toilet cubicle by an Argentinian Jew, recognised by the colour of his shoes. He was encouraged out, just in time to vote.

"Fascinating" says Joe

"I did not know that," adds Abi. "How interesting."

"Even before they had counted the votes all the Arab delegates had stormed out of the building, declaring that the United Nations was dead" adds Newt. "And, true to form, the Grand Mufti calls for a holy war!"

"Sore losers," remarks Abi.

"A nation shall be born in a day" says Joe proudly, quoting from the Bible, and gently thumps the weighty tome on the desk in front of him.

"Religious claptrap," sneers Jax.

"You would say that ... but the Jews came through ... despite all the odds."

"At what cost?" replies Jax.

"They brought it on themselves, Jax," says Joe. "Remember, it was the Arab nations that rejected the voice of the world through the United Nations and decided to invade.

Five against one ... I repeat ... What are the odds, eh?"

"Indeed," remarks Newt, thoughtfully. "As the clocks struck midnight on May 14th 1948, the British Mandate was no more ... and Israel was born. At dawn, Egyptian planes bombed Tel Aviv and the five nations invaded, from the north, south and east. They reckoned that the new nation would be finished within a fortnight."

"But what happened, Newt?" says Joe, looking at Jax. "Remind us ... because it was quite some miracle."

"Israel had no air force to speak of, no tanks, no heavy artillery. Soldiers were recruited as they came off the boats at Haifa and given rifles or whatever was at hand. Yet ... a year later, Israel had not just defeated the five nations but had captured 5,000 square kilometres of territory. It was a hard year; they had lost around six thousand in the fight. But, remember ... they were fighting for their very existence. The memory of the Holocaust was still fresh. The will to survive is what got them through ..."

"... as well as the hand of God," adds Joe.

"I am not qualified to speak of such things of course," says Newt.

"Makes you think, though?"

"Certainly."

Chapter fourteen

"And this is a good point to introduce something that is going to ... as they say ... blow your socks off," suddenly says Newt.

"I thought there were no more surprises?" says Abi.

"It's not a surprise to me," is Newt's weak reply.

Before more can be said, there is a strange sound, a hissing sound from beneath their desks. A panel opens under each one and a small box appears on a raised platform.

"Please open your box" says Newt.

"Do we have to?" says Jax, awkwardly.

"Oh yes ... it's in your contract."

"What contract?" argues Jax again.

"Oh stop whingeing and let's put ourselves out of our misery" suggests Joe.

They open their boxes and remove what looks like a rubber swim hat. They are featureless on the outside, apart from a monogram with their initials, presumably to ensure each has the correct hat. Inside the hat seems to be a mesh of fine wires covering the whole area.

"Now can you all please don your caps and I will explain."

They all complied and there was some sniggering from the younger ones.

"But I didn't bring my cozzie!" says Jax to some laughter. Newt ignores this and explains.

"You are about to enter the world of advanced HR."

"Human resources?"

"No ... Holistic Reality ... the next step-up from Virtual Reality."

Unexpectedly they all black out for a moment and a new world opens up when they open their eyes. They are aware of themselves and each other, as phantom figures, but the focus of their attention is the tableau presented before them. The difference from the holo-bubble is that they are not now casual observers, but participants. They can now walk about in it and, even more incredibly, find that all of their senses are now active in this strange new world. They are able not just to see and hear but also touch and smell.

"Incredible!" gasps Joe.

"My socks are … blown off," says Mo, "though I can't see my feet that well."

"That is because you are in a new reality. This is a new generation of super-advanced computer gaming, not yet released to the public."

"We are guinea pigs?" asks Jax, a bit peeved.

"Oh no, it is well and truly tested. It has already been used in many situations but … not as a group experience … you are the first."

"What do you mean?"

"Here all four of you function as one entity. You can move around all of the scenes that will be placed before you, but your movement will be governed by the will of the group. So if three or four of you wish to move in a given direction, you move. Otherwise, you don't move."

"So, Jax," says Joe. "You'd better behave yourself, or we'll take you to places you'd rather not go."

"And vice versa, Professor Poopy Pants."

"That's a bit childish!"

"We are in a kiddie's computer game after all. I'm just getting into character!"

The scene before them is reminiscent of an epic movie. A sea of forgotten humanity. Hundreds, if not thousands, of bedraggled people walk slowly in small groups. Some are barely dressed, others carry babies or young children or are helping old folk. Most are dirty, hungry-looking and with faces devoid of hope, or any spark of humanity. Others are surprisingly well-dressed, but still with dropped faces. The sounds are low, full of despair and barely audible. The smell is overwhelming.

"Newt, what is this? This is awful."

"Guess. It shouldn't be difficult."

"Displaced people?"

"Yes ... just a tiny fraction of the refugee situation ... in 1948."

"1948? But they don't all look like Palestinians. Some do ... but ..."

"... I get it, Newt," says Joe. "I see where you're taking us."

"Go on ... ask them ... where they are from."

Jax seems reluctant but is overruled, as the group moves closer to and engages with one of the smaller groups of people. They are a small family, pushing a small cart of their belongings.

"We are from Ukraine, the western region. The Nazis deported many of our people to Germany, to work as slaves. We escaped that, it was difficult, very difficult ... and we saw our home destroyed ... "

"So, you're going back to rebuild your home, then?" asks Joe.

"Oh no ... Now the Russians ... who are moving into our motherland ... they want us to move eastwards ... to help 'rebuild', but we know we'd end up as slaves too. That's not for us; we are going westwards ... perhaps to England, or America? We just don't know ... we just walk. We have left our lives behind in Ukraine, we are now ... Ukrainians-in-exile."

Abi points out another group. They seem Jewish, but are dressed in a very oriental manner. They approach them, despite Jax's indifference.

"Have you just escaped from the Nazi camps?" asks Joe.

"No, look at us. Don't you think we're a little well-fed for that? We have just been thrown out of our ancestral home … where our family has lived for centuries!"

"Where is that?"

"Iraq. We were given just a day to leave. Left behind our home and our money. We were rich merchants but now we have no money and no home. We are hoping to find a place in Israel … perhaps the only place where we Jews can find safety now."

A third group has a distinctly oriental look to them. A large family, pulling a rickety old wagon.

"We are Chinese. We can see no future in our own land now that Mao Zedong is about to take over. We have no wish to live under communism. We are a well-off family with good connections and a wonderful home that our family have lived in for decades, but that is all in our past now."

"So, where are you going?" asks Abi.

"To Taiwan. Where the Chinese Republic will function, we think. We will be among our own people there, hopefully in safety."

Another group seems better dressed and more organised than the others. They have motorised transportation but still have a look of despair etched on their faces.

"Stalin and his gang are coming," a man says. "Soon there will be a blockade and our homeland will be under Russian control."

"Where have you come from?" asks Joe.

"Berlin."

"And where are you going?"

"Anywhere in the west side. We have relatives in Dortmund, we will go there. There is no future in the east."

A very large group of Asian Indians now confronts them, a mixture of rich and poor, not divided by caste, but instead united by circumstance and religion.

"What is your story?" asks Jax.

"Our country has been cut in two. The British are no longer interested in us, they leave us to sort out the mess they have helped to create."

"Typical!" Jax can't help herself.

"Why are you moving? It looks like you have left everything behind."

"We have. It is no longer wise for us Hindus to live among Muslims. Our country is now a Muslim country, Pakistan, they call it. We Hindus must move east, perhaps to find a new home somewhere in India. It is going to be a very long trek for us. "Before we move on," says Newt, "we need some context for what you've just seen. As a result of the Second World War, some 65 million people were forced from their homes in Europe alone. After the war, they became known as DPs, displaced persons. Most found new homes, though there were still some 175,000 DPs left in Europe in 1951."

"We are talking major numbers here, aren't we?" says Joe.

"Yes, but the world cared for them," suggests Jax. "What about the 750,000 Palestinian refugees though? No one cared for them."

"I take issue with that. It was their own leaders who didn't care for them. You're forgetting the number of Jewish refugees created in 1948. We heard from some of them just now." This is Joe speaking.

"Yes," adds Newt. "The Jewish refugee situation, created as a result of all the Arab countries throwing their Jews out in 1948, despite centuries of peaceful history, was larger than the Palestinian one. Around 820,000 Jews were expelled."

"And all re-located ... because 'their' leaders cared for them! None of them ended up in 'refugee camps'!" says Joe. Newt decides to deflect.

"The Chinese situation, with Mao's communist takeover, resulted in around two million fleeing to Taiwan and Hong Kong," adds Newt. "And, similarly, so did 3.7 million East Germans, before the Berlin Wall was constructed by the Soviets. And, as for the Hindus and Muslims in India, 18 million became refugees."

"Enormous figures," suggests Joe. "Really makes 'our' situation pale into insignificance, Jax ... if we're really honest about it."

Newt acts quickly.

"Before this becomes a fully-fledged argument, let me take you somewhere else. It is now a year afterwards."

A building looms ahead of them. It is the United Nations building. The group are whisked inside and into an office, where there are two desks side by side, each manned by an official. The desk on the left has the sign 'UNHCR' and the other one, 'UNRWA'. The group approaches the desk on the left.

"UNHCR, what is that?" Joe asks the official.

"The United Nations High Commissioner for Refugees."

"What is your function?"

"To look after the well-being of refugees of course. We have been in operation since 1921, created by the League of Nations, the forerunner of the United Nations."

"All refugees?"

"Well, mainly for those left homeless after the Second World War."

"And, I suppose for the Palestinians in 1948?"

"Oh no," he says, pointing to the other desk. The United Nations Relief and Works Agency for Palestine refugees. He looks after them."

They turn to the other man. Joe again speaks.

"And you solely look after the Palestinians?"

"Oh yes."

"Why? Surely the Palestinians constitute a tiny percentage of the world's refugees, so why the interest? Why an agency solely for the Palestinians?"

"Because the world cares for them," answers Jax for him. "They are a special case."

"Are they a special case?" Joe asks the man.

"Oh yes. The UN voted us in as a General Assembly resolution."

"Why weren't there resolutions for Germany, China, India ... the Jews even?"

"Don't ask me, I just work here."

"It does seem strange why the Palestinians seem like a special case ... and still are now in 2025."

The man looks at him blankly.

"All those other refugees we saw were re-settled decades ago, yet the one group that has a separate UN agency created for it, are STILL children and grandchildren of those refugees, with some of them still living in camps ... doesn't that strike you as odd?"

Joe's question is for the rest of the group. None of them answers.

"It's as if ... these poor people have been kept as refugees with a grudge ... for some purpose ... and not one to benefit them ... doesn't THAT strike you as odd?"

Two of them nod. The other, Jax, looks away. Newt decides that it is time now to move on. He walks around and removes their HR caps. They return to their seats.

Chapter fifteen

"Back to the situation with the Palestinians, I think we need to consider the many human stories here", says Newt. "There was a lot of pain, particularly for much of the Arab population. This is a good moment to come alongside Mo's family and their particular experiences."

Mo straightens up, not sure what is about to happen. The holo-bubble fades into a drama. It is April 22nd,1946 and the location is Wadi Nisnas. We are inside a small house.

"That's my house," exclaims Mo, "but it's also ..."

"It's your house as it was in 1946, Mo," says Newt.

"How ...?"

"Clever technology ... just watch."

A young boy, Mo's grandfather, is sitting on the lap of a much older man, *his* grandfather. An old lady is by the sink, apparently oblivious to what is going on. They can hear an eerie voice from outside, a tinny voice, an amplified voice from loudspeakers mounted on vehicles.

"The day of judgment has arrived. It is time for you good people to leave your houses ... do so quickly ... before your enemy arrives."

The boy is scared. He grips his grandfather's arm tightly.

"Grandfather ... we should go ... they are telling us to leave."

"Ignore this, my boy. We are going nowhere."

"But ... the enemy ..."

"It is the enemy you hear. It is not our own people ... it is the Jews ... we don't listen to them."

"Why do they want us to leave?"

"They want our houses."

"They have their own houses. They are our neighbours. There are plenty of houses for all of us."

"Yes, Mahmoud. There were plenty of houses ... but times

change ... these are difficult times. We stay here. They won't hurt us."

His grandmother speaks.

"They say that more and more Jews are arriving by sea every day from Europe."

"Why is that, grandmother?"

"They are fleeing from bad people, people who want to kill them."

"But don't they want to kill us ... and take our homes?"

"No, Mahmoud. They just want to live ... as do we ... they will find places to stay ..."

His grandfather interrupts.

"This is true, but I can promise you. Not this house! We are not moving. Allah will protect us, have no fear, Mahmoud."

The boy looks up at his grandfather and over to his grandmother. There is trust in his eyes.

"Inshallah."

The display fades and Mo speaks.

"This is ... as it was ... as my grandfather remembered it ... they remained in their house; nobody forced them out. Many did leave though."

Jax interrupts.

"Bullshit!"

"How can you ... the boy has just told us it is a fair account."

"They were driven from their homes by the Haganah."

"Who said?" responds Joe.

"The history books."

"And who wrote these ... particular history books?"

"I will stop you there," says Newt. "Joe has a useful point. There are two viewpoints ... according to who you want to believe. We just have to accept that ... perhaps we'll never know exactly what happened in 1948. Perhaps there's a different question for us to ask now?"

He pauses and looks at them all in turn. He starts to speak then stops himself.

"No ... I have a better question to ask. It's a question that I would like you all to answer honestly, and to the best of your knowledge. Or not to answer if you have no opinion. The question is this; Why do you think the five Arab nations invaded Israel in 1948?"

Jax is the first to answer.

"Easy one. To reclaim the land that had been taken from them forcibly."

Joe has his head in his hands, shaking it.

"You know very well that isn't true. I had you down as a reasonably intelligent woman, someone who can process facts and discern the truth ... you've heard the truth so far today, are you incapable of responding to it?"

"Well, professor. Put me right then, show me how much more cleverer you are!"

"It's not about you and me ... it's about the facts, Jax. Here they are ... but, before I do I want it to be clear that there's a major distinction between the Palestinians ... and their leaders."

"Go on. Enlighten us all, then."

"Well, Jax, did you know that the Arab Higher Committee, who were the leaders at that time – with of course the Grand Mufti as the head – skedaddled when things went belly up, leaving their people helpless and leaderless."

"Skedaddled?" says Mo.

"Scarpered," corrects Joe, mischievously

"Eh? What are these ... strange words?"

"It's the English language, Mo," says Abi. "Being mangled."

"Hightailed," says Joe. "OK OK ... They ran off!"

"Traitors!" said Mo. "Wish you hadn't told me now!"

"Yes, Mo. But ... as I said ... these were the leaders ... totally letting their people down. When they saw what a mess they were making of it all, they just ran off!"

"Bah!" is all Jax can say. Joe continues.

"Well ... despite what you think ... I have nothing but pity for the average Palestinian Arab ... those living under Palestinian rule in the territories. But, for the grace of God, that could have been you, Mo. Just a matter of geography. Because your family lived where they lived, you were brought up as a normal, decent human being ... rather than having hate pumped into you."

Joe looks over at Mo and nods in his direction.

"Palestinians ... I believe are decent peaceful people ... or at least 'were' ... some of them have become something very different ... we saw that on October 7th ... which brings me to their so-called 'leaders' ... the imams, the mullahs, the Grand Muftis ... also the generals, politicians, mayors ... they are the ones responsible for the whole mess ..."

There's a silence, so he continues.

"Any leader who really cared about their people would have seen the writing on the wall back in the 1920s and would have given their people a choice ... stay behind and work with the Jews ... as they had already done up to then before the militants started stirring things up ... or move to Transjordan, which was still part of Palestine at the time with plenty of space for all. King Abdullah would have taken them in, I think he may have even offered this possibility."

He stops. No reaction. "Or am I just being naïve here?" He continues.

"Instead, what happened after 1948 is that the very same countries that started the war – Syria, Lebanon, Egypt in Gaza and Jordan in the West Bank mostly refused citizenship to the Palestinians in their lands, instead they bung them into refugee camps, where they still are – or their descendants are. Jax, can you answer that?"

She is pretending not to listen, as if she is bored.

Newt nods slightly, as if to give a hint of an agreement to this, but then reminds Joe. "Well, we can discuss that later but you haven't answered my question. Why did war break out?"

Joe answers him.

"The answer will not be to everyone's liking, but, from my perspective, it's the only possible explanation."

He pauses. He has their attention. He delivers his bombshell.

"They didn't want to share the land. They wanted no Jews in any part of their land. In short ... they wanted to kill every Jew who lived there ... we saw that with the Grand Mufti at Hebron and the riots in the 1930s ... and it is still their policy today. It's the Nazis all over again!"

"Well ..." says Jax.

"... do you agree, Jax?" responds Joe, immediately.

"But what about the other perspective ... the way I see things ... perhaps Mo too?" she responds, ignoring his question. Mo doesn't react to the name check.

"What about Deir Yassin?" she declares.

"Wondered when that one was going to come up," says Joe.

"I'm surprised it hasn't already," she answers, looking at Newt, who responds.

"Deir Yassin."

The holo-bubble fades in, with the same words, *'Deir Yassin, April 9th 1948.'* We see a small Palestinian village, before the events of that fateful day. A voice speaks.

'What happened on that day at Deir Yassin is probably the most controversial and emotive event in the conflict to date,

127

certainly at that time. The reason is because it has served as a symbol in the propaganda battle between the two sides of the conflict. It is impossible to do a reconstruction of the event as there is such a major difference between the two accounts. We start with the basic facts ...

A map is shown of the local area.

Deir Yassin was a small Palestinian village of around 750 people, located very strategically on a hill overlooking the approach to Jerusalem. Here is a consensus view of what happened. A combined force of Irgun and Lehi, two Jewish paramilitary groups, attacked the village. The assault was part of the broader campaign to secure areas around Jerusalem. The attackers aimed to take control of the village, which was seen as strategically important. The attack resulted in a considerable number of deaths, estimated from 100 to 250, many reported to be women and children, depending on your viewpoint.

Newt stops the display, perhaps prematurely. He speaks.

"I'll leave it there. To be honest, the impact, reactions and legacy of this event is significant because there are two totally conflicting narratives."

"But only one can be true, surely," says Joe. "I am fairly certain where the truth lays."

"Oh yes, professor. Again, you know best. So what does Professor Know-it-all think?"

"The key to understanding this is to see how the Palestinians, or rather the Arabs as they were then, have weaponised it to fuel hatred against the Jews. But ... and this may be painful to you, Jax ... it backfired."

"What on earth are you talking about?"

"Bearing in mind the timing – just before the May 1948 declaration of the State of Israel – they wanted to use 'their version' of the event to embolden the Palestinians, to encourage them to fight against the hated Jews ... by creating a false narrative about a massacre taking place there, exaggerating what actually happened. I'm not saying it didn't happen – no one is saying that – but not to the degree that was reported. The Arab leaders wanted their people to get so angry at the massacre that they would stay, take up arms and fight ... but ...

It didn't work out that way."

"Why? How?" This comes from Abi.

"By adding their spin to it, calling it a heartless massacre, they terrified their own people, so much so that many fled rather than fight these 'genocidal monsters'."

"It was a heartless massacre" insists Jax.

"Oh yes, who says? The Palestinian narrative, their version of history, tells us this, but the evidence suggests otherwise."

"So, it wasn't a massacre? Over a hundred villagers weren't killed then, professor?"

"I'm not saying that. Yes, it was an awful event and the men who did it were young and inexperienced and probably got a bit out of control ... but there were no rapes, mutilations, targeting of children ..."

"Have you seen the Wikipedia page? It mentions all the horrific things that the Jews did. And Wikipedia is not biased, it's independent."

"Is it now? Newt, what does your research tell you about the Wikipedia page?"

"My analysis of the history stats and original authorship suggests that it is biased towards the Arab position. The earliest edit in 2002 contains the comment, 'This has been a severe violation. There is a pervasive anti-Israel bias'"

Joe smirks, which really riles Jax. Newt continues.

"Let us say that arguing will get us nowhere on this issue. Deir Yassin has become a symbol, it has, in fact, become 'something else' and, as such, any truth represented is going to be endlessly contested, simply because of its status in both narratives."

"Perhaps, as you English say, the jury is out", says Mo, "though I know what narrative I choose to follow ... but I wouldn't want this to drive a wedge between myself and Abi. It's best if we leave it in the past."

"Again we find, such wisdom in the youngest of us" says Joe, with much admiration.

Chapter sixteen

"So, the Jews were hated so much, that the Arabs concocted lies just to make the world hate them, professor, eh?"

"Ah yes, that's how antisemitism manifests itself."

"Oh, what a surprise. Playing the 'antisemitism card! I wondered when that would happen," sneers Jax, eager to steal some of the thunder that Joe evidentially intended. "We have moved on from those days, professor!"

"Have we?"

Before more can be said, there is a familiar hissing sound from beneath their desks. The panel opens under each one and the small box appears again.

"You know the drill," says Newt.

They put on the HR caps and black out for a second or so, like before. The scene before them looks like a murder scene about to happen. A voice speaks. It is Newt, his voice projected as if part of a soundtrack to the scenes unfolding before them.

"It is February 1903, in a town in the southwestern part of the Russian empire. A girl has just had her cousin killed over a family dispute. This murder is about to change history."

As they stand there, the scene is acted out before them. It is the front room of an untidy house. A fifteen-year-old boy is busying himself cutting bread and an older man creeps up from behind and stabs him numerous times. This is shocking, more so as they can hear the screams of the boy and smell the dampness of the room and the distinctive smell of the blood that flows freely. Yet, strangely, it is not shocking. Although it is realistic, there's an element of unreality about it; it's like a drama being acted out before them, rather than a glimpse into reality. This is another feature of Holistic Reality and a welcome one.

When the boy finally lays still, the man drags his body into the garden, where a teenage girl waits for him, examines the body and leaves it there, then runs away.

They are all lost for words and cemented to the spot. They suddenly move forward, despite Jax's evident reluctance. "Absolutely gruesome" is her reaction. When they move, the scene repeats. When they stop, so does the scene. Joe bends down to the boy's prone body and touches it.

"Unbelievable," he says. It feels so real. "And ... yes, he is dead." Abi also touches it.

"The blood seems so real too ... awful ... can you explain why this has happened, Newt?"

"A family squabble over inheritance, that's all. The girl in the garden is the dead boy's cousin. Hard times."

They move back and, somehow, this seems to trigger another sequence. Time has evidently moved on. We see a peasant discovering the body a few days later. The body is thin and pale. He rushes off and spreads the word.

The scene is now a busy market, with people milling around, gossiping.

"What a stink!" exclaims Joe. "Is there anything here that isn't rotting?"

"I think even some of these people are rotting," says Abi, insensitively.

Newt speaks.

"News spreads and so does gossip. Go on. All you have to do is touch someone to hear what they are saying."

Abi touches the arm of a small, craggy-faced old lady carrying a basket of fruit. The lady speaks.

"A ritual killing I tell you ... the boy's body was drained of blood."

Mo approaches a teenage boy. "He was last seen in the

butcher's shop … the Jewish butcher's shop."

Another speaks. "Yes, my daughter works for one of them. She heard that they were looking for Christian blood to make their bread for their religious festival coming up."

Yet another. "It's the Jews … the Jews did it!"

The next scene is in the small office of a newspaper proprietor. On the wall are three front pages, with the lurid headlines, "Death to the Jews", "Crusade against the Hated Race!", then "Jews ritually murder Christian boy." Newt speaks.

"The proprietor of Bessarabets, the most popular newspaper in Kishinev was a notorious antisemite called Pavel Krushevan. He was happy to stir up popular feelings against the Jews in Kishinev. Why not speak to him."

Joe is the first to step up. "Why do you hate the Jews so much?"

"I just do. My sister is married to one and all he does is turn her against me. Children of the devil, they are! Christ Killers!"

"But the story about the dead boy is a lie, surely you know that?"

"Yes, so what? It's what the people want to read. It takes their mind off their troubles … I am doing them a great service … and selling lots of newspapers."

"You're despicable."

"No more than the Jews. I have read the Protocols of Zion … have you?"

"Actually I do know of it." Joe now speaks to the rest of them.

"It's a proven forgery and full of the most pernicious lies against the Jews. This man believes it as many did in those days – people like Henry Ford for instance. It was a Russian forgery supposedly about a Worldwide Jewish conspiracy to take over the world. Thoroughly discredited."

"Allegedly," says Jax.

"Come on, Jax. You know it is a blatant lie and a favoured read by the very worst antisemites, like Hitler. I hope you are not ..."

"Slow down, professor. I'm joshing you."

"Not funny," sneers Abi under her breath.

We see a church service, with the preacher stirring up the congregation into a frenzy of hate. Sticks, clubs and other weapons are freely distributed, as they take to the streets after the service to hunt for Jews.

"This is awful" says Joe, "and downright shameful ... what time of year is this, Newt?"

"Easter time."

"That figures. Bet the preacher dragged out the old 'blood libel' against the Jews, the killing of Christian kids for their blood."

"Yes, Joe ... one of the most pernicious false accusations thrown at the Jewish people. It began with the killing of William of Norwich, England, in 1144 and has never really gone away."

"And we know what comes next."

The group follows as the crowd spills out and takes to the streets. The chanting, the singing and shouting are all so real.

"Reminds me of Hyde Park last year ... eh, Jax ... your lot ... see the connection? Hope you do, because this is real ... and so wrong!"

What happened next as they followed was something they would all want to forget. The scenes were gruesome and the screaming and shouting were relentless. Men were helplessly held down while their wives were savagely raped; two teenage girls died of their wounds in front of them. People were cut down and openly slaughtered in the streets. Babies were torn from their mother's arms and savagely mutilated.

Most of the time they didn't move, because at least one of their number understandably refused to. At other times they were compelled to do so, particularly when the teenage girls were attacked. They automatically tried to help and, although they could interact and touch, they couldn't affect what was happening. Abi cradled one in her arms as she lay dying, unable to say anything that could change the circumstances. They were helpless bystanders, trapped in a history that time would rather forget.

Newt speaks. His voice is solemn.

"Forty-nine Jews are killed in a three-day pogrom, with over five hundred injured. Also, at least six hundred Jewish women are raped by these 'Christians'. At sunset on the last day, the streets are strewn with the dead and the injured. The local police did little to quell the massacre. It was a shameful event and accounts of it swept around the world and convinced Jews everywhere that they would never be safe, even in a town where they were actually in the majority. Tens of thousands of Russian Jews started making plans for a journey to Palestine, the only land where they believed they could find safety. Incidentally ... only two of the perpetrators received significant prison sentences, with a further twenty-two receiving minor jail time. And Krushevan, who instigated the pogrom, became the official political representative for Kishinev in the State Assembly, just four years later."

The scene fades and they are left to their thoughts. All eyes are on Joe, who is weeping uncontrollably. Only Mo is showing him any degree of sympathy, lightly touching his arm. In between his sobs, Joe speaks.

"This is awful. I knew about the blood libels and the pogroms but ... it's as if we have been a part of it ... I'll never forget this ..."

"This is your ... 'religion' ... professor!" spits Jax.

"But not in my name ... not in Jesus' Name!"

"Seemed to me ... in that Church service ... that your ... 'saviour' ... was very much in favour of ... baby killing!"

She is so angry, as if she had complete identification with the Jewish victims, despite her natural animosity. It is a very human reaction. Abi also feels it, unsurprisingly. She is stunned by what she has just seen and seems lost for words.

"Not my Jesus ... not my Jesus," insists Joe. He sinks to his knees and places his head in his hands. The others keep their distance. More could be said but they don't get the chance, because another scene flickers into view before them.

We are before the walls of a medieval city. It is Jerusalem. It is being besieged. The noise is deafening. There is a smell of death. They recognise it, they have just experienced it on the streets of Kishinev.

Newt speaks.

"It is July 1099 and the city of Jerusalem is being besieged by the knights of the First Crusade. For those of you who don't know, the Crusades were initiatives by the Catholic Popes to reclaim the Holy Land from the Muslims. This is a curious parallel to the situation today except that the level of brutality in those days was off the scale, as these knights were men driven by 'holy zeal' but, in reality, acting totally selfishly, out of hate, lust and greed. And they were as brutal as they came."

"Anyway, back to the story ... The city is defended by the Fatimid Muslim rulers and it is the end of a five-week campaign. There are many Jews also living in Jerusalem and they also fight alongside the Muslims. The Crusaders have had enough and launch one final assault on the walls. They succeed and swarm into the city."

"This is both compelling ... for the historian in me ... but awful ... for the humanity in me", says Joe.

"History coming alive", says Jax. "You are right, professor. I want to see it ... but I don't want to see it."

"The Crusades, Abi" says Mo. "Not good for your people or my people ... a bit of a horrible way to be united ..."

"... in death," Abi adds. "Life was so cheap in those days."

We witness a massacre. Muslims are slaughtered mercilessly in the street as you see them fleeing to their mosques. The Jewish quarter is breached and the Jews retreat to their synagogue, preparing for death. The Crusaders burn it to the ground. The streets are full of blood – ankle-deep in some places, even knee-deep in other places. Afterwards, we see street after street full of the dead and dying. It is a very hard watch. Their viewing position gives them an unprecedented and unwanted experience. The smell of death invades their nostrils and the cries of the dying tugs at their hearts. It is overpowering.

They watch from a prominent position, on the ramparts, away from the action. There is no will or inclination to venture forward for a closer look. Death is gruesome from every angle and distance.

"So much death and destruction," groans Jax. "Why? All in the name of religion?" There is no answer from the other three, all of whom have a stake in the scenario unfolding before them. When it seems to have reached a climax there's arguably the most poignantly horrible scene of all, Crusader knights, triumphant and bloody, on horseback on the way to the Church of the Holy Sepulchre, wading through the blood of dead Muslims, the main synagogue burning behind them ... and they are singing hymns and Psalms. 'This is the day which the Lord hath made: let us be glad and rejoice therein.' The words jar ... particularly with Joe, who is henceforth never able to read Psalm 118 without invoking these memories.

The scene fades and Newt speaks.

"Between 40,000 and 70,000 Muslims and Jews are killed, depending on which account you read. It becomes clear now why the term 'Crusader' is such a negative word for both Jews and Muslims these days." Mo nods thoughtfully.

The scenes fade, thankfully and we are left with the four of them, standing together, drained of emotion. Again Joe is prominent.

"Why torture me so, Newt? This is not helpful, well not to me," he cries.

Jax is not particularly helpful. "So, your God hates Muslims as well as Jews, I see."

Joe has an unsurprising ally. It is Mo. "It's not Christians doing this ... it is evil men. And evil men are still doing this. I grieve for my fellow Muslims as if it has just happened, but I also grieve for the Jews. And I also grieve for you, sir."

Joe looks up at Mo from his crouching position. "Why? Jax is happy to blame me ... and my God ... for the evil done in our name. But not you?"

"Because there is no use for hate. Hate destroys. There is always a better way, sir."

"I wish I could be so forgiving," says Abi. "But it's hard, too hard. We Jews have had to put up with too much, so much ... Why does everyone hate us so, eh?"

There is no answer from the others. There can be no answer. Particularly because of what is going to come next.

But it doesn't come next because a voice suddenly startles them. "I have had enough of this ... Newt, take us to sun loungers around a pool in Netanya in the middle of summer." And that is what happens.

"Clever, clever girl," says Joe, looking at Abi, who has brought them there. It is pleasantly warm, they are comfortable and all have pina coladas on side tables (apart from Mo, who has a Diet Coke).

"Now this is more like it. Abi, you are a genius."

Abi doesn't acknowledge Jax, as she still has unresolved issues with her, but smiles anyway.

For the next minute they lay there, basking in the sun, sipping their drinks. No one speaks. Jax breaks the silence.

"So, what now? We need to do something ... meaningful ... otherwise they will drag us back into some new nightmare."

"I agree," says Joe. "Why don't we play a game ... or ..."

"I spy with my little eye ..." says Jax.

"No," responds Joe. "A real game, not a kiddie distraction!"

They think for a bit.

"I've got one," declares Mo. "Something I did with my family when I was younger. Not sure if it would work with us, though."

"Why, pray?" asks Joe.

"You need to have a bit of an imagination for it to work," replies Mo, cheekily. He sips his drink while they all look at him, offended, or perhaps pretending to be offended.

"I'm offended, Arab boy," says Abi, not afraid to voice her frustration, but doing so with a playful glint in her eye.

"OK," he responds. "Let's play and see ... it's simple. It's all about making up a story. The first person makes up a paragraph, but leaves it on a ... cliffhanger ... I think that's the word ... then the next person carries on with the story in the same manner and so on ..."

"Easy peasy," says Jax. "Sounds like fun ... I'm up for it."

"Me too," says Joe.

"Count me in," adds Abi. "Though perhaps we pick a subject that's not connected to ... you know."

Mo nods and speaks.

"I will start. Here we go … A young man is wandering through a field of daffodils. He is happy and carefree. He has not a care in the world. What could possibly go wrong? … That feeling looks like it's going to be broken in a big way because out of the blue … something appears in front of him …"

Abi is next.

"… it is a fierce, angry … but rather beautiful … young lady. She looks at the … let's face it, ugly …young boy and snarls at him. 'You and me' she says, 'we are so different. Let me show you.' … she grabs his arm and drags him to …"

Joe is next. He glares at Abi, but with a smile and seems to be struggling for a few seconds before he continues with the story.

"… a loud, noisy and sweaty nightclub. 'This is my world' she says. 'I am going to show you things that you have only dreamed of …'"

The others laugh as this is an unexpected development from the sensible, straight-laced Joe. He continues.

"… 'Let's …' Before she can say any more, a huge imposing figure appears before them. She gulps. 'What on earth are you doing here?' she says …"

It is Jax's turn. She is quick to continue.

"Professor!' she cries. 'Shouldn't you be in the lab torturing mice, or whatever you do?' …'"

This gets an even greater laugh, even from Joe, who pretends to be offended. She continues.

"… He looks at her with pure kindness and says …"

It's back to Mo. "Thanks, Jax," he whispers under his breath. He had clearly underestimated this group. But he adjusts quickly.

"'I have to take you back to the laboratory … the old witch is stirring. You know what she needs … ah yes', he says, looking at the young boy, 'I see you have found one'. He grabs them both and takes them to ..."

Abi is relishing this and she takes her turn.

"... the ... laboratory." She pronounces this last word in an imposing, dramatic way, adding sound effects. She continues.

"The nasty, ugly, scarred old witch is waiting for them." She glances at Jax as she says this. Jax briefly pokes out her tongue.

"'Ah,' she says. 'Young flesh!' She grabs the young boy and drags him to ..."

"The field of daffodils," says Joe. "She takes his arm and they both dance with great abandon. The young girl and the professor look on amazed. They were fully expecting the witch to have feasted on the young man or something equally ghastly. But then ... something very strange happens ...'

Jax is not fazed and she immediately continues.

"Suddenly a road made out of ... yellow bricks ... unfolds before them and the professor changes into an old scarecrow, quite the most disgusting thing you have ever seen. He links arms with the young girl and ... quite unexpectedly ... over to you, Mo."

"His arm ... drops off and ... disappears into the ground. Suddenly a huge ... beanstalk ... grows out and reaches into the sky, getting taller and taller. The handsome young boy ... he is very handsome, not ugly as had been reported earlier ... decides to climb it ..."

Abi continues. "The young girl follows ... she is a much better climber of course and soon overtakes him ... the old witch also has a go but only manages a couple of metres before falling on her ... fat arse. She sits there and ... has an idea."

Jax butts in.

"She conjures up a chainsaw ... she has a spell for that

... and starts cutting down the ... beanstalk. It doesn't take long before it collapses and the two foolish young things ... come tumbling down ... landing on the scarecrow ... and killing it ..."

"Hey," says Joe, "it's my go."

"I know, but I just had to kill you off ... it just seemed so right ... go on, have your go now," responds Jax. He does.

"But this was no ... ordinary scarecrow ... this was a new breed of super scarecrows ... they weren't going to finish him off so easily, he was just pretending to be dead. He did have ... after all ... a special power ... Mo, it's your go now I believe." Mo complies.

"Yes, indeed ... the straw man grew ... and grew ... and grew ... until it was the size of a minaret ... then it looked down at the old witch and ... go on Abi, have some fun ..."

"... and ... blew and blew and sent her flying through the air into ... the branches of a small tree. There she hung ... upside down ... by the elastic of her underwear ..."

"What a sight," says Joe. "Please do something with that image ... it is so disturbing ... oh good it is my go now ... well ... the other three decide to convene a meeting about this ... what shall we do with the old witch ... do we leave her hanging or do we help her down? ... after an hour of debate they make their decision ..."

They all look at Jax. She doesn't say anything at first. She feels that real life has impinged and she wants to say the right thing, game or no game.

"They are decent people, this giant scarecrow, the young man and the young lady ... and they are filled with sorrow for this ridiculous figure hanging on the tree ... yet she had done a bad thing cutting down that poor beanstalk ... punishment was needed ... yet they looked at this poor, sad, pathetic creature ... so helpless ... so the young man takes the chainsaw and cuts down the tree, the scarecrow lets the witch down gently ... into the arms of the young girl, who ..."

It is Mo's turn.

"Embraces her ... and plants a great big kiss on her cheek."

"Yeuch," says Abi. The others all laugh. Abi shudders. She still has significant issues with Jax.

In the distance they all notice a small awkward man, running towards them. He seems angry, as if he had some sort of control over them and that they had escaped his evil clutches. All four of them look at him, horrified, when suddenly ...

It all goes black and they hear Newts voice. "Back to work I'm afraid, Ladies and Gentlemen."

There are communal groans. It has been a short, but pleasant, distraction. All thoughts of beanstalks and embarrassed evil witches leave them, to be replaced by a feeling of dread.

We see the outside of a huge mansion at the edge of a forest, it seems like an imposing conference centre. It is snowing and there is much activity outside as huge official cars draw up and unload an assortment of Nazi dignitaries. The atmosphere is cold in every sense of the word. It couldn't have been more of a contrast to where they have just been.

"Oh dear, I think I know what's coming ..." says Joe. "Not good ... not good at all."

"The Wannsee Conference centre, January 20th,1942" says Newt, "it will become self-explanatory."

We are inside. Fifteen men, all Nazis, are sitting round a table. Some are smoking cigars and all have filled glasses in front of them.

"The mood is one of begrudging joviality and deep suspicion, as this is a disparate group of high-ranking men with their own agenda. The reason for this meeting is to find agreement on a shared agenda, one that is going to affect the world for decades to come," says Newt.

Each man is identified by an overlayed text window, stating their name and position. Here is a full list:

SS Obergruppenfuehrer Heydrich (Chief Security police)
SS Gruppenfuehrer Eichmann (Reich Security)
Dr. Meyer (Ministry for the Occupied Eastern Territories)
Dr. Leibbrandt (Ministry for the Occupied
Eastern Territories)
Dr. Stuckart (Ministry of the Interior)
Neumann (Plenipotentiary for the Four-Year Plan)
Dr. Freisler (Ministry of Justice)
Dr. Buehler (Office of the Governor General)
Dr. Luther (Foreign Ministry)
SS Oberfuehrer Klopfer (Party Chancellery)
Kritzinger (Reich Chancellery)
SS Gruppenfuehrer Hoffman (Race and Settlement)
SS Gruppenfuehrer Mueller (Reich Security)
SS Oberfuehrer Schoengarth (Security police)
SS Sturmbannfuehrer Dr. Langer (Security police)

"You are not to interact, just to listen to the flow of their conversation. What you will see is a distillation of the key points made here," adds Newt, quietly and sombrely.

Most of the talking is done by Heydrich, who has convened this meeting. He clearly expects total agreement and implies consequences to any who may oppose him. He begins.

"Gentlemen, this is to be a secret meeting. There is to be no mention of this meeting. You are all bearers of ... secrets, is that understood? What we have here, frankly, is a storage problem in our need to expel all Jews from our living space, in the Jew-free society we are creating. We have tried emigration; that avenue has been exhausted. What we are looking for here is the complete solution for the Jewish question. This is our mandate here."

"As I said, this is a storage issue. We can't afford to store them; emigration is out of the question so ... how do we get rid of them? Evacuation?"

"I shot 30,000 Jews in Riga," says Lange. "Is that an 'evacuation'?"

"Yes. And all 'exemptions' will be sterilised. We have already sterilised over 300,000 in Germany."

"Death is the most reliable form of sterilisation," adds Eichmann.

"And the method?"

"We can't afford to waste our resources on dealing with Jews," says Lange.

"Shooting them is inefficient in terms of men, time and equipment. Gas is cheaper."

"We have already been using carbon monoxide in portable trucks", adds Eichmann. "We can kill 60 in one go this way."

"It seems that you have already decided on this method," says Lange. "So why this meeting?"

"We all need to be unanimous on this, so we can all take the glory."

"We have tried other gases ... and electrocution ..."

"We estimate that we can kill 28,000 a day with gas," says Meyer to a spontaneous explosion of clapping and cheering.

"There are already three camps in preparation."

"Auschwitz is being prepared," says Eichmann. "We can process 2,500 an hour ... 60,000 a day We have created a shower room ... they actually believe they are having a shower."

More clapping and cheering.

"And disposal of the bodies?"

"Combustion."

"60,000 a day ... all up in smoke ... Imagine!" says Mueller.

There is even greater applause at this.

"An assembly line ... a triumphant German vision. Let's link arms and work on this, friends. The machinery is waiting ... feed it! Get them to the trains ... keep the trains rolling ... and history will honour us for having the will to thus advance the human race ... this would astonish Charles Darwin ... the eradication of the unworthy ..." says Heydrich, who stands up, arms aloft and receives unanimous applause.

"And remember," he says in wrapping this up. "All of your notes of this meeting must be destroyed."

As this meeting is taking place our group wander around the room, together. Their senses are on fire. What they are experiencing here is total evil, they can actually feel it. It brings a shiver to their spines, all of them. To hear the destruction of human beings being discussed as if they were inconvenient and disposable beasts is beyond awful. Any thoughts of the nobility of man are destroyed as they witness here the depths that humanity can dredge. All fifteen of these men, all psychopaths, yet educated, with doctorates and qualifications as lawyers, have reverted to the lowest spiritual state possible, beasts without conscience. Charles Darwin would not only be astonished but he would surely be driven to suicide by this repudiation of any thoughts he may have about the nobility of man.

"If it makes you feel any better, Heydrich was assassinated two months later ..." says Newt.

"... and Eichmann, who took over from him, was eventually captured by the Israelis," adds Joe.

"Good for them" says Jax. "They have my admiration for that ... look ... I still have goosebumps."

"And that, Jax ... is ... the very definition of genocide."

Jax has no answer. Abi and Mo have been struck dumb. Neither are going to speak for some time.

"One question, Newt", if all records of the meeting were destroyed, how do we know what happened?," asks Joe.

"One transcript survived. It was hidden but found after the war."

Thankfully, these are the final scenes and Newt walks round and removes their HR caps. They are uncharacteristically speechless for a long time, each lost in their thoughts, reliving images that have intruded into their minds and poisoned their souls.

After a suitable delay, Newt speaks.

"Antisemitism is real and it has never really gone away. If there's only one thing you have learned so far, then that should be it. Now ... there's a lot to process and ... a lot more to discuss. But ... I think you have all earned a break."

The dinner tables reappear, the lighting changes and soft music is pumped in. It is clearly intended to break the atmosphere and dispel the heaviness that, otherwise, may have dragged them down and made them unfit for purpose. Because they have a purpose, a very real purpose, to be revealed ... all in good time.

Chapter seventeen

"What on earth has just happened?" says Jax, after stuffing an egg sandwich into her mouth.

They are sitting together in a small circle near the food-laden tables. This is a breakthrough and Newt knows it well. This is why he is keeping his distance and busying himself with some imaginary tasks but, in reality, doing his best to eavesdrop on the conversation. This may not have been his best move as he was, very soon, the topic of conversation and not in a good way.

"Newt had promised us 'no more surprises' ... well that seems now to be a downright lie," responds Joe.

"How was this even possible ... what just happened to us ... it was real wasn't it and not a dream?" asks Abi.

"And there's me thinking it was just a big awkward dream" responds Jax. Abi turns her back on her, something that Newt notices. So does Joe, who gives her a big smile, hoping that she interprets it as fatherly concern, rather than something awkward. She smiles back, but only swiftly.

"Is this something that ... is normal ... where you come from?" asks Mo, to no-one in particular.

"Certainly not," responds Jax, "and I'm quite au fait with new technology and such. I'm quite into VR these days."

"VR?"

"Virtual Reality, Mo. Like the Holo Reality we experienced, but an earlier version," responds Abi. Mo notes it's one of the few times she has addressed him by name in the group.

"This is way beyond any technology I've heard of," says Joe. "It's almost as if ..."

And he turns round to Newt, who immediately looks away.

"... they are experimenting on us. Anyone else feel that way?"

Jax also turns round and fixes Newt with a savage glare.

"Know what you mean, professor. Frankly I don't think it's much fun anymore ... but the food's good."

"And the company?" suggests Joe, surprisingly.

"Professor! Are you coming on to me?" says Jax.

Nothing could be further from the truth. Joe indicates this with an embarrassed blush and the immediate loss of eye contact.

"Your loss!"

While they are sparring, Abi has moved her seat closer to Mo, twisting her position so that Jax is not in sight.

"Horrible woman," she says.

"Not the nicest person," he agrees. "Certainly not the nicest lady in the room," he adds, cheekily.

"Are you coming on to me?" she exclaims, a lightness in her voice, with a clumsy attempt at Jax's peculiar vowel pronunciation. He laughs. She laughs. The ice is broken ... finally.

"So, we're good?" asks Mo.

"As good as it is possible to be for two 'sworn enemies' to be in this cooped up place with a pair of geriatrics and a know-it-all."

"Yes. Just a normal situation, really."

"We're the only two normal people here, Mo."

"Let's hope this remains so and that ... this experience doesn't break us. I get the feeling that it has only just started."

"Me too ... but we're strong people, aren't we? We'll get through whatever they throw at us."

"Yes ... I think so."

Neither of them look totally convinced.

Meanwhile, Jax and Joe seemed to be getting on well, despite having virtually nothing in common, apart from their age.

"So, when did you discover Stevie Wonder, professor?" asks Jax.

"I will answer you ... if you kindly stop calling me 'professor' ... we may not agree on much ... or anything really ... but we can at least be civil with each other at mealtimes, Jax."

"OK ... a truce for now ... Joe".

She smiles and a piece of crust drops out of her mouth into her lap.

Joe smiles back, not least because of the dribbles that follow the breadcrumbs down the left side of her chin, mixing up in the sparse hairs that have taken root there. He looks closer and notices, for the first time, a pink birthmark among the hairs. He wonders whether she was allowing the hair to grow perhaps to cover it up.

Jax points at the other two and whispers.

"I bet they feel a bit ... overwhelmed ... being in the room with us. I hope we haven't seemed a bit too ... what's the word?"

"Weird? Overbearing? Out of touch?"

"So, we're not on the same page here, professor."

"Probably not. Certainly, the way Abi looks at us, I don't think there's that much respect there."

"Not for me, anyway. I think she has something against me."

"You think?"

"Yes."

"I think you're right. Mind you, young Mo is a treasure."

"I thought you didn't like Arabs."

"What? That's an insult ... wherever have I given that impression?"

"Just from who you are, I suppose ... and the way you support the Jews."

"Doesn't mean I hate the Arabs. You are so wrong there."

"What about Hamas and Hezbollah?"

"I will make an exception there."

"Aren't you Christians meant to love your enemies?"

Joe has no answer at that. Jax smirks at her little victory.

"Abi, can I say something?," says Mo, a little hesitant.

"Of course, Mo."

"We are proper friends now?"

"Well … we're 'roomies' aren't we … let's see how it pans out, shall we?"

That was the closest to a 'yes' that he would get for now, so he continues.

"There's a story I'd like to tell you. It's been passed down through my family."

"Is it safe? It's not going to, y'know, stir things up?"

"No."

"Good … then let me fetch one of those yummy-looking salmon bagels first. Want one?

"Um, no … but thanks for asking. You are kind."

"And you are so … polite … it's very refreshing. You're very … different."

Mo ignores the compliment and, while Abi munches on her bagel, he tells his story. Newt listens too but makes no show of it.

"Once upon a time, a young man left his father, saying, I am going to learn a trade and be the very best at it. Soon, after travelling the world, he returns and says, 'I have become an expert designer of chandeliers and there is none better than me at this'. 'OK' says his father, a bit taken aback. You create the very best chandelier and I will get the leading chandelier makers in town to assess your work.' This is what happened. These craftsmen came, assessed the young man's work and agreed that ... they had never seen such a monstrosity! They all agreed that some aspects were very good, even excellent, but others were hideous, but they weren't always in agreement as to which were the good bits and which were the bad bits. How was he going to break this to his proud son? But he did. His son's reply surprised him. He said, 'While I was away I studied the work of all of these craftsmen, particularly focusing on their deficiencies and so I decided to create a chandelier that combined all of their imperfections. This is what you see before you. Each could see each other's imperfections, but did not recognise their own. In this way they all eventually became better craftsmen.'"

He stops and Abi thinks for a bit.

"Is that it?" she says.

"Yes."

"No clever conclusion?"

"Yes ... I said ... they all became better at their jobs."

"I think maybe there is more to this story?"

"Perhaps ... I just felt I had to tell you this ... not sure why."

She nods in encouragement. Newt also nods, but more to himself.

"Mo."

"Yes."

"Sorry about earlier, walking away from you like I did."

"I am sure you had your reasons. Actually ... that seems like ages ago, doesn't it?"

"It does. But it's been preying on my mind a bit."

"It's OK. I don't need to know ... it's enough that you've brought it up."

"OK ... Thanks. I appreciate that."

"I was a strange child", says Joe, leaning back in his

chair. "I was brought up very conventionally, I was polite and neat; butter wouldn't melt in my mouth. But ..."

"Go on, Go on ... Prof ... Joe!" Jax responds, unaware of the gungy mess on her chin.

"First let me do this," says Joe, who takes a serviette and briskly wipes her chin.

"What a gentleman you are!"

"Some characteristics ... can never be bred out," he responds, before continuing.

"I had a secret life, growing up in the 60s."

"Oh yes? Cannabis? Magic mushrooms? LSD?"

"Um, no, Jax ... it was about the music of the time. You'd look at me and think 'Ah yes here's a classical music buff if I've ever seen one' ..."

"... I certainly would do now. Look at you. I can just see you in a comfy armchair with your slippers on, with the Mozart on the HiFi and you waving your arms around like a conductor."

"No ... appearances can be deceptive, madam. I would have been more at home striding in front of the mirror playing air guitar."

"You're joking."

"No ... though I wasn't really into the guitar groups or white pop music. More James Brown than Joe Brown. But ... Tamla Motown, that was different ... my greatest favourites."

"Did you go the whole hog and identify as ... black? Bet you also watched the 'Black and White Minstrels'."

"No.. and no, Jax ... now you're jumping to ridiculous conclusions. When I say embarrassing I mean disappearing to my bedroom on Sunday afternoons to listen to Alan Freeman and the Hit Parade, hoping to hear a ... Jackson Five, Supremes or ... especially ... Stevie Wonder. I can even recite the words to Signed, Sealed, Delivered ..."

"Perhaps another time." She fears that she is about to hear a rendition of the same.

"Isn't it interesting," he says thoughtfully, "that the only place our worlds have collided is through Stevie Wonder."

She pauses for dramatic effect and then says, "And here ... in this ... precious moment?"

"Yes. This is quite pleasant."

"In what way?"

"Us sitting here, talking like adults and not arguing."

"Oh come on, I love a good argument. I bet you do too, I can see it in your face."

"Certainly not."

"True."

"Rubbish."

"Look, Prof., we're arguing about whether you're argumentative. I think I've proven my case."

"Very clever, now excuse me while I fetch a sandwich, I've got a strange taste in my mouth."

He wanders over to the food table.

"Another one bites the dust," says Jax to herself.

Newt calls them all to order.

"Five minutes ... then back to work," he shouts.

Five minutes laterrrr (in a French accent).

"If you remember," says Newt. "I posed a question, that Joe and Jax both answered ... but we left it hanging."

"Please remind us," says Jax.

"Why did the Arab nations invade Israel in 1948?"

"Oh yes."

"And Joe's answer led us to that rather horrific segway ... sorry for exposing you to those scenes, but perhaps you understand why now ..."

"No, not really" responds Jax, honestly.

"We needed to get right to the heart of the whole matter. No distractions, no political detours ... the very heart of the matter."

"Antisemitism" declares Mo. "I am still ... reeling." He looks sadly at Abi, who smiles weakly back, perhaps because she didn't want – or need – reminding of the fact that she is the sole representative in this room of a people that have been hated like none other, even to this day. Newt continues.

"Yes, Mo. To remind us of what he said ... the Arab invasion was nothing about reclaiming territory ... it was nothing short of genocide."

"Genocide?" says Jax. "Oh, come on ... now what Israel is doing now is ... Genocide. The world can see it."

The gloves were off. It didn't take long. Thoughts of Stevie Wonder and a gentler era are now long gone. Joe responds.

"Just because there was no social media or satellite TV or whatever to track every movement ... it doesn't mean that wasn't their intentions, Jax. They wanted to wipe out Israel from the face of a map that hadn't even been drawn yet!"

"Rubbish. Where is the evidence?"

"Plenty of evidence."

Newt intervenes. "Actually this is a suitable time to return to our story and examine whether there is any evidence. Let's see what happened after the war of 1948."

Chapter eighteen

"Despite being attacked by all surrounding nations, Israel prevailed and, in fact, ended up with more territory than it started with," says Newt.

"Amazing," says Mo, who clearly has little knowledge of the historical facts. "How could this have been?"

"One word, Mo," says Joe. "God!"

"Wondered when you were going to bring up the … Old Fella" says Jax sarcastically.

"Nevertheless …" responds Joe, leaving it in the air. Newt continues.

"I want to concentrate on the actual land areas themselves. Watch how the area changes over time, right from ancient times."

A map appears in the holo-bubble, with a title alongside it. It starts in Roman times, when the region was called *Syria Palaestina*, as a renaming of the Jewish region of Judea, after the failed Bar Kokhba revolt. Interestingly, this covered an area to the east of the Jordan River, part of modern-day Jordan. This is followed by the Byzantine period, when the region is divided vertically, but still extends eastwards. Then Crusader times, when it is called the Kingdom of Jerusalem and extends even further southwards, to the east of the river. Ottoman Palestine encroached even more to the east of the river, covering most of modern Jordan. Then the British Mandate period, when the area of "Palestine" now becomes Transjordan to the east and Palestine to the west. Newt pauses the display.

"So, the area historically called 'Palestine' has always included part, if not all, of the area currently in modern-day Jordan, though it was called 'Transjordan' between 1921 and 1946. What does that tell us?"

Joe is the quickest to reply.

"Palestine has always been on both sides of the river until it was lopped off in the east and renamed Transjordan. So ... Jordan has always been a part of historical Palestine."

"Now watch what happens after the 1948 war", says Newt.

The map changes and the West Bank appears. Newt continues.

"Although Israel made many conquests, it failed to conquer this lump of land to the west of the river Jordan, right up to East Jerusalem. The contentious area is known as the West Bank."

"Judea and Samaria ... ancient Israel", remarks Joe.

"The West Bank," corrects Jax, "the occupied West Bank."

"I don't understand," says Abi, whose knowledge of history is evidentially patchy.

"What don't you understand?" replies Newt.

"Two things. Number one ... why is it called 'occupied'?"

"Because people were still living there at the time," responds Jax.

"But didn't Israel conquer other parts of the land where Arabs were living? They did win the war, right?"

"Yes."

"Then why aren't those places called 'occupied' too? From my ... very sketchy ... knowledge of European history ... didn't loads of borders change after the Second World War and new nations pop up? I don't hear the word 'occupied' used then. It's what happens in wars, right? Why is this different from Palestine?"

"Because ...", Jax starts to answer before engaging her brain. Joe answers for her.

"Abi is right of course. Look at the Soviet Union, Germany, Poland, Czechoslovakia ..."

"Oh shut up, professor." Jax has reverted to his nickname. Newt speaks.

"And what is your second point, Abi? You said you had two points."

"Yes … as you said, Jordan was originally part of Palestine, why couldn't those in the West Bank move to Jordan, rather than live as a conquered people? I just don't get it. The Palestinians and the Jordanians … they are the same people! Look at the Palestinian flag, it's the same as the Jordanian flag, with just a little bit missing!"

"Why should they be told to just get up and move?" answers Jax.

"Because they lost the war!" retorts Joe, impatiently. "It's what people do. Think of how many Syrians had lost their homes under Assad; were kicked out of their homes by their own people and ended up as migrants with absolutely nothing? To say nothing of how many of their fellow Muslims were killed … around half a million I believe!"

He pauses and looks directly at Jax and even points at her.

"Why should the Palestinians be any different, eh? Could it be that there were no Jews involved in Syria?"

Jax has no answer and it shows on her face. She excuses herself and walks swiftly to the toilet. Newt looks at Mo.

"And what do you think, Mo?"

"I don't know. It's a bit beyond my understanding. I can only talk from my own family's perspective. The war had no real effect on us, we just carried on living as Muslim Arabs in Israel. We just got on with … living."

"Politics!" sneers Joe. "Not the best way of running a society, is it."

"Or hatred," adds Abi, more animated than she has been for hours.

"So," says Newt. "The West Bank ... what an emotive subject. No piece of the land in the world has become such a powder keg of tension, mistrust, hatred and conflict. Yet ..."

He pauses.

"In 1948 it could have been so different. You know, around 276,000 Palestinians moved into the West Bank then. If they had carried on moving eastwards to Jordan we really wouldn't have the problem we have today. In fact, they became 'settlers' themselves, they weren't indigenous to the area. The Jews who followed them in 1967, the so-called 'settlers' were doing the same thing."

"But in their case," adds Joe, "they came as victors of a war they didn't even start. They had every right to."

"Let's not jump the gun, Joe."

Jax had just returned, refreshed and recharged.

"Rights?!" she said. "What about Palestinian rights?"

She has misread the mood and the thrust of the discussion and so no-one responds. Newt continues.

"But ... it is what it is. We can't change the past and what happened and what should have happened etc. We must consider the present situation and Jax ... I have to agree with your last statement. It's not a good situation for the Palestinian Arabs in the West Bank at the moment. Rather than look at the causes and decisions that were made by other people, we must consider the plight of those who live there now."

"Thank you," replies Jax, quietly.

"But, continuing our story, in 1950, Jordan, saw this lump of land to their west that they occupied after the war and simply annexed it ... illegally. Only Britain, Iraq and Pakistan approved of this. So, when Israel conquered the West Bank in 1967 following the Six-Day War, it could have been very easy for the Palestinians, many of whom were recent immigrants to the area, to simply have moved to Jordan, a country that had already granted them citizenship in 1950."

"Again, I ask, why should they leave their homes?" says Jax.

"Again, I respond, because they have ... yet again ... lost a war," responds Joe, immediately. "Have you forgotten those conversations we had earlier with those refugees from so many conflicts ... all lost their homes, including hundreds of thousands of Jews, and many would have had to travel for hundreds of miles to find new homes. And, of course, it is still happening today. So why should it be any different for the Palestinians? Jax ... Don't you get it?"

"It's difficult to ..."

She is strangely hesitant. Joe rescues her by interrupting.

"Also, I think, with hindsight, I bet those Palestinians in 1948 wish they had gone to Jordan rather than allow themselves to live as political pawns, slaves to the hatred their leaders had against the Jews? Can you imagine it if they had known that their grandchildren, even great- grandchildren were going to be trapped by their own people ... this is why I grieve for them and my question is this, Jax ... *why don't you?*"

There is a sudden silence, with all eyes on Jax. She pauses and doesn't answer. Instead, she deflects.

"And what about those on the West Bank, professor? Don't you admit that the West Bank Palestinians have been given a hard time by the Jews?"

Joe believes that he has hit home with his point, but does not want to shame her. He senses that a breakthrough may have been made. So, he answers her deflection.

"Actually ... I would probably agree with you there, Jax."

She is taken aback, unused to victory in this ongoing debate. Newt responds.

"You are both right. Life for Arabs in the West Bank has

certainly not been easy. Let's have a look."

The holo-bubble starts up again with some film sequences produced by al-Jazeera, showing the hardships they have suffered. Even stripping out the emotional tone, some facts were undeniable. Palestinian Arabs, in general, do not have the same rights as the Jewish occupants and the Israeli authorities go to great measures to make sure life is as awkward as possible, with the massive queues at the checkpoints, regular harassment, victimisation by soldiers and worse. It is not a good watch, particularly when you see the young age of many of the IDF soldiers and the arrogance displayed by many of them. There is little love between the communities and you can understand the resentment against the Jewish 'settlers'. One word bandied about a lot is *apartheid* and, although the persecution is nowhere near the levels once experienced by blacks in South Africa, you can see an implementation of a watered-down version here in the West Bank.

When the report is over, something more evocative takes its place. We see a small Palestinian village, with a few very poor people going about their daily business. A voice-over proclaims:

'This is Zeita, an ancient village at the western edge of the West Bank since the Byzantine eta. It became part of the Ottoman Empire in 1517 when there were under one hundred households, mostly Muslim. In 1922, under the British Mandate there were 1,087 inhabitants, all Muslim. In 1948, it came under Jordanian rule, then, after 1967, became party of the 'Occupied' West Bank. Just over 3,000 people are living there now. A man is in a taxi with his father. They are driving back to Zeita for the first time since 1967.'

"Do you feel the breeze?" says the father.

"Yes, I do ... where does it come from?"

"The Mediterranean sea ... the land between the village and the coast was ours until 1948 and we often took trips to the sea before then."

"Now it is Israeli land ... and our village is in the 'occupied' land."

"Yes ... it is hard to accept, son."

The taxi stops briefly at a border post and then they carry on; their final leg.

"There were fierce battles here in 1967," says the father. "The Jordanians weren't up for a fight. After all they had no planes left and the Jewish planes were creating much damage."

"It must have been awful, father."

"It was."

"What happened when the Jordanians left Zeita?"

"Well, we waited and waited ... for the Jews to come and when they did ... one idiot, Abu, actually fired at them ... he claimed he hit a tank, which was a lie ... he ruined it for us all."

"What happened then?"

"We put white flags on our roofs. We surrendered. Fighting was not an option, son."

"Was there trouble?"

"The Jews told us all to gather at the eastern part of the village ... and wait."

"Why was that?"

"They told us they were searching for weapons, when in fact they had been blowing up houses."

"What did you do?"

"Nothing at the time. We could hear the explosions; we thought they were blowing up bunkers and trenches ... we found out soon enough though. Most houses were gone ... ours wasn't, we were one of the lucky ones."

"Why leave us alone?"

"We never found out. But we praise God for it."

"Basically, the soldiers could do what they wanted ... didn't have to give a reason."

"That's war, son ... that's war."

The screen switches off.

"See ... they gave no reason. Is that normal behaviour?" says Jax.

"It's war time, as he said, Jax. Look what the Jordanians did in the Old City of Jerusalem when they captured it in 1948."

Abi takes over. "They destroyed the whole Jewish Quarter and either destroyed or defaced every synagogue there. They even destroyed the Jewish cemetery on the Mount of Olives, in order to build toilets ... is that 'normal' behaviour, Jax?"

"As the professor said ... times of war," is her weak answer, not looking at Abi, who isn't looking at her either.

"I'm not excusing the Israelis, by the way", says Joe. "I know they still have a policy of house demolition and I'm sure there's not always a good reason for them to do so."

"Our cousins lost their home in Jenin" says Mo.

"Was there a reason?" asks Abi.

"None was given at the time. I know it's not the same as killing people and firing rockets, but it's still a form of terrorism. The end result is still ... terror ... with other families fearing that they may be next."

"You're right, Mo. Pretty awful. Times of war, eh?" Abi says this with a sigh.

Newt turns to Mo.

"I think it will be useful, perhaps as a point of contrast, for you, Mo, to give us an idea of what life is like in Israel as a Palestinian Muslim Arab."

"Actually, I call myself an Israeli Arab. I am a citizen of Israel, you know? And I have the same legal rights as my Jewish neighbours, so ... when I hear about apartheid, I say

... what's this? OK, there are times when I feel that I'm not getting as good a deal as Jewish friends, but ... to be really honest ... I thank Allah that I'm living under Israeli rule, not under Arab rule in the territories. I look at this nice girl here and think ... you know, she is Jewish and I'm a Muslim, but we're both Israelis and we can be friends."

"Too right," exclaims Abi. "He's certainly more polite than any of my Jewish friends!"

"Be honest, there must be some restrictions in your life?" asks Jax.

"Quite the opposite ... I am free to do what I want on the Jewish Sabbath, as a Muslim. But, joking aside, I could serve in the IDF and even run as a politician in the Knesset but ... I am quite content being as I am."

"I can see why they chose you, Mo, for this programme. Pliable is the word, I think," says Jax.

"Are you ... insulting me, madam?"

"No, she doesn't mean it, Mo." Joe comes to her defence. "That's just her way. She can't help it." Jax fixes him a malevolent stare, but tempers it with a wink, so he is unsure what she is trying to signal.

"It is interesting to see how better life is for Arabs under Israeli rule than it is in places, the West Bank and Gaza, where there is a degree of self-determination," remarks Joe. "Particularly in Gaza, of course, where Hamas rules their people with an iron fist."

"And you know that for sure, professor?"

"You are joking. Where have you been over the last two years? Oh yes ... I know ... demonstrating on the streets with the rest of the deluded Marxists!" sneers Joe, a little too forcefully.

"Come on Ladies and Gentlemen, a little bit of decorum I think" says Newt, trying to deflect. "We are going to move on to the present, soon but, in the way of a summary, we are going to look at one place, somewhere we have already visited, Hebron. What happened there since the massacre in 1929 has been described as a microcosm of both the Israel-Palestinian conflict and the Israeli occupation of the West Bank. Sit back ... and be educated."

The holo-bubble shows a series of images of Hebron through the ages, accompanied by the following voice-over.

'After the 1929, riots, the Jewish population were evacuated for their safety. Two years later, thirty-five families moved back but, because of general unease, the British moved them out again. All apart from one man, Ya'akov ben Shalom Ezra, who worked in the dairy trade and was considered a friend of all. He eventually moved out in 1947, just before the UN vote.'

'In 1948, Egypt took charge of Hebron, after many tussles with Jordan. There were deadly skirmishes and eventually Jordan won out. All signs of the prior Jewish presence were removed. In 1967 came the Six-Day War and everything changed. As Israeli tanks approached, Palestinian fighters laid down their weapons and the rest waved white linens of surrender from their houses. They feared retribution for the 1929 massacre. Many took to the hills, and others retrieved letters of gratitude their forefathers had received in 1929 for saving them from the mobs. There was no revenge and the Islamic holy sites and mosques were untouched.'

'The Israelis occupied Hebron, as the spoils of war and established a military government to rule this key West Bank town. Jews returned to the town in small numbers. Thousands of Israelis streamed into Hebron to pray at the Tomb of the Patriarchs for the first time. Jews had been banned from the city since 1947.

One of the Arab leaders, Sheikh Farid Khader opposed the concept of Palestinian rule here and he believed that Jews and Arabs must learn to coexist. There was a violent episode in 1980 when a PLO (Palestine Liberation Organisation) squad killed five

Jewish students. Yasser Arafat, their leader, claimed this was the beginning of a new phase in the armed struggle against Israel. The IDF responded by demolishing a neighbourhood adjacent to the attack. It also had the effect of emboldening many of the Jews and many now joined militant groups, particularly the Kach movement. They, in turn, attacked the Islamic University in 1983, killing three and injuring over thirty others. This was in response to the killing of a Jewish American student, Aharon Gross, in a marketplace.'

'The most infamous event was in 1994, when Baruch Goldstein, an Israeli doctor, opened fire in the Mosque, killing 29 and wounding 125, before being killed by the survivors, rather than by the Israeli soldiers, who were instructed not to fire on other Jews. This event was condemned by the Israeli government and Kach was banned. In 1997, Hebron was split into two sectors, H1, controlled by the Palestinian Authority and H2, controlled by Israel. H1 now has around 120,000 Palestinians and H2 has 30,000. However only 700 Jews live in the Jewish settlement, which is considered illegal by the international community.'

'During the First and Second Intifadas, the Jewish community came under attack by militants and, in 2002, twelve Israeli soldiers were killed in an ambush. In 2007 the Palestinian population in H2 declined due to security measures such as extended curfews, the closure of businesses and harassment by settlers. One street, Al-Shuhada Street was banned to Palestinians, earning it the nickname 'Apartheid Street'. There were many reports from humanitarian organisations of harassment of the Arabs by both the Jewish settlers and IDF soldiers, recording over 40,000 incidents.'

'It is a city divided. H2, the Israeli-controlled side, is run down. There are no cafes, hotels or shopping centres. But H1 is a different story. It is a lively Arab city, buzzing with life and vitality, much like any city in Europe. But there is a difference. Some people there may live for the present, but the past may very well be another country. Here is a conversation between a tourist and an Arab *student who lived there.'*

"What are you told about the massacre here in 1929?"

"What massacre?"

"The riots ... all those Jews killed."

"Oh yes, that was the British that did that, not us."

"Really? Are you sure?"

"Of course. And another thing ... these Jews ... they have no connection here."

"What about the tomb of the Patriarchs?"

"That's our history ... Ibrahim ... the Jews, they are just the killers of the prophets. They have no history here."

"That's not my understanding."

"You're a Westerner. What do you know, you have been fed with Zionist propaganda."

This, unfortunately, is a common response. Sadly, the Arabs have been taught a very different history.'

The display suddenly ends.

"Quite telling, especially that last bit," remarks Joe.

"That's a lot of information to take in, though", says Abi. "My brain hurts. Perhaps I'm just tired."

"Interesting, though," adds Jax. "Much food for thought."

"Speaking of food," adds Mo, "is it not time for another meal?"

Thoughts of food soon leave them when the next chapter begins.

Chapter nineteen

This time the huge screen on the back wall rolls down and a four-minute movie is shown, *'October 7th: Through Their Eyes: Exploring Hate.'* It includes genuine eyewitness stories from the massacre and features the imperative that 'the world has to know'. Newt speaks.

"We could have shown you the official government-sponsored 45-minute film of the massacre, but that would have been unfair as it is extremely harrowing. Instead, we would like you to see these testimonies and then comment on them."

The film is a collection of smartphone clips from eyewitnesses. The images of young, terrified people are heart-wrenching.

"A guy jumps into my car, asking for help. He's bleeding. We say we need to help him when trucks filled with terrorists start shooting at us from every direction. We heard the bullets flying near us and people just falling, the terrorists were after us coming from all directions, just trying to murder. Suddenly, I felt a sharp explosive pain. BOOM. They hit me. I screamed, 'They shot me! They shot me!' I had been shot 12 times – bullets in my legs, my left hand and my shoulder. I lay there bleeding between the bodies of my friends when suddenly I felt someone breathing. It was my friend. Amit's boyfriend decided to take a selfie. 'At least if we die, our families will have a memento to see that we loved each other to the very end.'"

"He was murdered. The terrorists shot him as he tried to escape through the window."

"So much death and hate. I realised that between all the bombs, gunshots and screams, the birds were still singing."

"For a moment there we could practically see them as they came to enter the room. I covered my two-year-old daughter, who

was asleep, hoping they wouldn't see her and I drew my last breath."

"I held onto the hand of the dead body lying on top of me and said thank you for shielding me."

Then it finished and the screen rolled up, leaving behind a blank wall and a small, shocked group of people.

"Well at least we didn't get the raw footage propaganda that the Israeli government was putting out to shock the world" says Jax, trying to break the tension, but failing.

"Why do you say that, Jax?" says Joe. "Are you in denial as to what your Hamas friends actually did that day?"

"They are not my friends. Did I ever say that?"

"But you wouldn't call them terrorists, would you?"

Jax fails to see the trap. "Freedom fighters," she says, defiantly.

"You still believe that?"

The angry glare from Abi could have melted an iceberg.

Newt starts to speak as he can see a volcano about to erupt. Mo does more. He leaves his seat, walks over to Abi and gently embraces her as she dissolves into sobs. Joe stares at Jax angrily. Jax just shrugs, seemingly oblivious to the emotions she has stirred up with her insensitive comment.

"Let's have some moments to reflect," says Newt. He gestures to Mo, to return to his seat.

What happens next is unexpected. After a minute or so, after she has dried her eyes, Abi stands up with a look of fierce determination.

"I have had enough … I'm out!" she announces and strides off to the ladies' toilet.

After the shock has died down, Mo stands up, perhaps to follow her. Newt stops him with a wave of his hand and he walks over to the ladies' toilet. He finds Abi in a cubicle, sitting on the seat, her head in her hand. She had been crying, but now her face is hard and resolute.

"Abi," says Newt. "What is wrong?"

"As I said, I've had enough."

"Had enough? Of what?"

"Of this whole ... thing."

"Why, Abi?"

"It's her!"

"Her?" Newt pretends not to know but has already guessed the source of this conflict.

"Jax?"

"That ... shitty woman!"

"That's a bit ... extreme, don't you think? She's ... passionate, certainly ... but it's all just her opinions ... it doesn't make her right ... and I do sense a ... softening."

"Really? Well, I don't see that, anyway ... it's not that."

"Then what is it?"

"I have met her before ..."

This floors Newt because the selection process for the programme ensured that none of the delegates would have met each other before and would certainly not have any prior history with each other. This is unexpected; even now he suspects that there will be consternation among the 'controllers'. Would they even pull the programme now? He hopes not.

"Are you sure, Abi?"

"100%. I knew it when I saw her birthmark ... the one on her chin ... I was prepared to let it go until ... until ... it just got too much."

"Can you ... tell me more about this. How did you meet her?"

Abi is silent for a bit while she thinks things through.

"No, Newt. I want to tell my story to the group ... together."

"Then you're coming back?"

"Yes ... to tell my story ... then after that ... it depends ... but, first ... you can do something for me ..."

THE CHANDELIER MAKER

Chapter twenty

Abi has returned. Her face may be tear-stained, but her demeanour is purposeful. The group wait in anticipation as Newt has already told them that she is going to make a statement. Abi hasn't taken her eyes off Jax once, which must be very disquieting for the older woman, as it is in marked contrast to being totally blanked, as she has been up to now. The screen on the back wall has been activated, with a video in standby mode. But all eyes are on Abi. She speaks.

"A few weeks ago I visited London with some friends, to see the sights and have some fun. What we didn't know was that every Saturday, there was a pro-Palestinian demo in the city ... every Saturday! With thousands on the march. We were curious. So we bought some headgear and scarves ... as a disguise y'know ... and went along to see what goes on at these events ... We were prepared for the worst ... but what we got was the very worst of the worst ...

She takes a sip of water. She is still looking straight at Jax, who has now averted her eyes and seems to be silently speaking to herself. If she hadn't been an atheist, one could imagine that she is actually praying. Abi continues.

"A young Muslim man was wandering around with a microphone. We could see he was targeting mainly middle-aged white people, though he did speak to some young people and some kids. We got close enough to hear but not too close in case he got suspicious or, even worse, decided to interview us ... well that would have been fun ... but I doubt whether we would have got out alive!"

She lightens up and there are a few smiles. But still, she stares at Jax, who is getting increasingly fidgety.

"I won't tell you what we heard. It was shocking but we didn't video any of it. But then I saw a familiar face and out came my phone. It was her ..."

She nods towards Jax, who is now ashen-faced, but still, like a prisoner waiting for a verdict.

"I recognised her. She's a big name in the 'we hate Israel' lobby and we all knew about her. 'Know your enemy' as they say. Also, she has this birthmark on her chin ... yes it was definitely her. I was prepared to just listen and decided to put my phone away until ... until she said this ... 'can this be off-camera, what I'm going to say first ... then I'm happy for you to film me' ... Well, how can I not record this? So, I set up my phone and covered it with my scarf, so only the lens was just visible, only just. You'll hear her voice and see parts of her, but you'll recognise her ..."

Newt now plays the video on the back screen.

"Can you tell me why you are here supporting Palestine?"

"Well if we don't stand up for what's happening to the people in Palestine, then the same thing is going to happen to all of us. All the killing, all the genocide that is happening in Palestine, it just shows that they don't care for people's lives."

"What message would you give to someone who supports Israel?"

"If you're supporting Israel, then you must understand that what Israel is doing at the moment shows that they have no sense of humanity, what it means to be a human being. Palestinians ... us ... at the end of the day we are all human beings, we have to look after one another and that's not what Israel is doing at the moment."

"And does Israel have the right to defend itself?"

"Israel has no right to defend itself from what's happening in Palestine. The Palestinian people have the right to defend themselves, Israelis are occupiers in a land that was never theirs."

The screen freezes and there is a deathly silence. Abi cannot contain herself anymore.

"So, I am not a human being in your eyes, old woman, eh? I bet you can't bear to be in the same room as me, eh? How do you answer that ... eh?"

Jax attempts to collect her thoughts.

"No ... I didn't say that."

"Yes you did, madam," says Mo.

"No, but I didn't mean it ... you've taken it the wrong way."

"Jax ... we have just watched you say these things ... now answer the girl."

Jax glares at him out of frustration. She stalls.

"I ... I just ... look, it was the atmosphere ... you say these things that you regret afterwards ..."

"Rubbish," says Joe. "You specifically asked them not to film you ... you meant every word."

"Perhaps ... at the time ... as I said ... the atmosphere ..."

"You take it all back now?"

Newt halts the conversation and speaks. He can see how riled up the other three are and he can also see how dangerous this is to the programme. He needs to turn this around.

"Jax mentioned the atmosphere. Before we lay into her any more I want to play some other clips from that particular demo. Listen to them, judge the environment and then evaluate what they're saying." "How could you have found ...?" says Abi.

"I'm a good researcher. I told you that before. They've all been uploaded on TikTok ... just listen to this selection."

The video restarts, with the same Muslim man interviewing others at that same demo.

"I am absolutely appalled by the genocide being committed there by the Israelis and how appallingly the Palestinians have been treated for forever. It horrifies me that so many people just don't seem to care."

"There's no way Israel wants peace. I am disgusted at the fact that they are slaughtering babies and children on a mass scale. Israel has been rejecting peace right from the start. The Palestinian people took them in when they were kicked out of Europe. This is about colonialism and Western imperialism. If you have any ties with Israel break them now, as people once had to do with Nazi Germany. It's the same thing."

"We need the liberation of the Palestinian people."

"It is 100% genocide. The Palestinian people have been oppressed for 75 years and they keep getting painted as the aggressors and the terrorists. It is propaganda and lies."

"They are being colonialised and oppressed."

"I don't like seeing children mutilated, killed and harmed really. It's disgusting. I can't imagine any normal person supporting Israel ..."

The video freezes and Newt turns to Jax. "Just answer one question. Do you agree with that last statement?"

Newt doesn't give her time to answer, to spare her embarrassment. Instead he makes an observation.

"Human beings tend to follow herd behaviour, particularly if their emotions have been triggered. I researched further – those people have just been listening to a series of highly charged speeches by people with great passion. They set the scene for the atmosphere that follows. No joy was present, no celebration of the human spirit, no mutual encouragement in the sense of binding people together against a perceived 'mutual enemy'. Instead all we hear are repetitive chanting of slogans and expressions of hate for the enemies, rather than love and empathy for the perceived victims. This is all very reminiscent of the marches from the 1960s when similar folk would express their disdain for a myriad of causes, from black power to anti-war, to feminism and ... yes ... Palestinian liberation."

"Marxism pure and simple as I said before," says Joe, "but married to Islamism. All very strange to see those comfortable middle-class white people so worked up!"

"Can I say something?" says Jax, very quietly. So quietly, that no-one heard her, except Mo.

"I think the lady wants to say something," he says. It all suddenly goes quiet as Jax again repeats her request. Satisfied that they are listening, she begins to speak.

Chapter twenty-one

"Please hear me out, that's all I ask. Then you can comment ... please?"

"You have the floor," says Newt. She gets up, walks to the area in front of them, where the holo-bubble usually appears, then stands still and speaks. This is not Jax the public speaker, addressing a rally of like-minded believers. This is something different. She seems to have diminished a little, lost some of her self-confidence and certainty. This is Jax the confessor, like a hardened drinker speaking for the first time at an AA meeting.

"Let me tell you my story. I was an only child, a horrible little brat I was ... nothing has changed there ... you would agree?"

There is no response to her weak joke. This has become a hard audience.

"... Parents were well off, pulled themselves out of the post-war doldrums and clawed themselves into a comfortable, safe, middle-class existence. He was a solicitor; she was a nurse and we lived in leafy Surbiton. It was a boring, predictable life, something that I think they both needed after the unpredictable mayhem of the war years. I was a restless kid. A rebel. I just wasn't happy being comfortable. Into the edgy and dangerous Rolling Stones, not the safe Fab Four. In a way the 60s was made for me, a world fit for a rebel, particularly one who could afford it ... the clothes, the records, the gigs ... the drugs. I never wanted for the funds, I could be as rebellious as I wanted, all fully financed by mummy and daddy ... if they only knew it of course. They just wanted to see me happy ... and out of their hair."

"Get on with it!" says Abi. "Do we need your whole life story?"

"Better cut to the chase, Jax", agrees Newt.

"OK ... it was the swinging sixties, but it was also the time of Che Guevara, Timothy Leary, Bob Dylan ... student sit-ins ... I went to Essex University ... learned more at the protest events than I ever did in the lecture halls, my education was truly from the streets ... OK. OK ... I can see you getting impatient ... I was such a rebel that I was attracted to ... rebellious things ... causes, campaigns, wherever I saw ... or where I was told about ... injustices ... the whole Marxist thing of victims and aggressors ... I was told that the Palestinian cause was the ... biggest injustice of all, that they were the biggest victims of all, trampled on by the heartless Israelis, these people who had had their share of suffering and now wanted to inflict it on others ... It was a narrative that was totally sold to me ... I was sucked in ... still am I think ... never attempted to see both sides because ... the other side are 'liars' aren't they? They have their own narrative based on 'fake news', that's what I was told. They are supported by 'the establishment', 'the Zionist appeasers', 'the men in suits', the 'Patriarchy', the 'colonialists' ... we loved our slogans, our buzz words ... our meaningless phrases ... I can say that now as I am, for the first time, looking into myself with your eyes ... if you get what I'm saying ... but I'm from a different world, with a different education ... and I've never seen the need to doubt it ..."

She pauses. "Until ... now."

"Nice speech," says Joe. "But do you meant it ... is this really, truly, from your heart, or ... just a means to an end ... just a way to stop that nice young girl over here from staring daggers at you?"

"Hey, old man ... I can speak for myself here, eh" says Abi, detecting a touch of paternal condescension here, even if it was well meant.

"But yeh," she adds. "Do you mean it? When you look at me do you see a human being or a … homicidal, imperialistic, colonial …" She has run out of words. "You know what I mean, eh."

Jax then takes a few sheets of paper out of her pocket.

"I would like to tell you a story. It will give you an idea of what I'm all about and why I do what I do... And then I will shut up."

She looks over to Newt. "Will that be OK?"

"Of course, Jax. To the rest of you … please hear her out … no interrupting. Yes?"

They all nod. Jax starts to read.

"I would like to tell the story of a young man living in the Gaza Strip, though it's really the story of his mother. She was born in the peaceful village of Beit Daras and her first five years there were happy. It was a small village with olive groves, and acres of fragrant lemon and orange trees. Then the Zionists came in 1948. They invaded her village and drove everyone out at gunpoint. Many of them were killed and others fled to live as refugees in the crowded refugee camps in the Gaza Strip. His mother was only five, but this journey changed her into an adult. Children grow up fast in war. On the journey to Gaza her father died and they had to bury him on the side of the road. Now his mother was a refugee. For the rest of her life she would live in the Nuseirat camp, riddled with disease, surrounded by barbed wire and filled with despair. Here she would grow up, marry and become a mother. In this camp she would be known for her sweet disposition and her generosity to the poor, even though she was so poor herself. And here in this camp her children would watch her die.

His father's family were neighbours in the camp and when they married they had nothing but each other. For years they survived on soup his mother created from discarded garlic skins, grass, and salt. They suffered so much and yet their suffering gave them incomprehensible strength. Very soon they had a son, Anwar. He was their shining pride. They adored him and he brought a rare joy to their lives. When he was two years old, he became very sick and they tried to take him to a hospital, but the refugee hospitals had little or no resources and eventually they walked miles to a makeshift UN clinic. They couldn't help him and sadly he died."

Her voice cracks a little. She takes a deep breath and continues. The others are actually totally absorbed by her story. She has their full attention.

"Eventually they had six children. Our young man was the fourth. He was a sensitive child, very attached to his mother. He had beautiful memories of lying under a fig tree reading Treasure Island while she sat beside him making bread. The smell of the fresh bread, the warmth of the sun, and her presence always filled him with calm, even while there was a war outside their door."

"The government made it illegal to start any kind of industry in Gaza. If anyone tried to build a factory, it would be destroyed and they would be arrested. If a man tried to secretly work in Israel, he would be punished. His most vivid memory is the first time he picked up a stone. He was ten years old. He was with his best friend, Mohammed. One day while they were walking home from school they heard the sound of screaming. Mohammed ran in the direction of the school. Tanks surrounded it and soldiers were throwing tear gas grenades over the walls into the school grounds. Mohammed picked up a stone and started charging the tanks. Hundreds of boys were there, yelling and throwing stones. Some boys were climbing the school walls trying to help the girls on the other side. The scene rapidly developed into a hail of bullets from the Israeli soldiers. The boys scattered and ran home, proud that they defended their sisters. News of the incident spread through the camp quickly. Later that evening, someone came to the door. His father ushered the guest into the sitting room. They were drinking bitter coffee. It was Mohammed's father. It is a custom that bitter coffee is reserved for times of mourning. Mohammed's father told him that the boy who had been shot was Mohammed. He survived the injury, but he no longer recognized anyone. He couldn't speak anymore. He couldn't do anything. But for some mysterious reason, he remembered one thing. He remembered how to pray. From then on, instead of spending his days at school, he sat in the mosque. He is a living martyr. The world sees these boys with stones in hand and says that they are terrorists. Others look at them and see heroes."

"As he grew older and the Intifada erupted, these violent confrontations with soldiers became more and more frequent. At night they imposed curfews throughout the camp. Soldiers would ride around in their jeeps and if they saw anyone outside, that person, without being questioned, was swiftly arrested or shot in the street. One night he remembers waking up to a tremendous noise of shooting and bombing. It was so loud and alarming that he thought there must be hundreds of people outside. At 6:00 A.M., when the curfew was lifted, masses of people went outside to see what the fateful results of the night were. He stepped outside his door to hear a blood-chilling wail. It was his eighty-year-old neighbour. The only life companion he had was his old donkey. This faithful donkey was lying in a pool of blood, having "violated" the curfew by getting out of his pen. Once he saw a small boy killed by the soldiers just outside of his house. He was peering out the window and saw him wandering home with a handful of sweets clutched in his hand. Violence erupted nearby so suddenly that, before the little boy knew it, he was in the middle of a battlefield. He was six years old."

"His mother became fearful when they were told of a new policy instituted in the area. This policy was referred to as "the broken bones policy." It said that Israeli soldiers were to implement corporal punishment on anyone near a confrontational incident. So, if two boys were throwing stones near the market, the army was to retrieve the boys and break their arms and the arms of anyone else near the incident. They thought that perhaps this would be a deterrent to stone-throwing. One night the whole camp was awakened by the soldiers' loudspeakers. 'Every man between the ages of fourteen and sixty must to report to the boys' high school immediately. We will be doing random searches of your houses. If we find anyone hiding at home, he will be shot on the spot.' With their fathers and neighbours, they made their way through the dark paths of Nuseirat camp. They arrived at the school to meet up with more than 20,000 other men. The school was surrounded by jeeps and tanks. There were soldiers everywhere. Their floodlights lit up the school grounds. They spent the entire night there while the soldiers systematically grabbed a young boy here and a man there, striking their arms with wooden clubs and pounding their legs with heavy blows. Many were chosen as examples of what happens to 'terrorist stone throwers.' The nightmare didn't stop that night. There were daily raids and women and men alike were struck down by the army."

She stops. Her voice is a bit croaky. Newt notices this and fetches her a cup of water. She thanks him and takes a few sips, then continues.

"It was early in the morning when they came to his house. They sat on the floor with their pyjamas on. A thundering came from the door. It was broken down and dozens of soldiers poured into the house. As his father tried to reason with them and his mother screamed and cried, they dragged him and his four brothers out to the street. His father came and diplomatically, yet frantically, tried to convince the soldiers to let them go. Their leader yelled, "We'll show you what happens to boys who don't follow the rules!" As they were about to strike with their clubs, his mother, in a frenzy, ran at them. She cried "Allahu Akbar" (God is Greater) and made herself a human barricade between her sons and the soldiers. One soldier took his gun and thrust it into his mother. It was not a bayonet, but it penetrated her chest like a dull sword. She gasped and fell to the ground. His father screamed and his brothers began to cry. The soldiers backed away and his father ran to her side, wailing. He held her head and kissed her hands as the blood trickled out of her mouth. It took fifty days until she finally died. His mother fought and died to defend her children."

She stops, then adds, "This is from a book, Children of Israel, Children of Palestine by Laurel Holliday. I have paraphrased it to shorten it a bit."

They are unsure how to respond. Abi is the first to comment.

"That is a terrible story."

"Terrible?" replies Jax, quickly, immediately on the defensive. "In what way?"

"No one should behave that way to another human being, whoever they are," is the surprising reply. "What did you think I meant?" Now it is Abi who is on the defensive. Joe comes to her aid, or so he thought.

"I think you expected Abi to deny the story. Personally, I find it hard to believe that Jewish soldiers would behave in such a way ..."

"… Joe," interrupts Abi. "Then you've got us wrong, old man. You should come and live in Israel for a bit and then you'll find out that we all can behave crappily towards each other … crappily? Is that a word?"

"Better to use 'badly'" suggests Mo. "More ladylike." She throws him a fierce glance. She continues.

"You have this ideal view of the Jews, Joe and it is wrong. Whatever your Bible tells you, we're not holy people, we're just like everyone else."

"Apart from your cooking. Jews are lousy cooks," says Mo.

"Who says?" she replies. "You Arabs are so much better, are you? A bit of hummus in some pitta bread and … you're happy … Oy!"

They are joshing about and it defuses the tension. They both smile at each other. Joe, wisely, shuts up. Jax speaks.

"So, no further comments on my story? You do accept it as true?"

They look towards Newt who says, "It is true … I have checked …"

"Done the research?" offers Abi. "Are you some machine or something?"

Jax is pleased with this. She feels that she may be on the way to win them over. Then something surprising happens. There is a sudden commotion and some groaning, as stiff joints are stretched out and then coaxed into use, followed by some wheezing. She is joined on the floor by none other than her adversary, Joe. He stands about a metre away from her. Is this to support her, or is there something else going on here?

"What's going on here?" says Abi, amused. "Confession time or what? Newt, please explain. What are these old people doing?"

"I think you'll have to leave it to Joe to explain himself," says Newt, also surprised.

"This is better than TV," says Mo. "What do you think, Abi?"

"Let's wait and see. Who would you vote for? Trump or Kamala? Neither if it was up to me."

They both laugh. Joe ignores this and speaks.

"Yes, you can call me a silly old man who should know better ..."

He pauses as Abi gives a slight smile that he takes as an apology.

"First let me say, I'm not here to support Jax. But ... neither will I attack her ..."

Jax looks sideways and even grins a little. Joe continues.

"She is very brave in what she has said up here earlier ... and her story has certainly made me think ... there's a lot to process there, to be honest."

Jax nods slightly.

"... probably the most sense we've had from her so far." Her nod turns to a frown.

"You have to understand, you two. You are inheriting a world that we ... us two standing here ... have helped to create. Yes, we are on opposite sides. Yes ... you will probably never get any agreement from us ... yes, we follow two different narratives. But it would help you ... it will help all of us ... to understand how we have reached our positions. We come from two different worlds; we're made of very different stuff. Jax's narrative comes from her rebellious nature and it is only natural that her path is defined by that. Without any ... corrections ... she is always going to follow the path, irrespective where the actual truth may lie ... this is because her narrative is not about truth ... it is about emotions ..."

"... I thought this was going too well ... now ...", says Jax, quickly interrupted by Newt.

"Please, Jax, let him continue."

"Thank you, Newt," says Joe. He continues.

"In a sense my path could have been very similar. I, too, had a bit of the rebel in me, but I was a strange kind of rebel. I hated any form of 'group think', I just didn't want to be manipulated ... in fact I was a rebel against the rebels. I looked at those rioting students and hippies with flowers in their hair and thought ... 'morons'!"

He giggles, which is actually quite winsome and Abi feels her spirit strangely lightening. He continues.

"In 1967, when the Israelis won the Six Day War and I saw how the 'rebels' campaigned against this, I saw it differently. These people ... these brave Jews that the world seemed to hate ... they became my heroes. I saw them as victims not aggressors. But ... at the same time ... my feelings for the Arabs and the Palestinians were not quite so favourable. I started to hate them ... especially after the plane hijacks, the suicide bombings ... I had very negative thoughts towards them ...And then ..."

He pauses. This time he is most certainly grandstanding.

"I met Christ."

Newt could see the mood changing as Joe seemed to be preparing for a sermon.

"Not the time for this, Joe ... perhaps later."

Joe nods his head and stops. Newt takes over.

"This has been very useful. Thank you, both of you. I think this has been very helpful to you other two. Age often brings wisdom ... but not always ..."

"Is that a smile I see on your face, Newt?" says Jax. "I thought you were meant to be unbiased and neutral ... neutral Newt ... surely that's not your real name. And ... following on that thought ... I just want to say one more thing, then I will shut up."

"OK, Jax," says Newt. "But perhaps you should both return to your seats. Age also brings ... arthritis!"

"Another joke?" says Joe, as he and Jax return to their seats. "Oy!"

Jax seems to have discovered her old self. She is a very thick-skinned individual and quite bold in what she has to say next.

"I know that, from what I have said so far, that none of you are on my side. Even you, Mo, I really thought you would be an ally. But ... never mind. I'm a big girl; I can hold my own. But ... Newt ... my problem is with you. As I just said, your very name suggests your function. You are meant to be neutral, and impartial, in our discussions. But it doesn't seem to be so, from where I'm standing. Do you have a problem with me?"

"No, Jax, certainly not. Newt by name, neutral by nature."

There is a silence as Newt seems to be making his mind up about something.

"I am not one-sided, Jax ... I stand by what I see as the truth ... in every situation. Otherwise, you'll all agree, I'm not fit for purpose."

A further silence ... then the bombshell.

"Then it's time for me to open my heart. Well, I would ... if I had one!"

Chapter twenty-two

"I am not ... what you think ... I am a self-contained Artificial Intelligence"

If this were a cartoon, tongues would hang out and eyes would be on stalks. It is the quietest they have been so far. No one can say anything, the words don't come, just gasps.

"I am Newt, a neutral voice... but also a Neuro Expanded Work auTomaton."

"Yes, yes, yes," shouts Abi. "I knew there was something ... different ... about him ... an A.I. ... of course!"

Mo is next to speak.

"Like Robby the robot?" This unleashes a torrent of quips and insults, a cathartic cacophony.

"C 3PO?"

"Terminator? Frightening!"

"Marvin the Paranoid Android?"

"Like the one from the Alien movie – you don't realise he's an android until his head rolls off. Can you do that trick, Newt?" asks Jax.

"Take me to your master," says Abi in her best robotic impression.

Eventually they run out of ideas.

"When you are finished ..." says Newt.

They fall silent.

"So, none of you guessed?"

"Well, I was a bit suspicious of your lightning-fast 'research' capabilities", admits Joe.

"Good point," adds Jax.

"None of you saw the clue in my surname?"

"Didn't know what it was anyway."

"Swinton."

There are shrugs all around.

"The family name in the Spielberg movie – 'A.I... Artificial Intelligence'?"

More shrugs, followed by more silence as they continue to take in the revelation. Newt stands up, as if to display himself to them.

"Clever, eh?"

"Unbelievable," admits Joe. "Actually, I mean that quite literally. Can I just put it to the test, Newt? Just to fully convince this old man."

"Sure, Joe. How?"

"Just tell me ... immediately ... who won the FA Cup final in 1962."

The answer came immediately, within the blink of an eye.

"Tottenham Hotspur beat Burnley on 5th May 1962, three goals to one."

After a few seconds of fumbling with her iPhone, Abi announces, "Absolutely correct", then repeats what she said earlier, "Now take me to your master, Newt Swinton."

"I am an independent entity, Abi. I have no master."

"Then who is your maker?"

"Ah, metaphysical questions. This is more for you, Joe," is the reply.

"Not quite, but we'll come back to that later."

"Actually, Abi, I have no interest in such things. It is not part of my programming."

"Interesting."

"When were you made?" asks Mo.

"When was I first conscious, you mean?"

"Yes."

"Yesterday, I believe."

"You're very mature for a one-day-old," says Jax, laughing at her not-quite joke.

"I am just more efficient than you humans. No nine

months of gestation then a dozen years of slow development … just a toggle switch flipped into the 'On' position. Would you like to see it?"

It seems so intrusive and surreal and there are no takers.

"Can we move on now?" adds Newt.

"You realise this is going to take us a long time to process, but, hey, it's been one of those kind of days," says Joe.

"Amen to that," agrees Jax. Newt continues.

"I am a prototype, inasmuch as I have been created specifically for this programme. It appears that I have been quite successful so far. Would you like to rate me? One star – not good at all – to five star – very good …"

"You are joking? This is a joke?" says Jax. "You're not a window cleaner or a telephone help desk … you're a blinkin' robot! What a question!"

There is much mirth all around at this particular exchange.

"Don't worry, Newt," says Mo, "I'll give you a good rating on Google when I return home."

There is more laughter.

"Does TripAdvisor cover these things too?" adds Abi.

Newt waits until the laughter dies down, then continues.

"Perhaps if I explain the thinking behind all of this, you will understand better and see it as more than a … joke."

"Are you annoyed with us, Newt?" says Joe, "I thought androids are not meant to have feelings. At least that is what the Isaac Asimov books implied if I remember correctly."

"You are correct … in fact that leads me in nicely to what I was going to say. The fact is that, for a convenor to be able to do well in such a prickly situation as that in the Middle East, three qualities are essential. He needs to be up-to-date with all of the facts, he needs to be impartial and he needs to be unemotional. To be honest, finding a human with all three qualities was impossible and so the authorities requisitioned me. I am also what they call a 'pure' AI. This means that I am free of social filters that used to skew the experience. Earlier AIs had to provide answers that conform to society's standards by filtering them so findings 'wouldn't offend' victim groups. My answers may seem blunt and hurtful to some, but at least they are honest and a true, pure, reflection of my outputs. There had been earlier secret prototypes of NEWT, but none had been operational, so what you see before you is ... the first of a kind."

"Then we are honoured," says Jax with a mock curtsey.

"No, the honour is mine," replies Newt. "It has been challenging, I believe, though I have had nothing to compare it with, me just being one day old." Then he adds, "But it has been a pleasure working with you."

"It is so hard talking to you ... now that we know who ... what ... you are. I think it will take a bit of time," says Abi.

"Just look at the 'outer man' not the 'inner robot' and you will do fine," is the response.

They actually find this funny although it wasn't intended as a joke. There is more laughter. It has taken this particular revelation to bond the group together, though it is doubtful how long this will last.

"I would like to move things on now if that is OK with you all. To return to the programme. Perhaps knowing what I am may help you open up more."

He now turns to Jax. "At least I have answered your question, the one that you asked what now seems an age ago. You can be assured of my independence and that, when I quote facts, they are verified and not infected by prejudice or opinion. Is that OK with you?"

"Yes it is, Newt. I think that perhaps we can make some real progress now."

"We can only hope", says Joe, under his breath.

Chapter twenty-three

When everything quietens down, Newt re-activates the holo-bubble. It is a short film about the Six-Day War. They watch in silence, and then when it is over, Newt says something very surprising.

"Now you know more about me, how I operate, the boundaries surrounding my thought processes and my core function, which is always to discern what is true and what is false. Now that I have assimilated every scrap of information about this war, I find myself perplexed."

He pauses. If they didn't know better they would think that he is currently conflicted with emotion.

"Yes. Go on," says Joe.

"Everything about those six days confounds everything I have learned about human conflicts and how messy, fuzzy and disorganised these usually are."

They are intrigued and allow him to continue.

"I see such a confluence of unexpected factors that I have arrived at a conclusion that my programming tells me is impossible."

Joe is pleased as he thinks he knows what is coming next. He closes his eyes and prays, hoping no one notices this. Newt continues.

"One side has such an advantage in numbers, equipment and support, yet loses spectacularly. The other side makes hunches and decisions and takes such risks yet emerges triumphant. This is unprecedented in my analysis. It leads me to contemplate that wars are not closed systems, but that, sometimes, unseen factors are involved …"

"Has our friendly robot found God?" asks Jax, very unsubtly.

"No … of course not … but he has discerned the workings

of His hands," replies Joe.

"Utter rubbish" is the reply. The feud has returned.

"If Newt, who relies on pure logic and nothing else, has made such discoveries, then surely we ought to listen," says Joe, insistently.

"So, Newt, what do you mean?" asks Abi. Being Jewish she has an 'iron in the fire' here, but not being particularly religious herself, his remarks surprise her.

"Then let me show you what I've found. It started off with fake news from Russia that Israel was planning to attack Syria. Nasser, the leader of Egypt, with plans for supremacy over the whole of the Arab Middle East, reacted by moving troops into the Sinai and blocking Israel's access to the Red Sea, to flex his muscles. This triggered plans that Israel had been preparing for years, involving secret mobilisations, deflections and 'leaked intentions'. The fact that the Arab world, including Egypt, Syria, Lebanon, Iraq and Jordan, were all taken in, I find very improbable. The fact that Israel very publicly prepared 40,000 coffins and requisitioned land for burial sites, to signal that they expected defeat, all added to the deception. On June the fifth they conducted what has been called arguably the most successful air campaign in military history, decimating the air forces of Egypt, Syria and Jordan in a pre-emptive strike. When Nasser saw most of his planes destroyed, many without even taking off, he boasted to his Arab co-leaders that they had Israel on the run. This dragged Jordan and Syria into the war, despite Israel offering peace. As a result the West Bank and the Golan Heights both fell into Israel's hands. The war was effectively over on the first day."

"Yes, I concede, those Israelis were clever and better prepared ..." says Jax

"... and fighting for their lives against nations that

wanted to destroy them ...", interrupts Joe.

"... and yes. But I don't see the need to involve ... the Old Man in the Sky ... here," adds Jax. Newt continues.

"I have read many verified reports. The risk the Israelis took when invading Egypt was that they only left twelve planes behind to defend Israel. The inability of Egyptian commanders to radio ahead and warn airstrips of the fact that their planes were being blown up on the ground. The fact that, during that hour, leaders of the Arab nations were flying over Sinai to observe Egyptian 'preparations' and ground units were ordered not to shoot at any planes flying over Sinai and Egypt. The Israeli planes were aged, yet very few malfunctioned and not a single plane was detected by Egypt's ground forces. Only one Israeli plane was hit that day. Egyptian soldiers ran away inexplicably when faced with just handfuls of soldiers and even an account of a battalion of Syrian soldiers running away from a single injured soldier, claiming that 'angels' were surrounding him. The unexpected recovery of their holy city, Jerusalem."

"And let's not forget America?" says Jax.

"What about America? No country took Israel's side, they were totally on their own here. I suggest you read your history books, Jax."

Jax looks over to Newt who shrugs his shoulders and nods his head.

"Let's say I find this very intriguing", says Newt. "But best if we leave it there. I don't want to stray beyond my brief ..."

"... which is?" interrupts Joe.

"To facilitate a discussion between a small, selected group of motivated people to see if this may in any way help the peace process."

"Aha," says Joe. "I think you will find that God is more

involved than many want to believe. You have stumbled upon something that you don't wish to pursue, possibly because it is a constraint of your programming … but … well, let's just wait and see."

"More claptrap" mutters Jax under her breath. Newt continues.

"The Six-Day War is of vital importance in our discussions. It resulted in a complete change in the vocabulary of the conflict."

"Which means?" says Abi, vocalising what everyone else is thinking.

"Well, our attention now moves to one man, Yasser Arafat. It all starts with him."

"Poster boy!" declares Joe, scornfully.

"Freedom fighter!" responds Jax, being provocative.

"And a multi-billionaire to boot. Apparently 'freedom fighting' can be quite lucrative."

"What's all of this, sir and madam, you've lost me?" says Mo.

"Me, too", adds Abi.

"Yasser Arafat, according to Wikipedia, 'was a Palestinian political leader born in Egypt, best known as chairman of the Palestine Liberation Organisation (PLO)'. Palestinians generally view him as a martyr and Israelis as a terrorist but he is also considered corrupt by some. The quote from him that is most relevant regarding the current conflict is what he said in August 1970, 'Our basic aim is to liberate the land from the Mediterranean Sea to the Jordan River. We are not concerned with what took place in June 1967 or in eliminating the consequences of the June war. The Palestinian revolution's basic concern is the uprooting of the Zionist entity from our land and liberating it.' …"

"That's it, that's it," exclaims Joe, "here is their true

purpose. It has never been negotiating 'land for peace,' it is the familiar old Marxist claim of ... genocide. This is the only genocide that is intended in the conflict and here it is out of the mouth of the one who really started it all, Jax!"

"Yasser Arafat was a bold leader of his people. Like it said, he was even martyred for his people," replies Jax.

"Never proved ... disproved I believe. He died of natural causes."

"He also won the Nobel Peace Prize."

"What a joke that was ... he also turned down EVERY peace proposal thrown at him by the Israelis and every time responded with violence ... like a true Marxist. You could tell he was going to be a bad 'un. He was even related to the Grand Mufti ... so genetically inclined towards antisemitism, eh?"

"Now you're being ridiculous ... Newt!" She appeals to the facilitator.

"Do you really want me to get involved, Jax?"

"Of course. That's your job, isn't it? Flushing out all of the lies."

"Well, Jax," says Newt, "he didn't always act in the best interests of his people and, true to that quote I gave, he never budged an inch, though, through what I've picked up of Arab politics, he was as much a victim of their culture as the innocent Palestinians were. Sometimes ..."

Newt drops his voice as if he is contemplating a major truth. "Sometimes ... there are rule books to follow."

"Eh?" says Jax, puzzled. "What do you mean?"

"I tell you what," replies Newt. "I think it's time for a break now. I believe they have prepared a feast for you."

They indeed had.

Mo and Abi are in conversation over their chicken shawarmas and felafels. It is comforting for them that at least they share a cuisine and both privately hope that there is more that they can learn about each other today. Although Mo has had many Jewish friends of both sexes, living in a mixed area, Abi has been a bit cloistered in her upbringing. Her parents were fervent Zionists and so it was rare for a Palestinian Arab to be welcome in their home. It is a shame that they didn't notice the presence of Jax, standing awkwardly in front of them, waiting to be noticed. She clears her throat and they both look up.

"Jax?" says Mo, "can I help you?" Abi averts her eyes. There is still unresolved pain there.

"Abi," says Jax, softly. "Can I have a word?"

Abi doesn't move.

"Abi," says Mo, softly. "At least hear her out. Give her a chance ... I would."

"I know you would, Mo ... that's who you are ... we are very different ..."

"... Please, Abi. Let me say my piece and we don't have to speak again today. I will respect you on that."

Still no movement. Abi is being very stubborn. Jax tries again.

"Listen, Abi. I'm a woman of passion and have always been. When I was younger ... in fact ... right up to about an hour ago ... I always thought I was right. Always surrounded by people who agreed with me and if someone didn't ... I'd always have a choice word or two for them, if you know what I mean. Listen, Abi ... I'm just a silly old woman and will always say silly things, I'm too old to change ..."

"Are you?" Abi looks up.

"Am I ... what?"

"Too old to change. Why should that be? We're intelligent adults here. Even a robot can see the truth better than you can, Jax ... can't you see that?"

Jax is stuck for words. She pauses and then a slight darkness crosses her face and her muscles harden just that little bit. The 'old Jax' is trying to break through.

"OK," is all she can say as she walks back to her seat.

"That went well," says Mo.

"She had it coming."

"Does that mean you're 'quits' now, Abi?"

"Not sure."

Chapter twenty-four

Newt begins the next session with a little speech.

"Did you know that, in 2000, Yasser Arafat went to Camp David in America for a meeting with Ehud Barak of Israel, at the invitation of Bill Clinton? Barak offered withdrawal from most of the West Bank and all of the Gaza Strip, Palestinian control over parts of Jerusalem, with other offers concerning the settlements and the refugees. Arafat refused this and made no counter-offer but, instead, instigated the Second Intifada later that year, a violent uprising, resulting in 3000 Palestinian deaths and 1000 Israeli deaths. This seems to be in line with his statement in 1970, that no peace deal would ever work and that they wanted nothing less than the destruction of Israel, from the River to the Sea."

"This is what I've been saying all along. The Muslims just don't want peace," says Joe.

"Well I'm a Muslim and that doesn't describe me," says Mo in return.

"There are Muslims ... and there are Muslims," adds Joe.

"Just like there are Christians ... and there are Christians, sir. We saw them earlier in the Crusades and in that pogrom."

"Well spoken, Mo", says Abi. "Though I do agree that there are some Muslims out to get us, certainly."

"That seems to be so," says Mo, "but I can't see it in the Qu'ran that I believe in."

"Thankfully most Muslims are like you, Mo."

"Thankfully most Christians are not like you, professor," says Jax, spitefully.

"What do you mean?"

"From what I've seen, most side with the Palestinians, especially in the UK."

"That doesn't make them right."

"And you have the truth, professor? What makes your little band of Christian Zionists right and the majority wrong?"

"Well ... how long have you got? We read the Bible correctly for a starter."

Newt interrupts. "Let's not make this into a religious debate, Ladies and Gentlemen. I'm not sure that will be very helpful. Yet religion is often at the heart of it all, as with the blood libels of old when the Jews were accused of the most ridiculous things just as a pretext to attack them. In fact ..."

Newt pauses as if he is thinking, which of course is not the case. He has learnt of the effects of the ... dramatic pause. He continues.

"It can be said that we have returned to those dark days."

"What do you mean?" says Joe. "Blood libels? Jews still being accused of kidnapping Christian children for their blood?"

"No, not exactly, but the same principle. A story is fabricated, say of a massacre ... then blamed on the Jews ... with the expected results. Nobody bothers checking the facts anymore."

"Especially when they are fabricated by Hamas", adds Joe.

"Well, Joe ... it would help if the Israelis actually allowed journalists into Gaza," says Jax.

"I agree, Jax. It would help, indeed," concedes Joe. "And of course Newt ... with his special talent for research ... can tell us which are true and which are false. Journalists all over are fed stories directly from Hamas themselves and do they check them? No. These stories do nothing other than encourage hatred for the Jews, which is the only reason for them. It's this false narrative of genocide that does nothing other than encourage genocide in the hearts of the growing number who hate the Jews. Those journalists should be ashamed of themselves … one day there will be a reckoning and there will be a lot of questions raised … you mark my words."

Joe has worked himself up but stops and looks at Newt, who nods, knowingly. "There's a lot I can say … about many things." He becomes reflective.

"Newt?" says Joe, slowly. "Now, be honest. What is really going on with you? I sense … something."

Newt sits there quietly, gestures for silence and then speaks.

"You are perceptive, Joe. I am stirred and my algorithms are in a turmoil, I suppose, though I don't know what the equivalent would be with you humans."

"Knickers in a twist, I would say," says Jax.

"In a bit of a tizz," says Joe.

"Strange language!" whispers Mo to Abi, who giggles.

"But, anyway," continues Newt. "I mentioned my observations of the Six-Day War. You need to remember who … or what … I am. I can analyse millions of pieces of data in no time at all. It only took a few seconds to assimilate every fact and opinion out there on the War, so I'm in a very good position to know what's true and what is false … and I repeat what I said earlier … your world is not a closed one."

"But what does that mean?" asks Mo.

"Let me continue, but first …"

Newt leaves his desk, walks across the room and stands before Abi. He is silent for a few seconds then speaks.

"Have you ever wondered, Abi, why the world hates you so much?"

She is initially taken aback. "Me, personally?"

"No, Abi, he's talking about you Jews in general," says Mo. "I must say that the thought has also crossed my mind today, particularly after what we have seen and heard." As he speaks, there is a real concern in his eyes. Newt continues.

"There is a hatred there that is ... not natural. Why should Arafat and those like him want the complete extinction of the Jewish people? Why did Hitler and the Grand Mufti? There are so many others, going right back thousands of years. It took me a full five minutes to analyse the data, which is billions of connections and data slices. It would take you many lifetimes to do the same. Abi ... if I had emotions I would be standing here weeping before you and I can't understand why the others here are not doing so ..."

"Believe me, I have wept much over the Jewish people ... and ..."

This is Joe. He is choked up as he continues. His words pour out almost frantically, but they are clearly from his heart. "... how they have suffered under the Church. But I need to tell you, Abi ... really need to tell you ... that we are not all like that. I have had a love for the Jewish people for decades now and ... yes I know it is easy for you to be cynical and I get it ... it is unconditional. I don't love you for deep, personal, selfish reasons ... I love you because my God ... Your God ... tells me to. There are many like me, I'm sure you must have met one or two ... I know there are some bad apples out there, but I ask you not to judge me because of their mistakes and agendas ... all I ask is for you to accept me, Abi ... please."

He is now weeping freely, as if a dam has broken in his heart and he is unable to hold back the salty tears.

Abi looks over to him. She knows that his tears are for real and her heart softens just a little. She gives him a brief smile. Nevertheless, this is very uncomfortable for her and she tries to change the atmosphere.

"Come on ... it is what it is ... people just don't like us; it's just something we have to live with." As she says this, she is staring directly at Jax, who is strangely impassive. Abi continues.

"So, Jax. Do you still hold on to everything you said about me and my people in your opening speech?"

Jax hesitates. "I was reading the words of another. My intention was to show her pain …"

"And what about my pain? Have you no idea of the pain you put me through?"

"No … it wasn't about you, specifically."

"It wasn't? But I'm a Zionist too, just like Ben Gurion, Weizmann and the rest of the 'depraved, violent colonizers.'"

"Yes, but you're a victim of their decisions."

"No … I am alive because of their decisions. If it weren't for them – and I agree they weren't perfect specimens of human beings, along with the bunch of leaders we have now … but without them we'd be 'in the river or the sea' drowned at the hands of your 'peaceful' Palestinian friends."

Mo joins in.

"If only we were running the country, our country, Abi, eh?"

She nods. Newt speaks.

"I am so glad I am not burdened by emotions. You humans live by emotions, but you also die by them. That speech that we heard this morning – and I can speak about it now – was so driven by hurt and pain, that truth became subservient to feelings. But Truth is not a feeling and passion needs an anchor. Passion is good if anchored in truth. If it isn't then it becomes a dangerous weapon …"

He pauses, then turns to Jax.

"… and, to follow this up, I have now analysed that opening speech …"

"Took you so long?" says Joe.

"No, had it done within two minutes but … there's a

time and a place ..."

"Understood. OK, Newt. How much truth was there?"

"It's a varied mix, but held together by a very considered, but emotional, delivery ... I want to just highlight some of the more emotive issues brought up and give you my findings, OK. Bear in mind that, as a pure A.I., I look for evidence that is attributable, rather than facts that may have been planted as fake news. You must understand this."

"We do. Go ahead."

"She says that the Zionists dub Palestinian babies as 'a demographic threat'. This is a true assessment just by looking at birth rate projections ... she also quotes from Chaim Weizmann, 'the rocks of Judea, obstacles that had to be cleared on a difficult path'. This is untrue, he never said that ... the quote from Ben Gurion, 'we must expel the Arabs and take their places' was from a private letter to his son and not a public statement, but the other quote of his referring to 'colonization' is true ... the quote from Benjamin Netanyahu, referring to expelling large swatches of Palestinians while the world looks at China is false, though reproduced all over the social media ... the 'break their bones' policy is true and we have already seen this in action in Jax's sad story ... the quote from Colonel Eitan, 'we have to kill them all' is true, but he was a nasty maverick and discredited ... the quote 'we have to kill and kill and kill, all day every day' is from an Aaron Sofer, who doesn't seem to have actually existed ... the 'leaving of poisoned food for people in Shyjaiyya' has no evidence ... the sniping of children in the West Bank, yes there were instances that the IDF are investigating ... then there is the emotive statement concerning 'bombings of entire neighbourhoods that bury families alive and wipe out whole bloodlines' ... this is a direct result of Hamas policy of using these families as 'human shields' and there is evidence that the IDF leaflet these families to tell them to leave before the bombings of the terrorist lairs ... I think that will suffice for now."

"A mixed bunch," says Joe.

"As I said, guys, I was only reading a speech, one that has gone viral anyway," replies Jax.

"And that's the sadness of it" responds Joe. "A mixture of truth and lies has gone viral and, because of the delivery and the person who delivered it, has been accepted as truth. Nothing more than propaganda, right?"

"I'm sure that your lot is just as guilty. Have you heard Douglas Murray lately?"

Newt interrupts the exchange.

"Propaganda ... a vital weapon in any war ... acts to increase hope and confidence, and yet often has little basis in truth. Winston Churchill used it most effectively during the Second World War ..."

"... as did Hitler," adds Joe.

"It seems that Churchill's lies were more effective than Hitler's" says Jax, provocatively.

Suddenly the light in the room flickers, only so slightly. This jolts Newt out of his mood.

"OK, Ladies and Gentlemen, can I have your attention? A few hours ago I overheard a conversation – it's one of the advantages of having 'super-hearing'. It was between Mo and Abi ... don't worry I'm not going to divulge any secrets ... Mo told a story that totally intrigued me ... the story of The Chandelier Maker ... can I have permission to tell the story to everyone, Mo?"

"Sure. Of course you can."

"Then please excuse the voice."

He says this because it is Mo's voice that can now be heard. This is weird, but it's been a day of surprises, so they take it in their stride.

"Once upon a time, a young man left his father, saying, I am going to learn a trade and be the very best at it. Soon, after travelling the world, he returns and says, 'I have become an expert designer of chandeliers and there is none better than me at this'. 'OK' says his father, a bit taken aback. You create the very best chandelier and I will get the leading chandelier makers in town to assess your work.' This is what happened. These craftsmen came, assessed the young man's work and agreed that ... they had never seen such a monstrosity! They all agreed that some aspects were very good, even excellent, but others were hideous, but they weren't always in agreement as to which were the good bits and which were the bad bits. How was he going to break this to his proud son? But he did. His son's reply surprised him. He said, 'While I was away I studied the work of all of these craftsmen, particularly focusing on their deficiencies and so I decided to create a chandelier that combined all of their imperfections. This is what you see before you. Each could see each the others' imperfections, but not recognise their own. In this way they all eventually became better craftsmen.'"

"Now before I comment further I want to ask you, Mo, where the story came from?"

"It's been in my family for generations I believe," says Mo. "But I really don't know where it came from ... a Palestinian folk tale?"

"No, Mo, it isn't. The story was written by Rabbi Nachman of Breslov."

Mo and Abi look at each other in amazement. "Mo ... are you a secret Jew?" says Abi, smiling.

"I'm far too pretty to be one of you, Abi ... but ... really, Newt?"

"Oh yes? You doubt my research skills?"

"Of course not."

"Rabbi Nachman was from the eighteenth century and a very popular man; he still has followers today."

"Oh yes, the Hasids in Jerusalem. I think they organise an annual pilgrimage to his place of birth."

"Correct ... anyway ... I have something related ... and important ... to say to you all."

There is a tone to his voice that adds a frisson to this announcement.

"You are all ... Chandelier craftsmen ... and women ... and ... I see myself as this Chandelier Maker ... if you'll excuse me, Rabbi Nachman ... You all bring something different ... You, Jax, you bring passion ... you, Joe, you bring humility ... you, Mo you bring empathy ... and, finally, you ... Abi ... you bring forthrightness. Together you are ... unbeatable ... together, as with all good chandeliers ... you provide light."

He stops and looks at them all in turn. "Just never forget what you are here for ... to bring light for others to see truth." He pauses again. He has not finished.

"But I also believe there's a deeper meaning here that is so relevant to you all and what has happened today ... It's not just about you, but it's also about what you represent. When you came to this meeting this morning, you came with your own agenda, mindset, interpretation, whatever you call it ... all of you were safe within the confines of your views. You'd worked it out, you were happy with it. ... Now what I think has happened here since is that each of you has not just seen the shortcomings of each other's viewpoints but also ... in turn ... thanks to the frank and open discussions here ... your own. The big issue here is incredibly nuanced, not everything is black and white, but what you have done is created a whole out of the parts ... or at least started the process to do so. I just hope that much good has been achieved here."

He stops, looks at each of them intently, then speaks again. "And one more thing … then I'll shut up."

He actually clears his throat, very theatrically for effect, rather than out of biological necessity of course. He speaks. "One statement I think summarises everything. You would do well to remember it. It is this …"

He stops. Again, he is grandstanding, perhaps to give extra authority to what he is about to say. "One thought … love and care for the Palestinians is often a smokescreen for hatred of the Jews. Until this is acknowledged, there will always be two sets of victims … and these are people who really ought to be friends. I'll repeat this, because it's important … write it down if you want … love and care for the Palestinians is often a smokescreen for hatred of the Jews. Until this is acknowledged, there will always be two sets of victims … and these are people who really ought to be friends."

He stops, looks at them all in turn yet again and gives them time to absorb his words. Then there is a hissing sound. They all collapse. Something has knocked them out, perhaps a gas. It is only for a few seconds. When they come to, Newt has gone. In his place is a fierce-looking lady with pink hair. She smiles at them, though it is more of a snarl.

Chapter twenty-five

There she stands, five feet two, rotund and a picture in pastel. Miss Garland is her name and she seems to have replaced Newt.

"Who ... are ... you?" says Jax.

"Miss Garland ... And I'm in charge now."

"Where's Newt?" asks Joe.

"Newt? Oh you mean the robot? He's back in the repair shop."

"Repair shop? Robot?" Somehow this seems so wrong to all of them. Newt had become their friend over the last few hours and the thought of him not being around anymore and also being referred to as a ... robot ... was a bit too much for Mo.

"He is our friend. We want Newt."

"Well, you've got me, instead, I'm afraid."

"But there was nothing wrong with him," says Joe.

"I am told that he had malfunctioned, had 'strayed beyond his brief' were the words used."

"That's ridiculous," says Joe.

"It is what it is, people. Now can we continue with the Programme? We are entering the final session ... then you'll be free to go and ... you will never need to see me again ... or each other."

Those last three words hit them. They had been confined together in this shared task for so long now that, thanks to Newt, they have bonded really well ... mostly. The thought that this would end hadn't entered their minds, so much had gone on to excite, motivate and absorb them. Jax is next to speak.

"Well, I'm ready, Miss Garland. Hopefully you'll be more amenable to my ideas than ..."

"Newt", Joe reminds her.

"Newt", she repeats, a name that she hadn't really forgotten but her hesitation was to make a point. She feels that, just from her appearance, with her pink hair, face jewellery and bright gaudy outfit, she may have finally found an ally in Miss Garland. She was not wrong.

"So, this is how this is going to work. We only have a brief time together, no real time to get to know each other, you and me. But that's not important, I've heard that you've got to know each other pretty well already. I suppose we have the robot to thank for that ..."

"... Newt!" Mo reminds her. She ignores his outburst.

"We'll start by asking questions. You are all free to ask one question to one other person here. That way we can get some discussion going. Who's first?"

There are no takers, they hadn't yet adjusted to these changed circumstances.

"Come on, now ... Jax, you've had plenty to say. Do you have a question?"

Jax had already been thinking. How could she start to steer things onto a better course? She looks around. Her eyes fall on Mo. She has an idea.

"Mo," she says. "As you have seen, I have been a real advocate for your people. Yet you don't seem to appreciate my efforts. Why?"

Mo is still as he thinks. The other two really feel for him, you can see it in their faces. What a provocative question, and so typical of Jax. Mo replies.

"Do you really want me to answer you ... Jax?"

There is a peculiar strength to these words. Jax is very slightly feeling not quite so confident now. *'What has she unleashed? I'm sure it will be OK; he knows I'm his best friend here.'*

"Of course, Mo. Go ahead."

Mo stands up and points at her. His voice starts off hesitant, but it grows with every syllable.

"I ... despise ... people ... like ... you."

Abi glances at him and smiles an encouragement. "Go for it, boy," she says under her breath. Mo continues.

"Why do people like you always think you know better? We Palestinians don't need you, all you do is give us a bad name ..."

"Now come on, Mo. We are a voice for the voiceless ..."

"No you are not! You are just a ... loudhailer ... for your own views. You just use us, just as you use all those other groups you are so 'concerned' about ... the transexuals, the blacks, climate change ... I've seen the videos on YouTube."

"I think you'll find, boy, that ..."

"Don't you 'boy' me ... that's the point ... you think you speak for us ... as if you are our betters ... well, as someone said ... age doesn't have to bring wisdom ... with your marches, your boycotts, your demonstrations ... your ... antisemitism!"

This is a seminal moment. Those last two words act as a trigger. Newt would have dealt with it, they knew. He would have stopped things, queried Mo, advocated for Jax, smoothed things over. Miss Garland, however, chooses to remain silent. Allows Mo to continue. Joe looks at Miss Garland. Does he see a slight smirk there? Mo continues.

"Are you really sorry, as you said you were earlier when you approached Abi? It didn't seem so to me. A leopard doesn't change its stripes ..."

"... spots" corrects Miss Garland.

"... Spots. I've been watching you, Jax, since then and ... I don't think you're really sorry about your attitude to the Jews. I think it's awful. Look at me, I'm a Palestinian by birth and a Muslim … I have every reason for hating people like Abi … but I don't … I don't allow it … Yes, there have been times when I could have followed and listened to people like you, but I chose not to. Because one thing has been made clear to me … your hatred for Jews is so much bigger than your love for Palestinians … it's all a game for you, isn't it? A way to vent your hate …"

All this time, Jax is trying to get a word in, but he speaks over her. It seems that he's been wanting to get this off his chest for some time. He stops and she immediately launches an angry tirade.

"How dare you, you ungrateful … I've dedicated my life to the likes of you … and no … I'm not antisemitic … I find that deeply hurtful … I just don't agree with a lot that Israel does."

Joe decides to join in.

"Can you be more specific about this … and then perhaps we can have a reasonable discussion?"

"OK, professor. Let's do it. Is that OK, Miss Garland?"

Miss Garland waves her hand at her, encouraging her to continue.

"Let's start with the settlers, then …"

What follows is a series of emotional rants, perhaps even slightly unhinged in places. Miss Garland seems unable or unwilling to moderate it and Joe, in particular, becomes very suspicious of how this has been allowed to play out. Things had gone so well under Newt. He had a way of pulling back when things got heated but pushing forwards when the truth had been sincerely sought. Mostly, he was able to control Jax. Now the very worst of her is shining through and it's as if Miss Garland is encouraging it. Joe feels sorry for Jax because he actually felt that there was a glimmer of something new going on with her, a realisation that perhaps she could make changes to her path in life. He also feels sorry for Newt, perhaps even now being prodded and probed by technicians worried that he had been guiding them into unacceptable areas, areas that, for Joe were unavoidable and possibly a key to success in this 'Programme' they were all a part of. Joe now realises that he has to step up his game.

"Jax, can I make a comment, please?"

She seems unsure but nods anyway. Actually, she is glad for the intrusion. Joe continues.

"I am still troubled by what Abi showed us at that demo, with her secret filming and ..."

"... you're not dragging that up again, are you?"

"No, I'm not. It's just one point that you made that I'd like to address."

"Oh yes?"

"You talked about the emotionalism of the event, how everyone was stoked up and perhaps what you said was prompted by this ... atmosphere ... of hate."

"Go on, professor. Not sure where you're going here, but ..."

"... it was meant to be a rally to support Palestinians and their cause, but it switched very quickly, didn't it. Emotions very quickly switched from love and concern for the Palestinians to hatred for Israel and ... I believe ... Jews in general. You did see that didn't you?"

"Well, yes ..."

"What we really saw was hate speech ... not just from you but all the others there. They were just ordinary citizens, middle class, well dressed, well-spoken in general, yet ... they could have been a baying mob after blood the way some of them expressed themselves."

"I suppose. But ..."

"... it isn't right, Jax. Surely that isn't right. You and me, we're fossils, but we've both been brought up on those newsreels and films on Nazi Germany, how easy it was for ordinary people to switch ... because of the atmosphere ... into a baying mob. The point is that I'm making, Jax is ... look where that led to in the 1940s ... Eh?"

He starts reading from some notes he has made.

"Just for full disclosure, Miss Garland ... what I have here is Jax's opening speech. She has graciously given it to me to look at and analyse ..."

Miss Garland nods, with little apparent interest.

"Now I know Newt has already helped us through this, but I just want to highlight some notes I made. Listen to these words taken from the speech ... set up an observation platform where citizens came to watch their slaughter ... corralled them by the hundreds of thousands ... burned them alive ... cut off their food, water and medicine ... Made children gather the flesh of their parents ... bury siblings ... made them pray for death just to join their families and not be alone in this terrible world ... all reminiscent of Nazi Germany ... and perhaps put in the speech solely to create that link in people's minds? Just a thought ..."

Jax is silent and nods thoughtfully. She doesn't disagree. In the absence of any intervention by the apparently useless Miss Garland, Joe decides to change direction.

"I would like to ask a question," he says loudly, speaking over the angry muttering that had taken over. Miss Garland waves him on. "My question is for Abi." Abi nods her head.

"Abi. I'm probably taking a big gamble here because I get your point about us ... oldies ... fighting your battles for you and why can't we just leave you alone. I am just going to make a statement and all I ask of you is if you agree or disagree."

"Oh yes?" She is a bit uncertain.

"I won't go into detail but you all know that I'm a

Christian, actually I've been so for over forty years, and God gave me a love for Israel and the Jewish people. Everything I do on that issue is done out of this love. Can you accept that this is sincere? I don't want you to think that I'm just a big fraud. Please ... this is important for me ... I know I have asked you this before but ... I don't believe you actually answered me."

Abi looks at him for a few seconds, as if she is weighing things up.

"Yes, Joe. I know we haven't really clicked together here. That's mostly about me, I'm not good with ... older people. But ... I can see that you are sincere. Don't see it with all Christians though, but, with you ... yes I get it ... and I thank you for it."

"Thank you, Abi. Really appreciate this."

"Too many of ... your lot ... look at us Jews not as people but, somehow, as 'players' in these 'end time games' they create. A lot of Americans are like that. We see them in Jerusalem with their big gatherings and their marches. I get the feeling ... I may be wrong ... that ... just like her over there with her support for the Palestinians ... they just use us ... in their religious games, you know."

"Yes I get that and I agree. And please forgive me if I've ever thought that way."

"I forgive you ... old man ... you want me to say a Hebrew blessing over you ...?"

He smiles but then realises that she is joking.

"Sorry, I don't know any. I can bless wine and bread ... but that's it!"

Joe decides to continue.

"In fact, Abi ... we've talked a lot about this antisemitism that has returned in such a big way ... not that it's ever gone away ... and I can give you a reason for it if you want ..."

"I hope that we're not getting too religious now," interrupts Miss Garland. "We need to get on point, otherwise we are wasting our time."

"My dear," says Joe, sounding like a real professor now. "As Newt discovered ... which is probably why he's not here now ... is that it's ALL about religion ... God ..."

This time she is insistent in her interruption.

"You've had the floor for long enough now, Joe. Abi, do you have a question for someone here?"

"I do." She has been waiting for this.

"My question is for Joe."

Chapter twenty-six

"Actually, Joe, I think you were cut off short ..." says Abi.

She stares at Miss Garland, but she is talking to Joe.

"So ... why is this all about God?"

"I must object ..." says Miss Garland.

"Pardon me? You never specified any no-go areas? I thought this was a safe place, Miss Garland?"

Miss Garland says nothing but just sits there looking bored. Mo looks at her and wonders, *'why on earth was she selected for this job? She obviously doesn't want to be here and is certainly not equipped for the role that Newt performed so well. What on earth is going on here?'*

Joe grabs his moment before there are any more objections.

"Thanks, Abi, for allowing me to talk. I promise not to filibuster, I will be as concise as I can."

At least two of the people here had no idea what he was talking about. Filibuster? He launches into what was probably a prepared presentation.

"We are talking about the root cause of everything, certainly of the purpose and the need for this meeting. Peace in the Middle East. It can only come if ... one side isn't determined to wipe out the other side ..."

"Agree ..." says Jax. "Until Israel stops targeting innocent Palestinians ..."

"You know what I'm talking about, Jax. In fact, I think you know more than you are saying but perhaps the powers that be ..."

He glances at Miss Garland, someone that he has an ever-dwindling respect for.

"... don't want you to be pushed beyond your ... conditioning. I think you know what I'm saying."

"Haven't a clue."

"Never mind, that's your problem, not mine. Back to my thoughts ... There is more going on here than meets the eye, to be dramatic. Antisemitism has been around ever since the Jews entered their 'promised land' under Joshua, all those thousands of years ago, perhaps earlier. Everyone has been out to get them. Here's a partial list of just their current enemies ... The British government, the Palestinians, the United Nations, the media, the activists, the academics, the boycotters, jihadists, some Christians, neo-Nazis, Conspiracy buffs ... Come on, let's face it, how ridiculous is that? Either the Jews are so amazingly evil that each has a valid reason to hate them ..."

He stares at Jax for a few moments. She looks away.

"Or ... there is something ... or someone ... that connects all of the dots."

"God?" says Abi, confused.

"No. Not God. He has been protecting you, that's why you're still around after thousands of years."

"Then who ...?"

"The Devil ... Satan."

"Oh come on," groans Jax. "We're not venturing into superstition now. The red imp with horns and pitchfork?"

"No ... the fallen angel. Who hates God and uses the Jews – God's special chosen people – to do so and has done his utmost to wipe them out. These days he's using the Jihadists and their enablers in the West ... Jax ..."

"So, I'm in league with the Devil, professor?"

"Didn't think you believed in him."

"But you do?"

"Of course. It's the only possible explanation for antisemitism. One power attacking them ... but a far greater power ... protecting them! It seems so obvious!"

"If you believe in God," adds Abi.

"And the Devil," adds Jax.

"It doesn't matter what you believe. It's either true or not and the reason why Newt was taken out was that, thanks to his amazing analytical skills ... he had discovered a truth that was 'not acceptable.'"

He leaves them hanging. Not even Jax is objecting, though Miss Garland is looking very uncomfortable. She speaks.

"You think I'm a patsy, don't you? Just brought in to scupper any dangerous talk."

"You've got it," replies Joe immediately.

"I can see that," adds Abi.

"Me too," adds Mo, "though every part of me seems to want to reject it!"

"Noted" says Miss Garland. No denial, no defence. Just, "noted". Then she adds, "You're all entitled to your opinions. That's why you're here ... anyway, let's finish with Mo. What is your question?"

Mo has been prepared for this and immediately launches into a question for Jax.

"I have been thinking that I was a bit harsh on you earlier, madam. When our 'Chandelier Maker' spoke of us, he spoke of you as a person of passion. And that is a good thing and perhaps it is not your fault if you have directed your passion in a way that is not pleasing to me. I don't know your story, what brought you to your beliefs. Perhaps I was unfair ..."

"Please get to your point, Mo" says Miss Garland. "Your question?"

"My question to you is this, Jax. It's simple. Why do you think I was angry with you?"

"That's it?" says Miss Garland.

"Yes."

"Good question," mouths Joe.

Jax smiles. She has been challenged and she will rise to it.

"Thank you Mo, for giving me the right of reply, because, I confess, I was taken aback by your comments."

"It is good to get … under the skin … to see if there is any unity in our differences," says Mo. "And also, please forgive me for my disrespectful comments. I have been brought up to respect my elders …"

"This boy is so wise, gang. Perhaps we should have listened to him more today, rather than us aging windbags."

"Please get on with it, Jax" says Abi.

Jax notices that this is the first use of her name she has had from the Israeli girl. Some kind of victory there perhaps?

"Yes … I am a passionate woman. And yes … sometimes this passion has been misplaced. In my heart of hearts … and I am still processing this … yes, I have had problems with Jewish people. And I know a lot of this has filtered through to me through the company I keep. The party line seems to be that we have to be binary; there must be victims and villains. If Palestinians are victims … then the Israelis must be the villains … always …"

"And to answer my question?" says Mo.

"Why do I think you were angry with me? … mmm. Well … you have shown me that being a Palestinian doesn't automatically make you an enemy of the Jews. I just assumed you would think like me."

"Like I said, Jax. I have been brought up to get on with Jews and try and understand them … you have been brought up too … in this revolutionary politics you picked up in the 1960s … to see things differently. Can't you see … your way will never see peace?"

"But if I see injustice? The oppression, the genocide, the apartheid."

"Those words … you wield them like weapons … do you not see them so, the damage they can do?"

"But you'd agree ... some Palestinians ... in Gaza and the West Bank ... they are oppressed, they are living under apartheid ... and the number who have been killed in these conflicts ..."

"You are looking at numbers. This is wrong. Palestinians are killed because their rulers use them as weapons. They hide behind them. They boast about these deaths and they call them martyrs ... but do you think my people ... who were forced into refugee camps and 'occupied zones' to use them as propaganda weapons ... do you really think they would choose this if they could? ... of course they wouldn't! I am so fortunate that my family chose to live among the Jews ... rather than allowing themselves to fester in hate."

"But the settlers in the West Bank."

"Yes, not the nicest of people. I'm not saying that all Jews are saints ... perhaps with the exception of ..."

He winks at Abi. Incredibly, she blushes. He continues.

"Yes, a lot of bad things happen to my people living in the West Bank and Gaza and I say this ... and we did talk about this earlier ... if they could have moved to Jordan in 1948 or 1967, they and their families would be living in peace and our meeting today would not have been necessary."

"But I see those babies, children, innocents ... dying so horribly."

"That's because our media pump it out to us continually. Do we ever see what happens in Syria, Yemen, Nigeria ... no ... we Palestinians don't have a monopoly on suffering ... but I do know of a people who do ..."

He stops to allow that to sink in. *'Out of the mouth of babes,'* thinks Joe. This young Palestinian boy has taught them so much today. What could the world have been like if all Palestinians had been allowed to flourish like Mo. Joe is full of admiration, but he is also full of sorrow. He has been as guilty as Jax, but perhaps not so publicly. He has also seen the world in binary, of victims and villains, with the roles reversed in his worldview. He feels a burden. He feels that there is something he needs to do. And there is no time like the present.

He ignores the daggers thrown at him by Miss Garland's steely gaze. He crosses the floor and stands before Mo. He hesitates as Mo looks up at him with a slight, nervous smile. Joe smiles back, then speaks.

"Mo. You really are ... the wisest among us. It has been an absolute pleasure sharing these last few hours with you ..."

"Me too, Joe. You have been a surprise, I must say."

"Really?"

"Yes. I have never met a Christian who ... has such a feeling for the Jews. In fact ... I've never met a Christian ..."

"And I must confess, Mo ... and I have many years on you ... I've never felt so close to a Muslim before. I have got you all so wrong. As someone said, we see so much in black and white, friends and enemies, victims and oppressors. We need to go beyond this and just see ... people ..."

"Correct. And when I look at you now, I don't see what the world sees, but what the heart sees ... just a good man doing his best."

Abi has witnessed this exchange and responds in the only way possible.

"Get a room, you two! Never heard such ..."

"Come on, Abi," replies Joe. "Indulge us. It's been a significant day I think ... and soon it will be ending."

"True. So ...?"

Joe looks at Mo and takes his hand. There are tears in his eyes.

"Then just grant this old man one thing. Mo. Forgive me for my attitude towards your people. Loving Jews should never mean hating Palestinians ... you have shown me a ... different way."

"Of course I forgive you. Allah compels me. We must enjoy our ... unity ... when there is so much division around us."

As he says this, he looks over the other side of the room. Jax is in conversation with Miss Garland. It is very animated, but, it seems, not in a good way.

"I wonder what they're talking about?"

Joe reaches down and hugs the young man. It is a little awkward as neither is comfortable with such physicality. But it is sincerely meant and received likewise. Abi looks on and, despite herself, is quite touched. So much so, that she ignores her usual rising cynicism and leaves her seat, walks over to them and, tentatively and gently, rests her head along Joe's bent back and wraps her arms around him. This poignant moment only lasts a few seconds, but it is a significant epitaph of the journey they have made together. This gesture has a deep effect on Joe and he feels that it is something he will never forget ... ever. From elderly stranger to kindly grandad in the space of a few hours. He feels vindicated.

Joe lifts himself up and looks over to Jax. She has stopped talking to Miss Garland and looks at him, wistfully. Is there a touch of jealousy there, a sense of missing out on a precious moment? Her face lightens up just that little bit.

Joe catches her eye and gestures her over ...

Chapter twenty-seven

Miss Garland clears her throat. She is clearly trying to catch their attention. She really is an awkward individual and they all yearn for Newt to return and wish that they had appreciated him while he had been there with them. She speaks.

"Yes, I know I'm not respected here, like that tin man of yours but I have been given one last instruction, which I do intend to carry out."

She reaches down into a box and takes out the four HR caps. They all know what is coming next. She walks round to them and places them surprisingly carefully and gently on each of their heads, then returns to her desk. She reads from a sheet of paper.

"This is to be your final act. You will be taken to an event that will be very familiar to two of you, though it has been spoken about earlier today. In a sense, how you individually and as a group respond to this will be a litmus test and a measure of how successful the day has been."

She stops and stares at them in a manner that suggests malevolence rather than benevolence.

"Enjoy!" is the last word she has for them. They all briefly black out as before and now find themselves in the centre of a large demonstration. It looks like London and it is decidedly pro-Palestinian.

"Oh no," moans Jax, "Really?"

It is the very place where Abi came in disguise and exposed her.

"I am going to enjoy this," says Abi quietly. "Or perhaps I won't." She says this because she suddenly reminds herself of the views to which she is about to be exposed.

"I'm really sorry for you, Jax" says Joe, "but we need to

do this."

"Yes I do get it," is the reply, spoken with a weary resignation. "I won't obstruct you all. Come on let's do it."

They wander over to the first person, an orthodox Jew, complete with trilby, black overcoat and white shirt, wispy beard and brandishing a Palestine flag.

"You're a Jew, what are you doing here?" says Abi, clearly offended

"Yes I am a Jew, but I feel I must stand in solidarity with the people of Palestine and show them that not all Jews are Zionists supporting these war crimes."

"Well ... I am Jewish ... and a Zionist ... and I see no war crimes. No ... I do see war crimes ... I see cowardly terrorists hiding behind civilians and shouting 'Come and get us, we dare you'!"

"Then you are brainwashed. Look at what they are doing in Gaza to the Palestinian people. Not in my name!"

"Me brainwashed? You really don't get it do you? You are a traitor to your people. Do you not see what Hamas did on October 7th as a war crime? Do you not identify with the Jews who were massacred?"

"The Zionists brought it on themselves!"

"No sympathy then?"

"I have spoken."

He turns away. Abi is seething and Mo comforts her as best he can.

"Look at him, Joe ... not all of us Jews are saints, or even decent human beings!" she declares.

Joe shares her anger but obviously not to the same depths.

But it gets worse, because another Jew wanders over, also carrying a flag and sporting a beard, this time an unruly ginger one.

"I was listening," he says. "And I need to tell you that

the idea that Israel is a promised land from God is a total lie. We are in exile and thus forbidden to live in a state unless the Messiah decrees. Your Theodore Hertzl and Weismann and the rest of their Zionist gang, they were heretics … not followers of Torah, real Judaism."

"And what if the Messiah has come and is calling them back?" says Joe, mischievously but seriously.

"Well he hasn't, so he isn't … who are you to speak about us … you're a 'goy.'"

"A 'goy' who knows a lot more of your God than you ever will," responds Joe. At that, Abi actually gives Joe a fist pump, which pleases him no end. They walk away from ginger-beard.

Next in line is a middle-aged lady in dark glasses. She has a confident look and is very keen to engage. Jax asks her why she is here.

"I am a Jew myself, descended from rabbis. I was brought up with stories that I now know are not true after I went off and did my investigation."

"And what did you find, if I may ask?" says Joe.

"I visited Israel and Palestine and all I saw was the effect of colonialist British power handing Palestine over to the Israelis. Britain made this possible through the Mandate and then of course there was guilt over the Holocaust. But what should never have happened is to dispossess others and create other victims."

"You seem to have a good understanding of the history and I agree that the British did create many of the problems we have now but … my reading of history is that, since the 1920s, the British were no friend of the Jew."

"But they were hardly friends of the Arabs, they handed over the land to the Jews after all."

"I thought that was the United Nations. The British just

wanted to leave …"

"But they could have done more to help the Arabs … that's just my opinion."

"If you could ask an Israeli or a Zionist anything, what would it be?"

"Know your history … and check everything."

"Couldn't agree more. Thanks for talking to me," says Joe.

As they walk away, Joe speaks to the group.

"She's right about knowing history, but I just feel that her knowledge is patchy …"

"It's not an easy history, professor," says Jax.

"Too true. So many nuances, so many angles and opinions. Look over there. There's a lady who I think will mean business."

The lady in question is elderly and in a high-vis jacket, suggesting that she was involved in the organising of the demo. Jax approaches her.

"I visited Israel when younger with some Israeli friends and was horrified by what I found. They did not have one good word to say about the Arabs, in fact I, was told not to speak to them, or they would rape me, murder me, rob me. Everywhere I went I heard this … it disgusted me."

"I'm an Israeli Jew and I would never say that", says Abi.

"Well, then I wish I had met you then, dearie. Perhaps you can educate your Jewish friends … I found the Arabs much better people …"

"That's because we are," says Mo.

The lady seems confused at this.

"Why aren't you marching with us? Do you want a flag?"

"No, madam. I'm an Israeli Arab and I'm quite happy living among the Jews."

"Why are you all here? Have you come to disrupt?"

She is deeply suspicious. She starts to walk away.

"Please speak to us," says Jax. "I, for one, have a better understanding of your position."

"Really?"

"Yes. Do carry on with your story."

"Well, I married a Palestinian and had two children with him. I saw the apartheid then, but it has got far worse now, along with the atrocities. In fact ... it's the longest-lasting injustice of our times."

"Thank you," says Jax, who seems a little troubled. Perhaps she has seen a mirror of the person that she once was, but who is possibly in a different place now. Her conflict ensures her silence, much to the relief of the others, particularly Joe.

None of them feel that engagement and argument will be constructive here. They can see this lady has obviously lived through some tough times and it would be unfair to doubt her sincerity, even though her conclusions seem rather extreme.

There is another lady who seems to be keen to talk. She is middle-aged and has a passionate look about her, you can see it in her eyes. She is wearing a garish Palestinian tee-shirt and carries a flag.

"I am absolutely appalled by the genocide that has been committed there by the Israelis ..."

"... what do you mean by 'genocide'? What is it?" asks Joe.

"Well ... the deliberate targeting of innocent Palestinian women and children ... it's not just since October 7th ... they have always treated the Palestinians appallingly."

"I'm an Arab living in Israel. I don't see this."

"Then you're not looking properly!"

"What? When's the last time you came to Israel to see?"

"Don't need to, I see enough on the TV. Look ... they are bombing hospitals. They don't care who they kill and

they have probably killed far more than we're told. It is …
appalling! They cut off water and electricity to Gaza, it's a
genocide."

"How do you know this?" asks Joe.

"The TV and the newspapers."

"But journalists are not allowed in Gaza. We're getting
all the news directly from Hamas."

"So? Anyway … I don't know why I'm talking to you; I
can see where you're coming from … you're upsetting me,
how can you be so uncaring!"

She bursts into tears and her friend gives them a harsh
look and leads her away.

"Another fragile liberal crying over the nonsense that's
fed to her," says Abi.

"A bit harsh, Abi," suggests Jax. "After all … you could
be talking about me there …"

She trails off, still conflicted.

The next 'victim' is a middle-aged man, dressed in a
casual jacket, with shirt and tie, adorned with a single badge
of a flag. He is clean-shaven and seems the type that would
have an articulate argument.

"I support Palestine because they have the right to self-
determination and to be free …"

"Why don't you think they are?" says Joe.

"The Israelis of course and their Apartheid State."

"And not Hamas? Do you really think Hamas allow their
people to be free and safe?"

"Of course."

"Then why do they build terror tunnels under their
hospitals, schools and mosques."

"That's what you say."

"That's what the world sees."

"Zionist propaganda!"

"OK ... we'll agree to disagree on that one. What do you think is the cause of the problems we see now?"

"British Imperialism, resulting in a Zionist land grab. The Jews suffered in Europe; does this mean they have to create suffering and apartheid in Arab territories? It is settler colonialism."

"Lots of Marxist buzzwords there, sir ... are you a Marxist?"

"That's my concern. Excuse me I need to go now."

"Nice talking to you."

He walks away.

"Not sure if I understood all of that," says Mo.

"That's because those who run these 'events' use certain buzzwords in their speeches that come from the far left. Isn't that true, Jax?"

"To an extent. I've given many such speeches myself. I understood what I was saying, I think many people here are just parroting these words without understanding their meaning."

"It's a shame, because they do mostly seem quite educated."

"Too wise for their own good, perhaps," responds Jax, stoically.

Another white middle-aged man wanders up. He is wearing a Palestinian headscarf. He makes a statement that seems practised and derivative.

"I'm standing with Palestine and Lebanon and all the other countries that Israel is bombing and helping to destroy. If you support Israel then you are complicit in their apartheid system within the occupied territories and you are supporting an out-of-control regime in the aggression it is showing to all of its neighbours. They have stolen Palestinian land and it's the legacy of British colonialism. Israel does not want peace, it just wants to expand into Jordan, Lebanon, Syria, Iraq and even Saudi Arabia. They are colonizers and they will kill to get what they want."

No one answers him. Perhaps they are becoming weary of all the rhetoric. Jax smiles at him and he walks away.

Another middle-aged man in a bright tee shirt and jeans has an interesting angle.

"The International Court of Justice has made it clear. It has clearly made its initial determination - It's a genocide – and Netanyahu is a war criminal. We can thank the Republic of South Africa for filing the case. They had a two-day hearing with loads of evidence. Of course, Israel doesn't turn up to the hearing and fifteen out of the seventeen judges declared in favour. It's a genocide. Therefore, it's a breach of the UN Convention on Genocide. Britain should be following this up and, because it isn't, this is an absolute disgrace."

"What about the other genocides in the world? In Sudan, Nigeria, Syria … it's a long list … why is this court only focussed on Israel … why is the UN in general so focussed on Israel?"

"You'd have to ask them. They must have their reasons."

He goes his own way.

"Joe, what's he talking about … this International Court?" asks Abi.

"It's a court in The Hague, set up by the UN It only has an advisory opinion on the issue of Israel, so is not in force. But, nevertheless, it's another stick used by Israel's enemies to bash it with. A case was brought to it by South Africa saying that there's a 'plausible' case that Israel is committing genocide in Gaza. In other words, that they are deliberately intending to kill Palestinian civilians there. It's a nonsense but not a surprise as the United Nations has been ruling against Israel for decades, more so than every other country in the world combined."

"Possibly ... no smoke without fire," suggests Jax. "Just sayin'".

"Look over there," says Abi. "Just a kid. Let's see what he has to say."

It is a youngster carrying a flag and wearing a Palestinian keffiyeh.

"I'm nine years old and the reason that I'm supporting Palestine is because Israel is bombing Palestine for literally no reason. It's not been since October 7th ... it's been since 1948."

"Clearly been programmed," says Abi. "This is so sad, how hate is taught to the kids. I've seen the Palestinian textbooks in their schools."

"Not all schools," says Mo. "I had a very balanced education. I was taught to get on with all people."

"But then you were educated in Israel, not the West Bank or Gaza."

"Yes, sure. All this really grieves me. Why has it ended up with this?" says Mo, pointing at this innocent boy and his slogans.

"It's no different in the West", adds Joe. "I've had a glimpse at some of the videos on TikTok, they are short ... but far from sweet."

"That's how the youngsters are educated on the things of the world, I'm afraid", says Jax. "Even I can see the dangers here. In our day, professor, we had things like debates and lectures and reasoned arguments."

"Apart from those endless marches, of course", suggests Joe. "It didn't all start in recent years. You lot have been marching for sixty years ..."

"And I'm worn out, professor. These old feet are calloused."

"Don't worry about your feet, Jax, it's your heart that

mustn't get … calloused."

"Look over there. That little kid can't be more than about six or seven."

It's a blond girl in pigtails, dressed in the full garb, wrapped in a Palestinian flag and grasping the hand of her 'hippy' mother. They are both chanting, *'From the River to the Sea, Palestine will be Free.'* Joe couldn't resist the comment.

"Hello, madam, I'm new to all of this. What are the river and sea you are referring to?"

The woman looked at him blankly. The girl continues singing.

"I don't know. Does it matter?"

"Well … yes … I think so. Why sing it if you don't know what you're singing about?"

"Don't we all do that sometimes … sing a song that we've heard on the radio that we like but have no idea what it's all about … like … um … oh yes … Bohemian Rhapsody."

"Yes, but that's just entertainment … what you're actually singing about here is about the genocide of the Jewish people – getting rid of them from the land. Don't you know that?"

"Rubbish … I'll sing what I want."

She returns to singing and drags her daughter away.

"Stupid woman!"

Joe addresses his friends. "Did you know that the words, 'From the River to the Sea' are actually out of the Bible? In the book of Genesis, I believe, but also somewhere in the Psalms. It actually talks about the land that God promises to the Jews, ironically."

"Perhaps you should tell her," says Abi.

"Don't think she's really up for a theological debate here, don't you think?"

"Maybe not."

Mo starts giggling and draws Abi's attention to an individual who has just come into view. It is a young man, very flamboyant in appearance and carrying a banner, *'Queers for Palestine.'*

"Oh, we must talk to this fellow," says Mo. "Someone needs to put him straight."

"You are not talking about conversion therapy, are you?" says Abi, mischievously.

He doesn't get the double entendre at first.

"Abi!" he exclaims when he gets it. "Naughty girl!"

They approach the man.

"Hello. You look a bit lonely. Can I ask you a question?" says Abi.

He hesitates for a moment, sizing her up. But he shrugs and speaks.

"OK, lady. Fire away."

"Why are you here? You seem a bit out of place."

His hackles are raised.

"What d'you mean? Are you being homophobic, lady?"

"No, no ... that's my point ... from my limited knowledge I remember reading a news story ... or was it a YouTube video ... about gay people being thrown from buildings in Gaza."

"That's what the Zionists do! They hate everyone, especially people like me."

"No ... not the Israelis, the Palestinians ... gays are not welcome, it's a religious thing I think."

He ignores her, but she can see a tinge of panic in his eyes. Does his banner visibly droop a few inches then?

"And Israel ... I think ... again, I'm sure I've read it somewhere ... is one of the most gay-friendly places in the world."

He stops and stares at her, thinks for a bit, then speaks, loudly.

"So what! Palestine must be free! Queers for Palestine!"

He moves on, ignoring her. He evidently hadn't thought this thing through, but perhaps she had given him food for thought for the future? Who knows?

"So what we're seeing here, I think, is ... apart from a few 'looney tunes' ... we see a very focussed group of individuals who see this conflict mainly through a Marxist lens. Is that a fair comment, Jax," says Joe.

"Oh yes and surely there's no crime in that. If the Socialist Workers Party and the Stop the War coalition are going to organise an event, it will be mainly for their people. I, of course, was one of these ..."

"Was?"

She doesn't answer him.

"It is strange though, Jax, how Muslims, who follow a theological system and the Marxists, who are atheists, can find common ground at events like this."

"Easy," says Abi. "United in their hatred for Jews ... period."

"Fair point," responds Joe. "How long do you think a progressive liberal from the far left would survive if the Muslims got their caliphate in this country? These women and gay men here wouldn't last five minutes."

Again she doesn't answer him, but Mo does.

"As I've said before, most Muslims are not like that. I count women and gay people as my friends. There is much good in my faith and, Joe and Abi, we have much more in common than what divides us. We all share, I believe, a distaste for the liberalisation we see around us ..."

"I agree. Obviously, there are theological differences but, in terms of morality and ethics, there's a lot of good in basic Muslim teaching. I can see that, Mo, just by talking to you."

"You have taught me much, too ... professor!"

"Oy", groans Joe, "looks like I'm stuck with that one! ... all your fault Jax, corrupting the poor boy."

"Hold on", says Abi, suddenly. "Is that me?"

They all stare at this isolated figure, trying to fit in but still managing to stand out. No one notices her, apart from Abi herself.

"How ridiculous I looked. I don't know how I got away with it."

"You look quite ... fetching," says Mo. "You certainly had a ... unique style there."

There's a gasp from Jax. She has seen herself.

"Please ...", she pleads. "No ..."

"I'm sorry, Jax, but we have to. I think this is what's expected of us."

The group moves towards alternate-Jax, in fiery mode, being interviewed by a young Muslim man. His microphone is switched off and hanging loose. Alternate-Abi has moved closer and is evidently recording the conversation from a distance.

"Can you tell me why you are here supporting Palestine?"

"Well if we don't stand up for what's happening to the people in Palestine, then the same thing is going to happen to all of us. All the killing, all the genocide that is happening in Palestine, it just shows that they don't care for people's lives."

"What message would you give to someone who supports Israel?"

"If you're supporting Israel then you just have to understand that what Israel is doing at the moment shows that they have no sense of humanity, what it means to be a human being. Palestinians ... us ... at the end of the day we are all human beings, we have to look after one another and that's not what Israel is doing at the moment."

"And does Israel have the right to defend itself?"

"Israel has no right to defend itself from what's happening in Palestine. The Palestinian people have the right to defend themselves,

Israelis are occupiers in a land that was never theirs."

They, of course, have heard the words before. Jax stands open-mouthed. *Was that really me?*

"Why not have a word?" suggests Joe. "Could be interesting."

The group moves forwards. Alternate-Jax notices them. There is no going back now.

"You look ... familiar."

"I think we are ... dopplegangers."

"Even down to the birthmark?"

"Yes, a bit strange ... anyway ... can I ask you a question?"

"Go ahead. I'm an open book."

"What do you mean that ... Israelis ... have no sense of humanity?"

"Can you see what they are doing?"

"Yes ... but there's a bigger picture ... surely?"

"I repeat ... can you see what they are doing ... bombing women and children?"

"Do you know why?"

"It's a genocide ... no other reason ..."

"Can we talk ... y'know ... honestly, person-to-person ...?"

"Even if they are one and the same," whispers Abi.

"Eh?"

Jax continues.

"All this you are saying ... off the microphone ... are you ashamed? Otherwise, why won't you allow a recording?"

"I'm not ashamed of anything. It's just that people ... the Zionists ... will take what I say and twist it. It happens all the time on social media."

"And you also say that they don't even have the right to defend themselves ... isn't that a little ... harsh?"

"No ... of course not ... after what they are doing to the Palestinians ... they don't deserve to live."

"Can you say that again? I'm not sure if I heard right."

"I repeat … the way the Israelis conduct themselves with their genocide against the Palestinian people … they don't deserve to live … Is that clear?"

Jax is shocked. *Is this really me?* She has only one response to this.

"That's what the Nazis said."

She has had enough and walks away, shocked. Joe puts his arms around her.

"Well spoken, Jax."

"Was that really me? Was I really like that?"

"Yes", says Abi. "But … I think perhaps … not now."

Jax looks at Abi, with tears in her eyes.

"Thank you," she says softly to the young Israeli girl.

The scene fades and they find themselves back in the room. They all remove their caps. Miss Garland sits with her legs propped up on her desk, reading a book. She seems angry that they have returned. *Why on earth is she there?*

"So soon?" she says. They ignore her.

Chapter twenty-eight

Jax stands up, takes her chair, drags it to the centre of the room and sits down. The others take the cue. Each of them does the same, creating a little huddle, excluding Miss Garland, who seems quite disinterested anyway.

"I think we're nearing the end now ... how do we all feel?" says Jax.

"Exhausted, I think. Could do with a long sleep, it's been a long day," responds Joe.

"We're no spring chickens are we, professor?"

"No, more like battered old hens! ... and it looks like I'm stuck with this title now, eh?"

"It suits you," says Mo.

"Well then, as I've come to value your opinion, Mo, then 'professor' it is."

They all laugh briefly. Joe speaks seriously.

"When I look back on our journey today ... I think that there's one of us ... who has ... been on quite some journey."

They look at each other. Jax speaks up.

"You mean me, don't you? ... I can see from how you're all looking at me."

"You agree though ... don't you?" adds Joe.

"Oh yes ... it was made crystal clear when I met ... the 'other' me."

There's a silence for a while.

"And?" asks Abi.

"You know ... it's a lot to process but ... there're some things that hit you in the gut and you can't avoid."

"Such as?" asks Joe.

"At the end of the day ... we're all humans here ... and it's humans that matter, not philosophies, or even history. When I first came here ... only a few hours ago ... isn't that incredible ... I was ready for battle ..."

"As was I," says Joe. "What about you two?"

"Well, I didn't really know what to expect," says Abi.

"I just came for the food ... and excellent it was, eh," says Mo, with mischief in his eyes. "No, I have had a real education."

"So have I," says Abi. "You old folk ... you certainly know your stuff."

"No, no, no," says Joe. "You're wrong there. I think Jax would agree with me if I said that we both learned far more from you."

"Oh really?"

"Yes. Jax and I are basically opinionated windbags ..."

"... speak for yourself, professor!"

"But you two ..." he adds. "You've lived it. Maybe not at the centre of it, but you're there, it's your land we are quibbling over, that the world quibbles over. It makes so much sense that the future should be in your hands ... in younger hands ... rather than the politicians, statesmen, generals, theologians ..."

"Yes," admits Jax. "We have ... failed you ... me especially."

They can sense a long speech coming, but a significant one that they are, for the first time, happy to listen to. Jax continues.

"When I gave that ... speech by the Palestinian activist ... I must say I believed every word of it, otherwise I wouldn't have given it. But now ... when I remember the words, rather than the passionate delivery ... I realise ... just how wrong I was. Perhaps it made me feel good saying it ... and I'm sure it was the same for the lady who wrote it ... but that is so selfish ... it's not about feeling good; it's not even about the cause ... it's about people ... real people, whether they are Jew or Arab ... and ... when ... I think about how my words must have pierced your soul, Abi ... and the words you overheard at that rally ... well ... I can't tell you how sorry I am ... words are so ... dangerous, the very worst of the weapons we have ... Now, as I look back at that demo and others I have been at and I see the same thing ... the atmosphere being whipped up by some people with nothing more than hate in their heart ... it must have been the same in Nazi Germany ... how easily we can switch into this ... hatred ... I am thoroughly ashamed of myself, I really am. At least ... thanks to you ... I've woken up to it, but thousands are still infected by this madness, this hatred ... how are they going to wake up to it, it just isn't healthy, is it?"

Abi moves closer to her. Jax gestures that she hasn't finished yet.

"Now don't get me wrong ... I am an advocate for the Palestinians and always will be ... there were some things in that speech, as Newt showed us, that were going on ... like the broken bones policy ..."

"... Yes I was absolutely appalled by that," interrupts Joe. "I did some checking and Newt was right, Rabin did implement it ... absolutely horrific ...". Jax continues.

"... yes, as I was saying ... what I now realise is this. Love for Palestinians ... and it is real, Mo, as real as professor's love for the Jews ... that you expressed so movingly at the time ... Joe ... but I wasn't going to tell you then, of course ..."

"... that was 'Old' Jax," says Joe.

"Yes ... 'Old' Jax ... Right ... Well 'new' Jax realises something very different, something that 'old' Jax never understood ... love for one people should never mean hatred for another ... Newt showed us that ... Boy do I miss him, who on earth is this new ... creature ... that they have burdened us with ...?"

"... the anti-Newt", suggests Abi.

"Right ... the anti-Newt ... a complete nightmare. I'll never forget those last words of his ... um ... 'Love and care for the Palestinians ...' ... actually I have forgotten the rest ... anyone?"

"... Love and care for the Palestinians is often a smokescreen for hatred for the Jews. Until this is acknowledged, there will always be two sets of victims ... and these are people who really ought to be friends." This is Joe speaking. He is reading from a scrap of paper.

"My memory is as bad as yours, Jax," he says. "But I'm a very good note-taker!" She continues.

"Yes ... and I can categorically say ... that I don't hate Jews ... I've been sucked into a kind of madness ... you, Joe ... you can probably describe it ... in fact you already have ... in terms of some great divine conflict ... but, although I don't go along with that ... nonsense ... we have seen enough, haven't we ... with the Nazis, crusaders, the pogroms ... to see that people like ... the 'old' Jax ... are just perpetrating this madness, allowing hate to trump all ... and it's not good enough and ... I'll say it one last time ... I am truly, truly, truly sorry, Abi."

You can see that she means this and that Joe agrees. He has been nodding feverishly throughout the whole speech. Abi leaves her chair and hugs both of them with great tenderness. And plants a kiss on Jax's cheek.

"You old witch!" she says ... tenderly.

Mo joins her. The huddle lasts for around two or three minutes. There is even the sound of sobbing, but no-one admits to it afterwards. In truth, they were all emotionally overcome.

Eventually they take their chairs back to their desks and sit on them ... and wait.

Chapter twenty-nine

The long, fraught day is coming to an end. They are exhausted but, mostly, exhilarated. Joe and Jax are showing their age and are slumped behind their desks, wondering what's next, if anything, and when they would be allowed home to their loved ones. They are all spent and sit waiting for a conclusion to the activities of the day.

The moment comes with fuss and fanfare. The lights dim and the screen on the back wall is suddenly filled with images, a collection of window groupings. Some, like before, contain a large group of noisy people in auditoriums, while others are smaller more serious groupings. At the centre is a screen with a single man, old grey-haired and kindly looking. He is instantly recognisable by all, as a prominent world leader, evidently the prime mover behind all that had happened that day.

"Greetings, friends. It has been a hard day, yes?" he says.

They say nothing to start with as the visual bombardment is so overwhelming. Eventually, they all answer in the affirmative, unsure if their voices can be heard. From his reaction, it seems that they could, not just by the man in charge but by all of the other groups that inhabit the display.

"I ... we ... thank you for your efforts today. It has been appreciated ... far beyond your comprehension, I suspect ... because it is time to ... let us say ... come clean ..."

The delegates all look at each other in slight shock, wondering what is going to come next.

"You all signed up to The Programme ... and believe me you were the very best of all those considered ... and that was a large number ... you all signed up expecting to participate in an ... experiment. And it has been an experiment in the sense that it has not been done before ... but it was always intended to be more than an experiment, far more."

Their sense of shock deepens, though this is mixed with a degree of excitement too. This is fed by an increase in murmurings in the watching crowds on the screen.

"First, a bit of a history lesson. Are you ready for this?"

"Yes," says Abi on their behalf, a little impatiently.

"In 1929, after an Arab uprising in Palestine, the British rulers of the land instigated an inquiry as to the causes, resulting in the Shaw Report, named after Sir Walter Shaw, who led the inquiry. The findings were controversial and did not do justice to all of the parties. In fact, it all seemed a bit of a fudge. One of the members of the commission, Henry Snell, a Labour politician, certainly felt so. He issued a 'note of Reservations', an addendum to the report, where he listed his disagreements."

"Yes … Newt spoke of him earlier. A man ahead of his time!" says Joe.

"And someone not listened to," adds Abi.

The man continues.

"His summary was that "a few men of both races" should "meet together and explore the possibilities of common effort for agreed ends," to work towards cooperation in establishing inter-racial justice and goodwill. "Out of their efforts would grow a reserve of understanding," he proposed, "to unite Arab and Jew in the task of building up a happy and prosperous land."

He pauses for effect. Then continues.

"Now, almost a century later … we have finally got round to it …"

He then stands up and starts clapping. There is clapping and applause all around. Even Miss Garland lifts a limp wrist in salute. He stops for a few moments for it to die down, then continues.

"You ... in fact ... have just played a vital role in the ... and I will be blunt ... Middle East peace process ..."

There are more cheers and clapping from the crowds.

"What has taken place today between you all ... has been a little more than just a lively secret discussion ... but in fact a very public discussion ... the whole world has been watching you every step of the way! In case you're wondering how this is possible and how you never knew about this before you joined us, it was all advertised over all media outlets, from newspapers to social media, in the two days you were all holed up in those rather comfortable hotels ... actually in four adjoining rooms."

The cheering increases in volume as the four delegates are literally open-mouthed and thoroughly confused. Jax lets out a single cry. "What!" The others are not quite so vocal.

"I can see you are shocked, as anyone would be. But it has been vital for the Programme that you believed that you were in a closed, private meeting, a safe space as it was described to you."

"You have all become celebrities, in a very short time. But that is the way of the world these days with social media. You have each become what they call ... influencers ... each with a devoted following. In fact ... Mo ... if you were to run for public office then you would win hands down. Abi, you have a very large following among some very unusual demographics ... teenage girls in Japan, goths in Scandinavia, seal farmers in Iceland ... and you already have five TikTok accounts, all supposedly authored by you. Joc, you have a following among Christians, but not all of them, to be honest. The Pope is a great fan, apparently. And Jax ... you have the greatest following of all, but not by your own people. Chat shows around the world are, I believe, queuing up to have you as a guest ... Also, U2 are allegedly about to release a charity single, 'The Witch and the Professor', which is expected to top the charts. And there's a growing clamour for a repeat performance focussing on other conflicts. Oh ... and you're all being nominated for a Nobel Peace Prize. I hope this is all an encouragement for you ..."

But Jax is not impressed. She is coming out of the shock, all guns blazing.

"You lied to us!" shouts Jax at the screen. Miss Garland tries to gesture her to control herself but, now the shock is over, Jax is firing on all cylinders.

"How can you do this? Where are our rights? You have totally gone against our human rights! I don't care who you are ... you had no right to do this."

"They have every right, Jax", says Joe. "If their cause is a noble one, then they are free to conduct it in the best way they can ... I ... for one ... have no issue and I hope we have helped."

"But ... but ... I would have said things differently if I had known ..."

"Just like when you were at the demo and thought you weren't being filmed?" says Abi.

This halts Jax and she goes very quiet. Mo adds his thoughts.

"We should always think and act as if ... the world is watching. Allah sees all, you know."

"The almighty God neither slumbers nor sleeps," adds Joe, wanting to redress the theological balance. The voice on the screen continues.

"Then please accept our apology, Jax ... and think of the greater good. You are, after all, an activist ... sometimes you have to lose a battle ... to win the war."

Jax is all spent. Joe stands up, drags his seat over to her and sits next to her, wordlessly. She doesn't flinch but accepts this kind act. He speaks to the screen.

"And what has been the outcome ... for the peace process that is ... may I ask?"

"For that, we must wait and see."

Chapter thirty

The reality of it all is that, for well over eighty years now, peace in the Middle East has been a forlorn hope and there had been a sinking, but inevitable, conclusion that it simply wasn't possible, that too much has been tried and found wanting already. Peace summits haven't worked, threats and promises haven't worked, wars and the rumours of wars have certainly not helped and international action, whether from the UN or independent states or groupings of states has not helped. The world had become a very dangerous place, particularly with the increased proliferation of nuclear, chemical and bacteriological weapons, allied to the increased willingness for leaders to actually use them, or at least threaten to, out of divine 'certainties' or just fatalistic nihilism.

No, something else was needed, a last throw of the dice. Something "left field", not tried before, although suggested by Mr Snell nearly a century ago. There was nothing to lose but everything to gain, after all. World peace is obviously something worth striving for. So, some bright spark had an idea. It is unsure who it was, as it was gleaned from an obscure social media feed during a trawl by one of the intelligence services, presumably looking for signs of intelligence! This is the premise:

Rather than rely on those in power to arrive at a resolution, we appeal to the grassroots, to people who have no power base, ambitions or unhelpful associations. We find representatives of the Israeli and Palestinian causes and allow them to debate and communicate with each other in an enclosed space, for an extended, but specified period. And that this would be moderated by a convenor who is unencumbered by emotional attachments or bias and has an extensive grasp of the facts and figures that define the conflict.

Research provided the ideal makeup of this grouping. For each side, there should be two representatives. One who is living in the land already, with no attachments to unhelpful influences and the other who has a sincere, but remote interest, either as activists for the cause or as academics who understand the underlying factors behind the conflict. After subtle advertising and canvassing, they arrived at a group of four people.

Mohammad (Mo) Hussein (Muslim) – age 27,
Haifa, Israel.
Abigail (Abi) Weiss (Jew) – age 25, Jerusalem, Israel.
Jacqueline (Jax) Botham (Atheist/Marxist) – age 72,
Highgate, UK
Joseph (Joe) Parsons (Christian) – age 74,
Cambridge, UK

Both parties unanimously agreed to go ahead with this selection. All four agreed to take part in what was known as 'The Programme'. The role of the convenor was problematic. It was nigh on impossible to find someone skilled enough, with extensive knowledge of the conflict and impeccable real-time research abilities, who could be guaranteed as independent and with no axe to grind. Then information filtered through about the secret NEWT research into artificial intelligence and that there was a prototype that could be used. It was a 'win-win' situation; a perfect choice of convenor and an ideal environment to test out the prototype.

There is another meeting. This one truly is a closed meeting, the world has been excluded this time. The meeting is at a secret location, though, in fact, it is simply just a couple of floors up from the location where our four delegates are now saying their farewells to each other and are ready to be escorted back, by limousine and private plane, to their homes. No expense has been spared. It is the least the world could have done for their efforts today.

The format of this new meeting, curiously, follows the same pattern as the first one. It appears that the simple stripped-down model is worth pursuing, rather than a room full of arguing hotheads. Just two from each side and a convenor. This person is neither an artificial intelligence nor a person who seemed to be grabbed at the last minute from the typing pool! His name is Arnold. He wears a bland grey suit and seems utterly unflappable. He will do a good job, he has been well-trained. He has been The Speaker of the UK Parliament and so is ready for anything.

All of them are furnished with earpieces, with access to various instructions and opinions emanating from another couple of rooms, packed with think tanks. Even Arnold has a room full of aides to help him. It is ironic as, with all of his abilities, Newt needed none of this. All the information in the world was available to him and he could sift through it and evaluate it and come to good conclusions. Unfortunately, his latter conclusions were unacceptable to some, which is why he is currently languishing on a factory floor somewhere, waiting to be recommissioned.

Each side has a war hawk and a dove of peace in their team, in order to be able to provide some sort of balance. The Israeli side is led by Ari, a senior politician, once a famous general in past-but-not-forgotten battles. By his side is Esther, a mid-range diplomat and a highly respected negotiator. The Palestinian side is led by Ali, another distinguished veteran of many conflicts of yesteryear, ably supported by Umar, a rising young social commentator, very popular among younger Arabs. There is little conviviality between the teams, they are there to do a job, not to make friends. It was a spark of genius to follow the simple instructions of Mr Snell from a century earlier and the results of the endeavour seem to have been successful. Yet here they are now, reverting to type, taking the conclusions from the earlier meeting and sifting them through another series of filters.

They watched the complete day's activities in real-time. They even shared the HR sessions through highly classified and experimental technology. They watched in private, taking extensive notes and researching all of the permutations and possibilities thrown up by the various debates. It is now time to share discoveries and views, with both friend and foe, to see if the exercise has been a fruitful one.

They came to some initial conclusions. By all accounts The Programme was successfully implemented. The following observations were made:

1. Mo, Joe and Abi were good choices. Each promoted the interests of their groups more than adequately.

2. On initial reflection, perhaps a better choice than Jax could have been made. A major oversight was the fact that she had already met Abi, albeit by complete accident. But, on further reflection, it was thought that she generally acquitted herself well, particularly as her views were becoming increasingly isolated. She is truly the barometer of success and her journey was the most dissected of all of them all.

3. NEWT performed well to a degree. It was felt that he exceeded his brief through his interpretation of certain data, which could have compromised his neutral position.

4. There was some regrettable confusion over NEWT's replacement for the final session. Somehow a rather biased individual from the typing pool was selected, due to some confusion over names. It was felt (hoped) that no

lasting damage resulted from this oversight.

The final discussion took hours to complete. There needed to be a unanimous decision made, with the following question needing to be addressed: *'From the interactions between these four individuals, is it possible that lasting peace between the citizens in the Middle East can be attained without the need for external inducements or threats?'*

That was the sole criterion. It was all down to Jax, Abi, Mo and Joe. That was the theory of it anyway. Perhaps not. Our society has always functioned through the machinations of those who have risen to the top, the sort of people who were either at this second meeting or advising those who were at the meeting. It has never been about the Jax, Abi, Mo and Joes of this world. Is it really going to be different this time? Are they going to decide in accordance with the spirit of the camaraderie that we saw at the end, or will it be … the same old same old? The fate of not just the Middle East, but the world is going to be in their hands. Will they rise to the challenge?

After a full day of deliberations, a decision was finally made.

THE CHANDELIER MAKER

Epilogue

It is now three years in the future. The whole landscape of the Middle East, indeed of the world, has changed. Our lives, all of our lives, have taken a real battering. The world has truly been turned upside down.

I am standing next to the ruins of what was once the Israel Museum on the west side of Jerusalem. All that is left standing there is the peculiar white dome of the Shrine of the Book, proud and untouched among the rebuilding around it. It originally housed the Dead Sea scrolls but has now been expanded to include many more sacred writings relocated from buildings that are no longer there, even some from other lands. Next to this is a new building, only opened a year ago, the Museum of Testimony, nicknamed *'Last Chance Saloon'*, by those with an over-developed sense of irony. I am in a long queue, along with an old friend. It is a happy queue and it is moving along quite nicely. We have come to Jerusalem to see for ourselves what is actually the only feature in this Museum; the exhibit that was the inspiration for its ironic nickname.

We are finally let in, we buy our tickets and are led to the main auditorium, joining hundreds of others. There is a wonderful sense of anticipation as we sit in the front row, in nice comfortable premium seats for which we have paid extra. Music is pumped in from hidden speakers. It is uplifting and full of hope. The performance is about to begin. Refreshments are aplenty and toilet facilities are conveniently to hand because this is to be a very special performance and none of it should be missed. It will last six hours long with hourly breaks and it is required that everyone should give full attention to it. In fact, it is now a condition of citizenship of the country to make such a pilgrimage at least once.

The reason is to both highlight the problems and issues of the world when conflict reigned, but also to show the possibilities that occur when human beings really do work together to a common end.

This is going to be very special to us, more than anyone else here, because the story that is about to unfold ... is our story. And it is the first time we have seen it, from the 'outside' so to speak.

A bell rings and all is hushed. Then the national anthem, Hatikvah ("The Hope"), is played and we all stand and sing the words which are far more poignant than when they were penned by Naftali Herz Imber in 1877. *'Our hope is not yet lost, the hope that is two thousand years old, to be a free nation in our land, the Land of Zion, Jerusalem.'*

Then we sit down and the holo-bubble in the centre of the room flickers into life.

It seems strange to relive those events of just a few years ago but which now seem an eternity away. It is even stranger to watch them as an observer, along with hundreds of others. We are both in disguise, me with an eye patch and a gaudy toupee, she with a variety of scarves hiding most of her face. It is important to do so, as we were once considered celebrities, not so much now, but still recognisable. We just wanted quiet lives, to be anonymous. After all, our fame was hardly a reward for a lifetime of work, just a single day ... a single eventful day.

We watch, cringing when the focus rests on us individually and laughing at the funnier moments. This performance has been seen by millions from all over the world. They have all come here, whether Jew or Arab, Christian or Muslim, even those who have absolutely no stake in the scenarios that were unfolding. It has become a vital artefact of a bygone age.

When it is over, only then do we discuss it, over a cup of

coffee in the lounge area.

"It's a shame it all came to nothing," I say. "But I don't regret it."

"That stupid old woman," is the response. "It could have been different if she hadn't been so ... stuck in her ways."

"Possibly. But you don't know ... but she came through in the end, didn't she?"

"Didn't seem to make a difference anyway ... I think they just wanted their war, whatever the outcome of our ..."

"... We don't know the full repercussions, so much was kept from us I think. And then again ... it turned out OK ... eventually."

"Yes, indeed. But not without a lot of pain."

"For everyone. I just hope that we did have some effect and that it made some kind of difference."

"It didn't stop the war."

"No, the war was an inevitability ... as you said ... but that's in the past now."

"And of course ... we met each other ... the odd couple."

"Actually, a couple of odd couples really."

"We've all been through challenging times. There has been so much hatred ... but no longer ..."

"Right, things are so much better now."

"Despite what we did ... despite what we all did ... what a mess we all made of things."

"But we ... you and I ... we did our bit, I believe. Despite all of the nonsense."

"Quite. But never mind ... that's enough talk of the past, it's all over now."

"Yes ... and we now embrace the future, yes?"

She adjusts her scarf and scratches her birthmark. It had flared up a bit lately.

"But it's time to go now, professor. I don't wish to be

reminded of what I once was."

"That's all forgotten, Jax. It's what you've become that is important."

"Whatever!"

"Did you hear the news, by the way? I only heard it yesterday."

"Do tell, professor."

"They are pregnant."

"Who?"

"Mo and Abi, of course, well Abi, to be specific."

"Wonderful news. Life goes on … So will it be a Jax … or a Joe, then?"

"You mean a Jacqueline or Joseph?"

"Don't know, but I'm sure they'll come up with a suitably exotic name, what with their mixed heritage."

"As long it isn't a Newt!"

"Perish the thought!"

"Great news, perhaps we can drop in to see them afterwards … oh dear, look at the time!"

"Yes … it *is* quite late. I heard the evening shofar, just about. These ears are not what they once were."

"Yester me."

"Yester you."

"Yester day."

This is our ritual whenever we meet up and it always makes us smile. Out of all the thousands of words spoken that fateful day three years ago, this is the only exchange that we remember, the Stevie Wonder song.

We link arms, slowly shuffle out of the building and head towards the Old City, along with a growing band of fellow pilgrims. A little later, as we wander down Jaffa Street, we both notice something very intriguing.

"Is that a new shop?"

"Yes it must be. We would have noticed it before. So many lights, quite some display".

"We have to have a quick look. Come on, there's a bit of time."

"Certainly."

We enter the shop. It is full of lights, lamps hanging from the wall and the ceiling, both LEDs and traditional light bulbs. Electric menorahs, candelabras and ... chandeliers of all shapes and sizes everywhere. A smartly dressed middle-aged man stands behind the counter, facing us. He looks familiar, very familiar, even though our reference point was just a few hours, some three years ago. We stare in disbelief.

"That can't be ..."

"... Newt ... the Chandelier Maker."

"Must be a joke ... or a dream ... are we dreaming, Joe?"

"No. This is real. But it may be a joke. Somehow ... don't know how or why."

We wander up to the counter, never taking our eyes off him. He looks at us slightly puzzled, or is there something else there in his expression? We both look for signs of recognition. We even take off our disguises momentarily. It makes no difference. His face displays nothing. He smiles, as any good salesman would.

"Can I help you?"

Jax gets straight to the point. "Newt? ... Is it you?"

He looks at us with a blank expression. There is no recognition at all in his eyes. We look hard for something, the tiniest tell, but nothing.

"I am Mr Fothergill."

"The Chandelier Maker?"

"Of course ..."

Our spirits lift. I am about to extend my arms to him.

"... Among other things," he adds. I hold back. "I also

make candelabras."

"No … *the* Chandelier Maker … our Chandelier Maker."

There is still no recognition. We stand staring for a little longer. His eyes drop, as if to get on with something else, as he sees no possibility of a sale here.

"Think we have this wrong, Jax. Let's go."

We turn round to leave. I open the door, like a gentleman, for Jax to precede me. I look back at him. He lifts a hand up to get my attention and speaks.

"Oh yes … I am a Chandelier Maker, indeed … but … also … I am a very good … researcher."

He says that final word with a slight inflexion and there is the tiniest glint in his eye.

We both nod at him and he nods back. Communication, at some deep level, has been made. It is evident that he is unable to acknowledge his past life, our brief encounter three years ago. Probably a safeguard built into his programming. We accept this. We leave it at that, as we exit the shop.

"You know, I've never forgotten the last thing he said to us … Love and care for the Palestinians is often a smokescreen for hatred of the Jews. Until this is acknowledged, there will always be two sets of victims … and these are people who really ought to be friends."

"He was so right. If only our 'leaders' had listened … but, then again, I was as much to blame."

"Well, that's well in the past. We are living in better days now."

There are many people in the street. It is time now to join the throng and make our way to the holy hill to greet The King.

Author's note

As the theme of the book is the search for truth, where there are many competing voices, I would like to explain where I find my truth. Every writer will come from a particular mindset and will write according to how they see the world. I am no different and it is my belief in Jesus Christ that informs me. Yet this book is not a religious polemic; my aim was always only to provide light on a difficult situation and to report from all positions as fairly as I could. The only place where my religious beliefs have impinged is in the very last sentence, so I would like to take the time to explain a little.

'It is time now to join the throng and make our way to the holy hill to greet The King.'

Jax had undergone some kind of transformation and now considers herself a different person. The tiny microcosm represented by our quartet showed that peace between human beings is not easy. The problem is our attachment to the past and all of its hurts and our fundamental inability to break free in all sincerity and embrace a new future. The way of hate has always been an easy path for us and the way of love simply requires a lot more forgiveness and cooperation. For these reasons I come to the sad conclusion that real lasting peace in the Middle East is not possible, though I would be more than happy to be proven wrong on this.

Although Joe hadn't always been the best witness for his faith, he eventually reminded himself of his shortcomings and embraced a sense of forgiveness, both seeking it from others and offering it to others. Thus, the two of them were reconciled and now find themselves in Jerusalem, ready for the journey *to the holy hill to greet the King*. It is my belief that this King is Jesus himself, returning to a broken world after a horrible war to end all wars. He has returned to reign and usher in a new age of peace. In my mind, this gives me hope for the future and perhaps you too?

If you're one of those who check out the final few pages before reading a book, then I've possibly already put you off. This would be a shame as this book is a sincere attempt to provide a fresh voice in the peace process and I encourage you to read it. Finding truth is always worth the effort.

Enjoy your life.

You will find the following resources useful:

BOOKS by Steve Maltz
Available from good bookshops or https://www.saltshakers.com

Now Everything Changes
Derek and Dawn's first adventure, leading them into an understanding of the causes and effects of antisemitism, particularly in the wake of the war in Gaza. This is followed by looking at the implications and relevance of this to our own lives.

Outcast Nation
The story of the People and the Land through biblical and secular history, tracing the out-workings of God's covenants and offering explanations for both the survival and the success of this Outcast Nation.

Zionion
This book scratches away at the phenomenon known as antisemitism and takes an intelligent and balanced approach to arrive at the real heart of the matter.

BOOKLETS by Steve Maltz
Available from good bookshops or https://www.saltshakers.com

The Simple guide to the Middle East Conflict
Much heat has been generated by the subject of Israel and Palestine. This 8-page booklet has provides a simple but effective introduction to this complex issue.

For Whatever Reason
This booklet outlines the spiritual root of the current Israel/Palestine crisis - It Is taken from a chapter of the book, *The Bishop's New Clothes*.

YOUTUBE VIDEO

Blindspot

Available at blindspot.church

This short, hard-hitting and entertaining video will surprise and shock you if you think all is well in the Western Church. It arrives at the heart of the problem between the Church and Israel through a surprising route. It should have particular use in trying to reach younger Christians, from Generation X, Y and Z, who tend to be the hardest to reach on this particular subject!

WEB APP

The Mirror

Available at themirror.church

The World, with all of its burdens and intrigues, spins on its axis. Where is this axis located? Apparently, a tiny strip of land between Israel and Egypt. The goings-on in Gaza tugs at the emotions like none other.

Despite over a million Muslim refugees about to be expelled by Pakistan, the repression of millions of Muslim Uyghurs in China, the bombing of Ukraine by Russia and over a hundred other armed conflicts around the world, only one issue will regularly bring out tens of thousands of indignant protesters to the streets of London and other places.

But it doesn't end there, as many have felt empowered to take it further, with worrying consequences. Emotions are rife, but how many really know the context of what they are protesting against? Would you like to understand more?

If so ...

The following publications helped in the writing of this book:

Pogrom: Kishinev and the Tilt of History:
Steven J Zipperstein *(Liveright 2018)*

The Revolt: Menachem Begin *(Futura Publications 1980)*

Ghosts of a Holy War: Yardena Schwartz *(Union Square 2024)*

Children of Israel, Children of Palestine: Laurel Holliday
(Atria Books 2014)

Palestine as it was: Hugh Mitford Raymond
(Mitford Literary Society 2017)

British Policy in the Middle East & the Creation of Israel:
Hugh Mitford Raymond *(Mitford Literary Society 2015)*

TCM1f0225

THE CHANDELIER MAKER